IN THE DARK

Also by Carol Brennan

•

HEADHUNT
FULL COMMISSION

IN THE DARK

Carol Brennan

G. P. PUTNAM'S SONS • NEW YORK

G. P. Putnam's Sons
Publishers Since 1838
200 Madison Avenue
New York, NY 10016

The author gratefully acknowledges permission
to reprint portions of lyrics from the following:

"If Love Were All" (Noel Coward), © 1929 WARNER BROS. INC.
(Renewed). All rights reserved. Used by permission.

"You're the Top" (Cole Porter), © 1934 WARNER BROS. INC.
(Renewed). All rights reserved. Used by permission.

Library of Congress Cataloging-in-Publication Data

Brennan, Carol.
In the dark / Carol Brennan.
p. cm.
ISBN 0-399-13940-0 (alk. paper)
1. Parent and child—California—Los Angeles—Fiction.
2. Actresses—California—Los Angeles—Fiction.   3. Murder—
California—Los Angeles—Fiction.   4. Los Angeles (Calif.)—
Fiction.   I. Title.
PS3552.R3777I5   1994   93-42287 CIP
813'.54—dc20

Printed in the United States of America
1   2   3   4   5   6   7   8   9   10

ACKNOWLEDGMENTS

Anita Diamant: agent; editor of first resort; patient friend.

Phyllis Grann and Leslie Gelbman: whose quick enthusiasm for this book made my year.

Nancy Lucas and Susan Glass: loving critics.

Frank Peters: arbiter of *le mot juste*.

And Eamon: always *primus inter pares*.

For my children, Richard and Joanna,
with my love—then, now and always

All colours will agree in the dark.

FRANCIS BACON
"Of Unity in Religion"

"*N*o!" She hears her mother's voice—frantic with a wild edge that scares her. It penetrates her sleep. She opens an eye and can't for a second or two make out anything in the dark. A sharp pop—like Tommy McClusky's cap gun, but a little louder even.

"*Ooohhh my God!*" Her father—moaning, almost crying. Another pop, then nothing. She jumps out of bed, bare feet instantly icy as they hit the flagstone floor. A third pop. Her heart bangs hard, a clenched fist punching its way out of her chest.

"*Oh Jesus, the kid! Where's the kid?*" A new voice, hoarse, croaking. Man? Woman? She can't tell. Footsteps overhead, back and forth. Now they sound like they're heading for the door to the stairs—to come down and *get* her. She hears herself whimper as she stands there in her faded blue nightgown, frozen to the cold floor. She bites her lip to keep from hollering for her mother. The footsteps move closer. "*Emily. Emm-i-lyy!*" The voice knowing her name heightens her terror.

Suddenly, her body knows before her head what she must do. The upstairs door creaks open. She bolts for the sliding glass doors to the garden. Turns the lock. The footsteps start down. She feels sick in her stomach. If her heart pounds any harder, she knows she'll throw up. She slides the door open just enough to slip out and push it all the way shut behind her. That's important. She knows from when she plays hide-and-seek it's always a dead giveaway to leave the door open even a crack.

She runs fast now toward the storage shed in the far corner of the garden, where they keep the lawn chairs and her bike. The sharp stones cut her feet. She trips and falls down hard, scraping her knee right through the nightgown. Up fast. Can't stop.

The rusty hinges of the shed door don't want to move. She pulls harder, knuckles scraping raw against the rough wood. She hears the strange voice again—down in her room now. It's muffled through the closed glass doors and she can't make out the words. Come *on,* she prays silently. The door creaks open and she dives gratefully into the cold, damp shed, pulling the door shut.

She feels her way in the pitch-dark past bikes, past chair frames. She begins to shiver violently, shaking too hard to move. Her body has escaped her command, won't obey her. Stop it, Emily. Stop it, now! She starts to punch her open palm with her other fist. Over and over and over with all the strength she can summon, to regain control—know what's real. Her hand is real. Her fist is real. She can make them act on each other. She starts to come out of the nightmare, reenter herself.

She stumbles on a sheet of heavy canvas, gropes for an edge and crawls under it, panting. She makes herself concentrate on breathing slowly in and out. She doesn't let herself think about what might have happened to her parents. She knows it is something terrible. She closes her eyes and begins to speak softly, the way she does when they're fighting upstairs and she can't stand to hear it.

"Once there was a girl named Emily," she tells herself. "She was only nine, but when she grew up . . ."

Hats, badges, strong hands lifting, carrying her thin, numbed body. Blankets, rough and scratchy, smell like the doctor's office.

She wakes up in a high, white bed with a white curtain pulled most of the way around it. She half remembers dreaming of water—hot water, all over her. Now, tucked tight into starchy sheets and heavy blankets, she is exhausted and very hot, her mouth so dry it's hard to open.

A man she doesn't know is sitting on a chair next to the bed. He stands up and walks close to her. He has a square face with freckles and a squashed, Silly Putty nose. Freckles on his head, too. She can see them through the few strands of rusty hair. His tie is green—the exuberant green of the Saint Patrick's Day parade. He smiles. "Hi. Feelin' better?" His brown button eyes are friendly.

"Where's Mommy and Daddy?" As she says the names, sobs, suppressed in the terror of the previous night, well up in her sore, swollen throat. She starts to cry and can't stop. The man doesn't try to make her. He pats her shoulder and mumbles "There, there" and "Okay, okay" till the racking sobs lessen into intermittent hiccups. Then he hands her a Kleenex.

"Do you remember what happened, Emily?"

She nods. Then she tells him all of it. He does not interrupt, just listens with a few uh-huhs like she's doing well, telling him just what he wants to hear.

"This other person," he says, his thin, reddish lips twisting in a funny way she doesn't like, "you're sure there was another person?"

"Yes." She feels an instant wave of anger—betrayal. Doesn't he believe her? "With this creepy, hoarse voice," she says emphatically.

"Okay. Was it a man or a lady?"

She thinks about that. She's good at voices. They play back in her head and then she can do them herself. She even fooled her best friend, Susan, once on the phone by pretending to be their teacher, Miss Ebbs.

This voice had sounded sort of like the witch in *Snow White*. But it'd also sounded like a record her parents played sometimes of a singer they liked. She'd thought it was a lady, but Daddy had laughed and told her it was a man called Mel Tormé.

"I don't know," she answers. "I just don't know."

CHAPTER
ONE

$\mathbf{A}$ ringing telephone at three a.m. does not usually bring good news. This one brought the news that Mike was dead. I listened quietly with the frozen calm that sets in when suspense is abruptly broken and worst fears confirmed. The LAPD cop on the other end had to ask a couple of times whether I was still there. I did not bother to correct him when he called me Mrs. Florio.

"We think it could be Teamster enforcers. They can be, uh, hard guys," he said, his voice turning sheepish, uncomfortable at broaching grisly details to the bereaved. "Are you . . . Do you have someone you can call to stay with you?"

"I'm okay." I sounded to my own ears as though I were speaking from the bottom of a well.

"I need to come to talk to you, Mrs. Florio."

"Come ahead. I don't think I'm going to go to sleep."

"One-three-five Columbine, right? That's out where? Just past Santa Monica?"

"About twenty minutes. Down the canyon, a little road just along the beach." The beach. It was so important to Mike to live on the beach. To be able to run into the waves for sunrise swims, his long, brown arms piercing the cool, jelled water in slow, rhythmic crawl strokes. My breath caught in my chest with a sharp pain.

"Forty minutes or so. You sure you're going to be okay?"

I was sure of just the opposite. "Yes."

I hung up the phone and crouched there in Mike's big chair, my tangled thicket of hair curtaining my face, knees to chin, arms wrapped around—a huge fetus about to die of pain, rocking back and forth, wanting only to disappear into the soft, tan leather. Then the shakes started and I was punching fist into palm again and again to stop them, just as I had the night my parents were murdered. But no tears. I felt them, a boulder in my chest, lodged there, not able to rise. Maybe I didn't deserve the relief of tears. The cop on the phone had said Teamster guys, but I knew better. I knew that Mike was dead because of me.

It had happened ten days ago—whacked me with that mix of surprise and inevitability that accompanies the invasion of the terrible just when life seems wonderful.

Mike was out driving a job up to San Francisco and wouldn't be back till late. I'd popped into a Westwood movie to take another look at *Running Fast*, my first appearance on the big screen. It was a nice, meaty little part and I wanted to see the movie again, alone this time. Nadia had pointed out some nuances in my performance that I hadn't realized were there. "Your ahnger is intrusive in the reconciliation scene, Amily," she'd said last week in class. I'd debated her hotly, but any actor fortunate enough to study with Nadia Gregoriu takes what she says pretty seriously, and I wanted to check it out.

Just as the lights dimmed, I heard it—a number of rows behind me. ". . . *old-fashioned, like Mother.*" It was so entirely unexpected that it took maybe twenty seconds to reach the right part of my brain. When it did, my head spun around, ears perked like a hunting dog's, straining to hear more. Silence. Then a trailer for a new cop-action movie drowned out any possibility of hearing more. But in the segue to the next promo, it spoke again. ". . . *wouldn't alter . . . just plain chance. . . . Well, we'll see what hap-*

pens next chapter." Innocuous snatches of conversation, but in a voice I'd never forget or mistake, not even after twenty years. Its androgynous hoarseness was burned into my memory, into my dreams, where I'd hear it, and I'd kill it. Or it would kill me.

I felt the back of my neck go damp and icy with sweat. The person who owned that voice had always been "it" to me, never "he" or "she" but a kind of floating, disembodied evil. But there it was, quite real, all the more horrible for the ordinariness of the setting. The man or woman who had killed my parents was sitting behind me watching a movie, chomping popcorn, maybe, chatting about books and mother. My temples pounded with a furious rush of blood.

I twisted in my seat, eyes narrowed in a futile effort to study and memorize nameless faces in the dark. The theater was almost filled. The picture had gotten good reviews. It took me a full five minutes of mind-racing up and down blind alleys to realize that unless it spoke again, there wasn't a damned thing I could do. Make them shut the theater? Call the police? "A voice, huh? You heard it how long ago?" The way the people in charge speak to children—and nut cases. I'd heard plenty of that years ago back in New York, when I'd still thought that if I could just tell them persuasively enough, they would do something. But they hadn't. They never had.

The voice didn't say another word.

Then I got an idea. I'd grown up to look a great deal like my mother. Maybe my sudden appearance on the screen would shock it and it would do something. . . .

Just before my first scene started, I got up and stationed myself at the exit and waited. No gasp, no sound. Two teenaged boys left. Then I spotted a rotund fortyish couple hurrying up the aisle. My heart scudded. One of this dumpy pair? Was it possible? As they walked out she was complaining of a headache and he, rummaging around in his pockets, reported that he couldn't come up with an aspirin. Both their voices were disappointingly average.

After the movie, as the theater emptied out, I examined each face that passed by me and listened hard. They all looked blandly innocent. I didn't hear the voice again. But as I felt the blood tingle thick and hot in my hands, I knew that everything in my life had just changed irrevocably. I'd learned something there was no way to forget or ignore. Whoever had killed my parents was here in L.A.

I drove home and poured a stiff scotch over a couple of cubes while I paced the house, waiting for Mike. For the first time in three years I wished I had a cigarette. My mind blurred under a pelt of questions. Was this some crazy coincidence? Or had the voice followed me out to California, stalked me all these years? But why? If it wanted to kill me, why hadn't it? And why had it murdered my parents?

I'd hidden out from that question, left it back in New York, resigned to living the rest of my life with it unanswered. Finally, in the past few years I had begun to unclench, shed a few prickles, lose some of the guarded tension. I'd started being easier with the good times, quit grabbing at them so frantically, mauling them in a way that reminded me uncomfortably of my mother.

I owed that to Mike, as I did most of what was good in my life. After all, he'd brought me up, in a way. I was twenty when I met him, a mass of ragged edges. I'd fled New York at eighteen and come to Hollywood to be a movie star—a reckless girl with three things going for her: an offbeat, angular face some thought beautiful; an odd talent for imitating the way other people sounded; and the freedom that comes with nothing to lose.

Two years later it happened for me. Rick Lind, an actor important enough to do it, had twisted Bruce DeRenkin's arm to put me in his new picture. DeRenkin had given in, but he took it out of my hide every day on the set.

It was a small part, but a big break for me. I blew it. One day after a brutal barrage of sarcasm: "Miss Silver, did you perhaps go to *drayma* school back in New York? Miss Silver, you do not *need* to have a motivation. Just hit the fucking marks and let's see those cheekbones." Snicker. He raised his voice and addressed the crew. "I bet Rick Lind prefers our Emily's *other* cheeks—less bony. Ha ha." That was when I let him have it with the violence I was usually able to keep in check. No thinking, just knee action.

Everything froze for a second. DeRenkin, doubled over clutching his crotch. Me, knowing instantly in my throbbing head and sick stomach what I'd done to my barely budding career. I heard one of the crew members quip ironically the traditional phrase they use to cap the filming of each actor's final scene: "Finished in the movie, Emily Silver." Finished in *any* movie.

I turned and ran, hitching up the tight skirt of my costume, through the giant soundstage and out the door, as though pursued by demons—no idea of anything except to get away. Then I saw the truck, its back gaping invitingly open, unloading scenery. No one minding it for the moment. I jumped up into the cavernous trailer and made for a dark far corner. I crouched there panting, grateful for the cool blackness, ready to spend the rest of my life sheltering right there. Suddenly, I felt the engine rev up and carry me away.

The driver's name was Mike Florio and he laughed himself into tears when I surfaced and told him how I happened to be stowed away in his truck.

"Best story I've heard in years," he grinned, white teeth gleaming in his olive face. "Right in the *coglioni,* huh? I've worked on a couple of DeRenkin shoots. It couldn't've happened to a nicer prick. Okay, so where do you live, Rocky? I'll take you home."

Up till now, with Rick Lind. But no way I could go back there—not after he'd stuck his neck out for me with DeRenkin. "I guess I don't have a home," I said, surprised at my mouth, which had started to smile.

"Great. I'll take you home with me."

The beginning of the good times. Nine years ago.

* * *

I've said that Mike brought me up. And he did. He was seventeen years older than I, old enough to be lover and father both. A born father—a born lover, too. Mike had perfect pitch for priorities; it was his greatest gift. He always knew what was important and what could be skipped. He tried to teach me, and I tried to learn. Some of it stuck, but I wasn't a natural at it the way he was.

That first night I spent under his roof, he taught me to make linguine with red clam sauce. We ate it on his deck listening to the crashing waves and drinking rich, dark Chianti. The second night, he taught me to make love, which was as different from what I'd been doing since I was fifteen as his clam sauce was from something that came in a can. We never actually discussed my moving in permanently. I just did it. And when my first tantrum came, as it was bound to, Mike didn't throw me out, or turn his back, or bait me. He gathered me up in his powerful arms, held me hard till the flailing stopped, and, for the first time, told me that he loved me. After I'd calmed down, he leaned back against the fridge and surveyed the damage.

"Rocky," he said with a moderate sternness, "you clean every string of that pasta off the floor. I find one you missed, or a sausage, or a pepper, I'm gonna kick your ass from here to . . ."

"The bedroom?" I asked with exaggeratedly wide eyes, hoping hard that his ears would translate it to the "I'm sorry" that I felt but couldn't say.

"Now that's not a bad idea," he answered after a beat, and reached for my hand.

In the nine years we'd been together, my career had taken a path far from spectacular, but one that pleased me. I'd played Strindberg and Shaw and Shakespeare on stage mostly for love, with a healthy helping of TV thrown in for money. And now this movie. Mike's business had grown from two to six trucks. Somebody else might've traded the driver's seat for one behind a desk by now, but he continued to drive at least a couple of jobs a week himself. Though I sometimes nagged him to stop, I don't think I really wanted him to quit driving. Part of what I loved about Mike was that he did real physical work, maneuvered a huge tractor trailer as though it were a compact wagon, hefted weighty cargo with the grace of an athlete.

He'd built most of this beach house with his own hands. It'd been little more than a shack when he bought it twelve years ago, and expanding it had been his pleasure. And I'd taken pleasure in watching him apply the sure hand of an expert to Sheetrock and flooring and plumbing and double-glazed windows—things that would leave the sleek actors and pale writers I knew, the downy Yale undergrads of my teens, entirely copeless.

In so many ways, Mike came from a different planet from the one I grew up on, and even though I remained a resident alien in his world, I felt more comfortable living there— safer than I'd ever felt before.

Finally, just before one, when I was ready to pour a third scotch and start to ransack the house for a desiccated, deeply stale cigarette, I heard Mike's car pull in. I ran out the door and threw myself at his chest, craving the solid, warm feel of it. He wrapped his arms tight around me. "Some reception. I thought you'd be asleep. Hey, what's the matter, Rock, you're trembling."

"Just hang on to me for a second, Mike, okay?" I said into his chest. He did. We stood there not talking, his strong, blunt fingers massaging my back, playing each rib like a skilled pianist. Finally, I stepped back and looked at him. The gray that had begun to salt his black hair, the sun wrinkles around his shiny, black eyes—these were special charms, ones I was grateful for. I took his hand and led him into the house.

He put on a fire and we sat, curled up together on the red sofa in front of it while I told him.

"All right," he said after a minute. "Good." He nodded

slowly, as though in conversation with himself. "This's been let go too long. I'm gonna fix it now. No way my girl's having nightmares for the rest of her life."

The nightmares. In daylight, I was Emily Silver, actress, lover of Mike Florio, doing very nicely thank you. But in the dark, without warning, my screen would flash the horror film, and I'd become again the child of murdered parents, fleeing, searching, never knowing. I'd hear the voice coming for me. Some nights I'd run in terror, but others, I'd turn hunter. The dream always ended the same way. A single shot, releasing a geyser of scalding blood which would envelop my body like flames. When I screamed myself awake, Mike would hold me, stroking, patting. He was right, it had been let go too long.

"I need to do something, Mike, but what? Go to the LAPD and tell them that somewhere in Greater Los Angeles there's a creature with a funny voice that killed two people in New York twenty years ago?"

"I guess not. What did the voice say? I mean tonight, at the movies." Despite my ears' excellent memory, the sequence of the disjointed bits I'd overheard gave me some trouble, and I had to shuffle them around a couple of times before I got it right.

He frowned in concentration for a moment, his brows knitting to form a single, deep line above his nose. "We need a link—something. And the something's not in L.A., it's in New York."

I felt myself stiffen. I hadn't been back to New York once since I'd left eleven years ago. To me, New York meant my grandmother, and even now, cradled as I was in Mike's arms, she scared me. Much as I'd fought, defied, hollered, I had to admit she still scared me.

"I guess I need to go there then, see what I might turn up," I said, my gut jumping as I spoke.

"Hey, knock off the 'I.' I say 'we,' and it's we, got it? Somebody has to go to New York, but not you."

"No, Mike, I should—"

"You're too close to it, Rocky. You can't go. I'm not saying you wouldn't be up to it. Hey, aren't you the kid who gave it to DeRenkin in the balls?" He grinned, trying to make me feel better.

"I can. I can handle it in New York, Mike. I *will* go."

"No. I say you won't." That tone. The command of the Italian male. It always triggered combat.

"And I say *you* won't."

We had one of our battles about it, loud and short, as they usually were now—but entirely verbal. I didn't fling spaghetti platters anymore. In the end, Mike came up with a different idea. He knew some guy in New York who was good at "nosing out things." I hadn't much liked it. A stranger. How would he even begin?

"Same as I would, but better. He knows the cops up there. If anybody can get hold of those police records from twenty years ago, really do some digging, he's the one. You're gonna tell me everything you remember from back then. Maybe there'll be a hook. Someone your folks used to know who moved here. I'll call Dev tomorrow and brief him. We'll see what he can turn up in a week or two. And then I can start to poke around out here."

"Hey," I said, "knock off the 'I,' it's 'we.' "

He grinned and nuzzled my neck. "You snagged me, Rocky. 'We.' That's what we are, we're a we. For now, anyway."

I knew what he meant. He'd said it before—that one day I'd be ready to fly away and he'd have to push my ass out of the nest. Hearing it always made me mad and sad and scared. "Not for now," I said firmly. "Forever. What'll it cost for this guy in New York?" I asked, more to change the subject than anything else. "I want to pay."

"Not a thing," Mike answered with the faintest smile. "Not a damned thing. Dev's my goombah. A mick, but my goombah."

That had been ten days ago. I'd raked my memories, pretty sketchy ones, impressions, names, while Mike took notes—handed over brittle old Xeroxes of newspaper clippings: "SOCIETY DOUBLE DEATH," describing the official version, the one the police had accepted: that my father, in a boozy fit of temper, had shot my mother and killed himself. Going through it all again after so many years—the terror, the grief, the fury at no one, *no one* believing me—left me rubbed raw.

Mike's thought that the voice might be connected to some old family friend sent me combing the local phone books for dimly remembered names, but I came up empty and discouraged. Then, yesterday afternoon, Mike had called from the road and left a message on the machine that he had news—something might be about to break—and that he'd be home before midnight and tell me about it. I'd waited—pacing, jumping out of my skin, furious at his delay. Along about two, I'd started getting scared. It got through to me how crazy and stupid it was for a pair of improvising amateurs to try to close in on a successful murderer, no matter how much time had elapsed. I should've gone to the police, no matter what.

Now the police were coming to me. Too late.

CHAPTER
TWO

BY the time the doorbell rang, my shakes were gone. I was as dead calm as I'd been on the phone, which seemed a bit uneasy-making for Sergeant Stivic, a slightly overweight man about my own age, who'd've looked at home lopping off lamb chops on a butcher's marble slab, wiping his chubby hands from time to time on a stained white apron.

I don't know at what moment I decided not to level with him. I think it was when he told me exactly what they did to Mike. He hadn't wanted to, but I'd insisted, ravenous all at once for every detail, needing to see each atrocity, feel each jolt of punishing pain.

They'd broken his fingers and his arms. Then they'd bashed his skull with a jack handle and left him, their job finished. Stivic figured there were two of them. I knew it. I knew that no one guy, no matter who, would've been able to do that to Mike, who was fast on his feet and good enough with his fists to have been some kind of boxing champ in the Navy. He'd been in brawls before with Teamster thugs and competing truckers—came away with a broken arm one time, a broken nose the next, but he'd always left the other guy at least as battered.

Stivic seemed sold on his version of what had happened: union toughs. His assumption made sense, given Mike's record of skirmishes with the Teamsters about who could or couldn't drive his trucks when, where, and for whom. I just didn't believe it for a second. The coincidence was too great. No, the voice had struck Mike down because of what this Dev had uncovered. Listening to Stivic reluctantly recite his description, I grew colder and colder. My blood turned icy; I imagined I felt it freeze solid. No more running away. I would be the hunter now.

I answered all Stivic's questions. Yes, Mike had talked about recent troubles with the union. No, I didn't know any names. (That much was true—Mike had never wanted me to.) No, Mike and I weren't actually married, though we'd lived together for nine years. Yes, he had a sister in San Francisco. Parents, both dead. Yes, I felt up to identifying the body. And no, I preferred not to do it from a photo. I wanted to *see*—to bear witness.

"You know, Mrs. . . . Ms. Silver, you look kind of familiar."

I got that a lot. My TV work, and of couse the new movie—parts big enough for people to place the face but not the name. "I'm an actress, Sergeant."

"Ah, sure. I think I saw you on *L.A. Law,* right?"

"Right."

Later, as I was coming out the morgue door after having nodded that yes, the slaughtered animal on the slab had been Michael Vincent Florio, I saw Stivic and another cop standing around in the corridor. ". . . wouldn't mind pokin' her myself." "Not me. Good-looking, but she'd probably freeze your dick off. Little wacko, too. Wanted to hear every last detail. Then she wouldn't even do a photo ID, had to come *gaze* at him."

I slipped past them out the door and went home.

Mike was a one-day, bad-news story in the papers and on TV. He'd been neither a movie nor a mob celebrity, and as far as the police were concerned, his death wasn't exactly a mystery, even though they didn't have anyone they could lay hands on and arrest. But, as Stivic told the reporters, that was often the way it went when you were "dealing with pros." The *Times* followed up with an editorial on the recent escalating violence in the local trucking industry. Mike's death hadn't been an isolated incident.

He was buried in San Francisco as a Catholic, from the church where he'd served Mass as a boy, St. Dominic's. The Mike I knew had had little use for the church, so I suppose I could've protested, but why, really? Mike no longer cared and his sister, Angie, cared very much.

I considered skipping the whole thing. I wasn't ready to mourn. A fortunate numbness blocked anything I might be feeling, except cold fury. Considering what I'd determined to do, it was a useful condition. In the end, I went to Mike's funeral for only one reason. It was my best hope of finding out how to contact the mysterious Dev.

I flew up with Trip Colby. I'd known Trip even longer than I had Mike. He'd landed in Hollywood six months before me, from Cedar Rapids. He'd been Walter Grody, until this very butch agent decided that Trip was a pretty sexy name and that Grody didn't make it at all. Trip looked like everybody's idealized, sun-streaked California beach boy. Peel back that layer and you found an ambitious, damned good actor who during the past two years had made a jump-start on becoming a star. I didn't have lots of friends, and Trip was by far the closest—a piece of undeserved luck which I didn't quite understand and tended to take for granted.

I'd argued with him about coming up to San Francisco, said I really didn't need him, I could manage. He'd just smiled that smile—the one that gladdened the hearts of studio accountants—and told me to stop being such an asshole. As it turned out, he was a godsend. He steered me through the flowers and incense, and shielded me from having to look at the coffin. I'd lived with the truth of Mike's life and stared at the truth of his death. I didn't think I could bear a painted, sanitized fiction, laid out on pleated satin.

I watched the funeral as though I'd wandered into the wrong movie. The priest intoned. Angie and her daughter, Tiffany, wept loudly. Mike's drivers bore the coffin down the aisle and back again—huge Hank, little Jerry, and the others, their stoic faces belied by reddened, watery eyes. Mike's Aunt Clara sat beside me, stone-still, her bright black eyes as dry as my own.

Mike used to call Clara Santangelo, his late mother's younger sister, "the iron broad." She was over seventy now, and kept her hair as fiercely black as her eyes—those Santangelo eyes, just like Mike's. He'd told me the family legend: Forty years ago, Clara had been on the arm of her first husband when he was gunned down in a mob turf battle. She had run into the street, fist raised, her blood-soaked fox coat flapping behind her, trying to catch the killers' car. Twenty years later, she'd slammed the door on her second husband when she learned that he'd ordered the hit. She'd gotten the family's first divorce, taken back her maiden name, and dared the inflamed ex-husband to do something about it. He hadn't.

Trip drove Clara's car out to the cemetery. She and I sat in back. She took my hand and held it. Neither of us said anything for a long time.

It was Clara who finally broke the silence. "It's bullshit, Emily."

"What?"

"What the cops say about Mikey."

"I don't know," I said, not daring to look at her as I spoke. "They seem pretty sure it was the union."

"Nah. Wouldna killed him. Smacked him around, sure, but not this. Mikey wasn't important enough to kill."

"I don't know," I repeated. There was nothing else to say that wouldn't recruit her into it, activist that she was. And I couldn't do that—not to her, and not to Trip, whose eyes were fixed firmly on the road, but who, if I knew him, was taking in every word. I was convinced that poking around in my grisly past had killed Mike. I wasn't going to let it kill anybody else. Except probably me.

"Your hand's like ice." She leaned over to study my face and must've been troubled by what she saw. "You levelin' with me? You have any other ideas about who did him, you oughta tell me. Hey, I know nothin'll bring him back, but I believe in an eye for an eye. May not be enough, but it's all we got." Her two hands placed themselves on my cheeks and turned my face eye to eye with hers. "I can make it happen," she said, black eyes confirming the words.

Easy to just hand it over, dump it in her lap. But I'd have hated myself for the rest of my life. "No other ideas, Clara," I said stonily. I was aching to ask her about Dev, but I couldn't right then. She was a sharp old lady. She'd've known the question wasn't casual.

"You made him happy. He was a wreck after he left Franny. Guilty. Beat himself up somethin' terrible." Mike's had been the second divorce in the family. "I thought it was gonna be strictly one-night stands for him after that. And it was, till he met you. You were good for him."

I felt my eyes fill up for the first time since I'd learned of Mike's death. In some ways, Clara knew him better than I did. She'd been his main support through an agonizing divorce from the coked-out Fran. It was Clara who'd threatened to cut his hands off if he gave over another dime, who convinced him to leave San Francisco and make a fresh start in L.A.

And Clara thought I'd been good for him. Something loosened inside me. For a split second it felt as though the glacier would melt, and I ached to lay my head on her solid, capable shoulder and give way to hot, cleansing tears. But I knew that if I did that, I'd be lost. So I squeezed her hand and stared at my lap.

"Thank you," I said, my voice coming out husky.

"Nothing to thank. Ya know, I don't know too much about you, Emily, even after all this time." She held up a hand, fingers blunt and square like Mike's, against a possible interruption. "And I don't need to. I know you where it counts. I can see past your funny, fancy school way of talkin', and how you snap and close up sometimes—even that pointy, society face of yours. We're the same kinda people, you and me. And Mikey." I thought I heard her voice crack, but I wasn't sure. "Not like that sugar-coated bitch sister of his. That one's gonna split a gut when she hears about the will."

Clara was Mike's executor, so she knew that three years ago, right after his mother's death, he'd changed his will and left everything to me. Money, house, business: all told, a very decent sum—not in my grandmother's terms, but more than enough to be a substantial cushion for an actor's uncertain income. I'd felt funny about it though. Not because of Angie; she and her husband had inherited Florio's Seafood Shack on Fisherman's Wharf and were prospering. Besides, I didn't like her a bit more than Clara did. But money and wills summoned up unpleasant memories of my grandmother, and anything that smacked of her was something I wanted to block out.

I remembered the evening Mike told me about the new will. I'd just come out of the shower in the mood for a session in bed before dinner.

"Sit down, Rocky, I got something to talk to you about."

"I don't want to sit down. I want to lie down." I unwrapped my towel and stuck a still-damp breast in his ear.

"Not now," he said. Unusual. "It's important. About money."

I made a face. "Well, if it's about money I'm all ears." I climbed on his lap facing him and started to unzip his fly. "Well, maybe not *all* ears."

Before I knew what was happening, he'd flipped me across his lap and laid a single whack on my bare ass, hard enough to make me yowl. I jumped up and went for him, fist clenched in fury. "That hurt, goddamn it!"

He caught my wrist. "It was meant to." He held my shoulders and sat me on the sofa. "Money's serious, Rocky. Anybody but a kid raised rich like you's smart enough to know that. Now, listen up."

The complete Mike-ness of it made me smile, in spite of everything else. I held on to that memory like an amulet to get me through the burial.

Back at Angie's fussy house, family and friends sidled around the massive, phony Spanish furniture socializing, drinking, eating—eager to confirm, with just a tinge of nervous guilt, how glad they were to be alive. Trip caused a sensation. A movie star! Angie and her eighteen-year-old Tiffany simpered at him through their tears and then whispered cattily behind their hands about my untimely new romance. I came close to laughing out loud at an over-heard snippet from Angie to one of her friends. ". . . and would you believe her bringing him to the *funeral?* I mean, my brother not even cold, and her carrying on already with . . ." I could've told them that Trip's desires ran in an entirely different direction—toward a gifted British scene designer, one Anthony (silent *h*) Newland-Wragg, at the moment. But of course, I didn't.

I circulated methodically, purposefully striking up conversations with as many people as possible, using every device I could think of to casually bring up the name Dev. Nobody, including Clara, seemed to have the least idea who I was talking about.

CHAPTER
THREE

My agent, Bernie Clegg, was furious with me, with reason. Spielberg had just called with a hurry-up request that I test for his new movie. The actress originally cast had come down with appendicitis or gall-bladder trouble or something. He'd seen *Running Fast* and was, quote unquote, intrigued.

A balloon of sheer elation inflated inside my chest and almost carried me off. It would be a real step—hell, three steps—from a little low-budget sleeper like *Running Fast* to Spielberg. The only hitch was, if I got it, shooting started immediately. Desire. I felt it in my hands, my stomach, my skin. At that moment, it superseded everything in the world, except the one thing that made the answer no.

"For Chrissake, you crazy or what!" Bernie's four-pack-a-day rasp exploded in my ear. "Look, I'm not heartless, I get it about Mike." He tried for a mitigating softness that would acknowledge my bereavement. It didn't quite work. Bernie was a man of one emotion at a time. I understood that. I wasn't too different myself. "He was a great guy, okay? But work's the best thing for you now. Hey, you can't bring him back."

"It's not a question of that." I closed my eyes and concentrated on distancing myself, trying to make it easier to relinquish a prize I'd worked feverishly to win. "I have urgent family business in New York," I said tonelessly.

"Not as urgent as this! You realize how many years you lost after you pulled that stunt on DeRenkin? No one would touch you. Remember?" I remembered. "But *I* took a chance on you, didn't I? Old Bernie took one look at that face, those cat eyes, the bones, and said to himself, 'This one's on the money.' You even got some talent—not that it matters that much."

I gritted my teeth and didn't let a word out. At that moment, I was terrified that if I did, the word would be "yes." And Mike would've died for nothing.

"Look, Silver, I nursed you along here for ten years, got you the dribs and drabs, the Norwegian plays in Seattle, the TV bits. Know what my commissions were? *Bupkis.*" True, I acknowledged to myself with a twinge of guilt. "So I finally got you back in the movies." Lie! Nadia Gregoriu did. The director of *Running Fast* was her old friend and former student. Bernie overstepping, grabbing undeserved credit, had an oddly tonic effect on me. My moment of wavering was over.

"No, Bernie. I'm going to have to pass it up."

"This is Spielberg, cookie. *Spielberg.* Got it? If you're too dumb to know what's good for you, think of me. You owe me, babe—big time."

"I understand how you feel, and—"

"The *hell* you do! You are one crazy pain in the ass. You know that? Two zillion broads woulda kissed the ground for the chance you had when you were twenty. A DeRenkin movie, for Chrissake. But no, he *offended* the great lady and she kicked him in the balls." I clenched my jaw. Even now the memory smarted. "Some great lady. A little *pisher* is all you are—still are. You're gonna spend the rest of your life in plays by dead Norwegians! What do I need you for? Answer me that."

But he didn't wait for an answer. He hung up.

I poured myself a refill of cold coffee and took it over to Mike's big tan chair. He'd been dead less than a week, yet with his vibrance gone, everything in the house seemed petrified and covered with the dust of disuse, as though nobody'd lived here for a very long time. My eyes went from object to object, dully surprised that Mike could be dead with his running shoes sitting by the door, laces pulled loose, set to slip into; *Newsweek* lying on the coffee table, opened to the article he was reading; Frank Sinatra discs stacked on top of the CD player, ready to slip in.

I drank the coffee, feeling sick.

Florio Trucking was located west of L.A., where rents are cheap. I didn't go there much, but from time to time I'd drop by, and when I did, I enjoyed the insider feeling of listening to the driver chat—shoptalk, quips, rough jokes, banter between the guys and Lucy Caspar, Mike's secretary, who also served as a kind of Wendy to this small tribe of lost boys. But Mike had been neither boy nor Peter Pan. He'd enjoyed to the fullest the perks of being a grown-up.

When I arrived, Hank, the only driver not out on the road, was resting his huge rump on the radiator in Mike's office talking with Lucy, who was bent over Mike's desk going through a stack of papers. Her task probably would've been easier if she'd just sat down in his chair, but I was glad she hadn't.

We looked at one another for a beat. I'd seen Hank yesterday at the funeral, but not Lucy. She'd been too distraught to come up to San Francisco. She was calmer today, but her long, wise, rabbit face was blotched with red and her pale blue eyes small and moist under swollen pink lids.

She and I embraced silently, two tall, thin women, fused for a second by the current of mutual grief flowing back and forth between them.

Hank broke the silence. "Hey, Emily," he said softly. His voice was surprisingly light for his size.

"Hey, Hank." I walked over and kissed him on the cheek. There aren't many men I have to stand on tiptoe to reach, but Hank Maston was six six, and wide as a sequoia. He'd been one of six men to carry Mike's coffin, but as I'd watched them proceed down the church aisle, it almost seemed that Hank was bearing the burden alone, his dark, almost black, face dulled with isolated sorrow.

Hank had been a tight end for the Rams. After a season and a half, he'd racked up his knee and spent the next six years trying to bury his outrage with the help of various substances, some of them illegal. He'd almost buried himself instead. Two years ago, he'd quit all of it and come to work for Mike. They'd gotten very close—not in the way of spending great stretches of time together, but in the way of understanding and trust. Mike's will stated that Hank and Jerry Staleigh, both of whom had been with him since the beginning, jointly were to be able to buy the business from me according to some lawyer-accountant formula.

"I guess we ought to talk about what happens next with this place," Hank said.

"Not necessary. Why don't you just keep on truckin'," I said, attempting a smile. "It's going to be your shop, anyway—yours and Jerry's—as soon as Bondino and Mike's Aunt Clara get the estate sorted out. I called Bondino this morning and told him to get papers ready so that I can give you authority to write checks and things. I'll sign them before I leave."

"Leave?" Lucy asked.

"I'm going to New York. I . . . I might be gone a long time."

"Well, maybe you got a point, Emily," Hank said, his face making clear that he didn't think so. "But you can't run fast enough to lose grief. I tried it, and I bet I run a lot faster than you do."

I shrugged. Better to let them think what they were thinking, that I was looking for a change of scene as a quick feel-better fix. "Either of you ever hear Mike mention someone named Dev?" I asked neutrally.

Hank shook his head. "You asked me that yesterday. What's up?"

Before I could construct an answer, Lucy chimed in. "I think so," she said, her forehead furrowing. "Just a second." She pulled out the pencil she habitually carried stuck into her wispy bun of hair and started flipping through a pad on the desk. "Yes. I thought I recognized the name. He called a couple of times last week."

I moved in quickly in my eagerness. "Where? Let me see." Too quickly. A suspicious look crossed Hank's broad features, but he didn't say anything.

I forced myself to damp down. "Something personal," I explained lamely, "an old friend. Mike would want him to know about . . . what happened. The cops have been here, I guess."

"Four times," Lucy said. "Been through every piece of paper in this office. Left an awful mess. Wanted to know about back-and-forths with the union—certainly enough of those—and relationships with other truckers."

"Also wanted to know if Jerry and me were in a rush to have our own business," Hank said with a bitter smile. "Enough of a rush to do Mike."

I made a face. "For God's sake, that's ridiculous!"

"No, it's not," Hank said mildly. "Not true, but not ridiculous. Folks kill for a lot less reason. Anyway, I was in Vegas when it happened, and Jerry, he's just a shrimp. Mike woulda broke him in half."

"I need this Dev's phone number, Lucy."

"I don't have it, Emily. He never left a number. Said Mike knew it." Shit!

"Then it'll be in the Rolodex, right?"

It wasn't. No Dev. No Devlin, last name or first. This was a setback and a half. Stupid. *Stupid!* How could I have not gotten the goddamned *name* from Mike? Because you didn't know he was going to get killed, that's why. I went through the Rolo, card by card, and copied every 212 number on it, no matter what the name. There were seven in all.

I told Hank and Lucy I'd keep in touch and to leave a message on my home phone with Dev's number, if he called.

Hank, who'd silently monitored my research, fixed me with skeptical eyes.

"So you're going to New York to deliver the news in person to this guy you don't even know his name?"

"Mike would want me to," I said in a tone suitably firm for lying. If Mike's ghost were corporeal for five minutes, its single act would be to chain me to the bedpost rather than let me track this one more step.

"Watch your ass, Emily," Hank said, taking my hand between his mitt-sized ones. "And holler if you need help."

I took Mike's gun out of his top dresser drawer and held it in firing position, two-handed, just the way he'd taught me. "You're alone here some nights, Rock, you never know." No, you never do. I tightened my grip for just a second and let out a deep breath I wasn't aware I'd taken. Then I put the gun back under the socks. No way I'd ever get it on the plane. After one more unsuccessful search around the house for Dev's number, I packed.

Trip and Anthony took me for a hamburger and deposited me at LAX in time for the 9:30 United flight to JFK. I was relieved that both of them were there. That way we could keep the conversation trained on movies, laugh a little, not get into why I was going to New York, except that it was something important I had promised Mike I'd take care of. I didn't mention the turned-down Spielberg opportunity. If I had, Mike's ghost wouldn't have needed to bother chaining me to the bed—Trip would've tackled me and done it himself.

We did have a few minutes alone together when Anthony went off to the men's room. "You know, E.S.," Trip said, his face losing its smile of a moment earlier, "I'm not deaf. I'm not stupid. And I am worried about you."

"Sure you are, Triplet, I'd be worried about you, too."

My attempt to gloss over wasn't working. "That's not what I mean and you know it. You're acting weird in a different way. I heard you stonewall Aunt Clara at the funeral, and the last few days, you've been walking around like Hamlet stalking his stepfather. I haven't pushed, but you want to talk to me?"

"No," I said quietly. If I'd been able to talk to anyone, he'd have been it. I wanted to let him know that, but I couldn't think of any way to do it that wouldn't make things worse.

CHAPTER
FOUR

BIG, anonymous, and not glitzy or expensive, I told the cabdriver. He took me to the Ramada, right across the street from Madison Square Garden. The fluted columns that flanked the door were a vestige of its grander origins in the twenties or thirties. So was the elegantly engraved sign proclaiming its original name, the Pennsylvania Hotel. It used to be called something else when I lived here, but I couldn't remember what.

Though I was numb-faced and a bit queasy after the sleepless all-night flight, I felt exhilarated. I was here now, ready to start. A nut on a suicide mission, you might say, but why not? I had as powerful a motive as any zealot commando or kamikaze. My country had been invaded— twice. I may have been a laughably inadequate avenger, but I was the only one around.

I felt a sense of sharpened reality, a consciousness of every move I made, heightened by danger, by the possibility I was under enemy surveillance. Did the voice yet know I was here? Had my phone been tapped? Was the secret force of agents tracking me? I wasn't afraid. I didn't much care what happened to me. I just didn't want it to happen before I'd found my nemesis, finally looked in its face—and killed it.

New York seemed surprisingly the same as when I'd left, except for the man who tried to wash the windshield when the cab stopped for a light and the ones who just knocked on the driver's window and stretched out their hands. They were new, as they were in L.A.—but there were more of them here and they looked sadder, maybe because it was cold. The driver and I doled out a couple of contributions. "Don't do no good, you know," he shrugged at me. "I know," I said.

I settled into my institutional-beige plastic hotel room, stretched out on the slightly concave mattress, and thought about what to do next. It had occurred to me that Dev might be just as dead as Mike by now. But I didn't want to believe it, so for the moment I chose not to. I had to know what he'd uncovered. Otherwise, my chances were cut to almost zero. I had no starting place, so I'd be playing blindman's buff and would certainly make disastrous blunders. What the hell was the mystery about him anyway? It wasn't as though Mike had made a secret of his identity. I just hadn't asked. So why wasn't he in the Rolo? I flashed a mental snapshot of a double-0-something type with a limp, his collar turned up and a copy of the *Paris Trib* under his arm.

I reached for the phone and checked in with the answering machine at home. No message from Dev. I dialed the first of the New York numbers on Mike's list. Twenty minutes later, I'd finished the calls with disappointing results. "Dave who? I think you have the wrong number." When I asked for Mr. Devlin, that rang no bells either. I reached three individuals, two answering machines, a law firm, and a stock brokerage. In each case, I said I had news of a family emergency. I didn't mention Mike's name. Why, I wasn't exactly sure—instinct just said not to. I left my name and number with the law firm and the brokerage, both of which promised to check their files of former employees and get back to me. Right—and pigs have wings. I'd call them both later, and the two answering machines that night. If they were all dead ends, I'd start on the column and a half of Devlins in the Manhattan phone book. My last resort, I guessed, would have to be the police, who could at least tell me whether anyone named Devlin, or something close to it, had been killed during the past five days.

I unzipped the bag I'd brought and hung up the stuff that needed hanging up. I hadn't brought much. I didn't share Trip's passion for clothes, and anyway, Angelenos don't tend to own a lot that's suitable for February in New York. I'd shivered in my cotton trench coat while waiting in the taxi line at Kennedy. Absurd, but the great detective's first assignment was going to have to be shopping.

I stripped and got into the shower—always a secure, safe spot for me. I'd discovered the bathroom as an ideal refuge when I was growing up in my grandmother's house. No, even before that—in the little Chelsea duplex where I lived with my parents.

My father was a playwright and my mother an actress. They laughed and they hugged sometimes and they argued passionately about the theater with the changing stream of friends who came and went. They also fought. He drank and she pretended everything was fine, until she couldn't. Then she'd explode and he would, too. Sometimes, I'd hear the door slam, which meant he'd gone out. *Bastard, bitch, failure, lunatic.* I'd learned the words unwillingly, and too young—along with others, harder to grasp: *philanderer, castrater, remittance man.*

But I adored my father. Drunk or sober, he was one of those magic people who make everything more fun than it ought to be, every trip to the grocery or walk to school an adventure. He wasn't especially handsome—medium height; horn-rimmed glasses; curly red-gold hair, inherited, like his poor eyesight, from his mother. But he had something more powerful than looks: a kind of incandescence, a way of focusing a beam of distilled delight on someone, and making that person feel like its source—fascinating and special and beloved.

Years later, I'd wondered if that quality came through in the plays he pounded out at the round oak dining table always too covered with papers to eat off. I remembered being taken to see several in narrow Greenwich Village basements, but the only thing I recalled about them was my mother, striding confidently around the stage, her slightly smoky voice making every word sound important.

What I remembered most about my mother was how talented she was. That and the nervous tension that seemed to color her every offstage move. I'd taken her maiden name, Silver, when I moved to California—maybe hoping that I'd be as good an actress, or maybe just needing to stop being Emily Otis. At unpredictable times, her reflection looked at me in a mirror, or her voice came out of my mouth. I don't mean a mere resemblance. I knew from the newspaper photos that we looked alike. But occasionally, it was Celia in the mirror, Celia talking. And when it happened, it jarred me. But the kinds of specific memories I had of my father eluded me where she was concerned. All I could summon up was a strong sense of discomfort, laced heavily with guilt.

The ring of a telephone interrupted my shower reverie. I dashed, dripping, to catch it, realizing only as I picked it up that nobody but the people I'd just placed calls to knew where to reach me. "Emily Silver," I announced tensely into the receiver. A brief pause, followed by the sharp click of a hang-up.

I bashed my forehead with my fist hard enough to hurt, and sat down, still wet and naked, on the bed to make all the calls again. The two machines still answered and none of the other seven admitted to having made the call. My scalp tingled. Okay, it's in motion. Good.

I towel-dried my hair, put a little cherry-flavored gloss on my chapped lips, and pulled on jeans, a sweater, and a pair of cowboy boots. Then I belted my inadequate trench tight and headed, hands balled up in my pockets, for Macy's, only a block away. Every few steps, I caught

myself turning around surreptitiously to check whether anyone seemed to be following me. By the time I reached "The
Biggest Store in the World" I was feeling foolish and inept.
I had no damned training in what I was trying to do, except
watching suspense movies, and so I was aping somebody in
one of them. It played better on the screen.

Fortunately, Macy's wasn't big on sales help eager to show
me "fabulous pieces." I just grabbed at what looked likely,
and quickly acquired a couple of skirts and sweaters, black
tights and pumps, a long pearl-gray overcoat, a soft wine-
and-black-striped wool scarf, and fur-lined black leather
gloves. I wore the new stuff out of the store and returned
to the hotel. No messages—not in New York, not in L.A.
But I hadn't really expected any.

I had to give it till tomorrow to see if any of my phone
messages reached Dev, before I called the police or even
tried to trace my parents' old friends. That left my grandmother as the only logical place to start now. My eyes
blinked shut, trying to overcome a wave of . . . what? Fear?
Stop being an ass, Emily. You say you're not afraid to die,
but you're afraid of *her?* Talk sense!

Cordelia Tucker Otis. I'd barely known the woman when
she came to the hospital to collect me the day after my
parents' death. Once a year, on Christmas morning, the
ritual: Starting when I was three or four, MacNiff, her
chauffeur, would pick me up in her long black car and take
me to her big limestone house on East Sixty-sixth Street.
There I'd joylessly exchange a flat box of hand-rolled han-
kies, which she probably didn't use, for a pair of hand-
smocked dresses, which I never wore except on Christmas
mornings. Then I'd have to eat poached eggs with gucky
sauce, prepared by Mrs. MacNiff, her housekeeper, and
try not to look as eager as I felt to get home and begin real
Christmas.

I went along with it all on best behavior, because my
father let me know it was important to him. "We're counting
on you, Goose Girl," he'd say with that melting, crinkly

smile of his. "You help bring home the bacon." I'd known very well what he meant, even at four. I'd heard my parents battle enough about money to understand that it was a severe problem; that my mother's temp work—temp so she could always be available to accept the acting assignments, which seldom came—couldn't completely support us; that my grandmother gave my father money, and we couldn't afford to offend her. I never questioned that my father did not have a "job job," as my mother did, but stayed home with me and his typewriter, filled ashtray to one side of it, filled tumbler of scotch to the other. I was just thrilled to have his company.

So when my grandmother appeared at the door of my room in St. Vincent's, her emphatic chin upthrust, her light-struck glasses obscuring her eyes, to tell me that I was well enough to leave what she disapprovingly called "this place" and come home with her, I knew for sure that my parents were truly dead, and that my life was over.

I was to be a prisoner in her dungeon, trapped amidst dark, polished wood, gleaming silver, sparkling crystal, and endless rules. I retaliated by becoming a nine-year-old des-perado—the chancier the caper, the better. I was most often caught and punished—at home, at school—but more than willing to risk that for the occasional, delicious satisfaction of getting away with it.

I began to dial her house, my finger balking at the very familiarity of the long-neglected number; I hadn't forgotten it. I slammed the phone down midway through. No, I wouldn't call. I'd go to the house, just show up—use the element of surprise as an edge. I'd need any edge I could find.

I walked east, rehearsing how I might approach her, adult to adult, in a way that wouldn't get the heavy, carved walnut door slammed in my face. Without quite thinking about it, I turned up Madison and within a few minutes found myself on Thirty-sixth Street in front of the Morgan Library. The old pirate's place was as gorgeous as ever, commanding the block as though it always had, always would. I stopped and looked and remembered. With almost no hesitation, I walked up the steps and became twelve years old again.

J. P. Morgan's library is a great deal larger than my grandmother's house and far more ornate, but after a sixth-grade school trip, the houses and their owners melded in my head. Over the next few months, I returned here often to wreak hidden revenge on both my cold, exacting grandmother and the canny swindler, twins in some way—powerful, unentitled possessors.

The East Room holds the journal of Sir Walter Scott, confiding his mortification at becoming suddenly bankrupt, his unbearable pain at visiting the home he loved and was about to lose. It had seemed to me an obscene violation— the greedy producer of nothing but money acquiring the private anguish of the writer and displaying it publicly, another prized trophy. Emily Otis teamed up with Sir Walter in a mission of sabotage: two captured artists fighting back.

Now I handed the woman my five dollars and made straight for the corridor right outside J.P.'s personal library, my heart beating unexpectedly hard. Was it still there? Yes! They'd polished over it, but I could see on the rich, dark wood paneling the ghost of my work—carved painstakingly, secretly, deeply with the sharp point of a nail, a seraphic smile on my face for each passing guard. *W.S. & E.O. hate you.* And repeated again, again, again—four times in all. I felt a surge of recalled criminal joy.

I jumped like a scalded cat at the touch on my shoulder and wheeled around, heart in my throat, head in the past. I'd finally been caught.

"Yes?" I said icily after a recovering second.

"Emily Silver?"

I didn't answer, just stared at the asker. He was slim, wiry. You could see that through the worn Burberry belted around him, collar turned up framing his face—a triangle

IN THE DARK · 45

ending in an improbably squared-off chin. Maybe five ten, maybe thirty-five, maybe older. Thick, straight black hair and brows, skin tinged with gold—not, I thought, from the sun. What were remarkable were the dark purple eyes, heavily fringed, and the mouth, wide, thin-lipped, as ascetic as the eyes were voluptuous. He took a step to the side and I could see a slight stiffness to the movement, an imbalance.

"My God, you *do* limp," I said before I realized the words were out of my mouth.

"Where'd you go to charm school?" he continued, his lips curling slightly.

"Sorry." I felt my cheeks burn red. "You are Dev, aren't you?"

"Only to a few people."

It took me a while to grasp that he'd followed me here, or to be able to think a straight thought of any kind as I stood there face-to-face with this man I'd come back to New York to find. I should've felt surpassingly relieved—and I did, in part. But I also felt exposed. This stranger knew things about my life I didn't know. Dangerous things. A shudder of unreasoning anger blindsided me. Why was Mike dead and this man alive?

"Why don't you fucking tell me what's going on here? Why did you just drop your bomb and disappear? Why the hell didn't you call? You followed me here. You goddamn *followed* me like some CIA spook!" I started out in a hissing whisper, which escaped my control and turned up its volume.

He held out his hand in a stop sign. "Quiet down. I've got some questions too." His tone was equable, but the set of the square chin truculent. "First off, why are you in New York? Mike said he wasn't going to let you come."

It dawned on me then that he didn't know, and the realization stopped me cold. "Mike is dead," I said quietly. "The police think it was the Teamsters."

He didn't say a word, or move—just looked straight at me. I felt my own frozen shock reprised as I watched his.

The purple eyes darkened to bottomless blackness as they stared into mine. But that could've been just a trick of the light.

"I've been in Toronto. I just got back this morning." He spoke calmly, tonelessly, his mouth not moving much. The words seemed to be coming from somewhere else.

Simultaneously we noticed the guard, a round-faced woman of indeterminate age, lingering near us. She ambled past reluctantly. A nugget of human drama on a slow day in a boring job wasn't to be ignored.

"Let's get out of here," Dev said, turning abruptly and striding toward the lobby. His stiff leg gave a defiant roll to his gait. I followed him, running to keep up.

CHAPTER
FIVE

"Where are we going?" I asked as I slid into the taxi seat beside him.

"My place." I waited a moment for him to say more, but he kept silent, his eyes trained on the scratched plastic divider, studying the back of the driver's head.

"Look, what did you find out that got Mike killed?" His silence refueled my anger. You might say I had no cause to be angry at him—this man who'd put his own life at risk for nothing but friendship. But anger was my accessible emotion for all tense occasions, hanging there ready for me to slip into, like a favorite, much worn sweater.

"Maybe nothing," he said absently. "I have got a request," he added, his tone taking on an edge that had nothing to do with requesting. "Be quiet and let me think for the length of this cab ride."

"But—" I stopped myself. Rein it in, for Christ's sake. Give him a little time to absorb Mike's death. You've had five days. He hasn't had five minutes. "My goombah," Mike had called him. *A mick, but my goombah.* So I let my urgent curiosity claw at the inside of my own skin, and watched downtown Manhattan go by through the grimy cab window.

All at once, we were on a bridge leaving Manhattan. I turned to him and risked speaking. "Where do you live, New Jersey or something?"

"You've been out west too long. Brooklyn."

"Brooklyn?" I don't know why I was so surprised.

"Uh-huh. Haven't you heard the rumors." A slight smile. "Life exists in seven-one-eight country."

Seven-one-eight country. Brooklyn. Maybe he'd been in Mike's Rolodex all along. I'd only looked for 212's.

The cab pulled into a wide, quiet street of old, fairly large houses, each distinctively different from its neighbors. It stopped in front of the third house from the corner. The scene looked as though it had been transplanted from nineteenth-century London—or at least from a movie about nineteenth-century London, which was as close as I'd ever gotten.

"Not very far outside of Manhattan," I said as he paid the driver.

"Here in Brooklyn Heights, we think of that the other way around."

He unlocked a bright-blue-painted door and I trailed him up four flights of darker-blue-carpeted stairs to his apartment. It wasn't an apartment really, more like a large loft, a bare-bones kitchen along one wall. Its ceiling followed the house's roofline—high peak in the center, sharply slanting eaves toward the sides. Arched front windows looked out on the East River; rear ones faced a garden.

The place looked unfinished somehow, as though someone were just finishing moving in or out, and it seemed even bigger for its uncarpeted, glossy pine floors and spare furnishings: well-worn dark blue sofa, Eames chair, double bed tucked in a corner under the eaves, long, low pine shelves jammed with books—old, new, tall, short, thick, thin. I had the idea that even a quick once-over would tell me something useful about this enigma called Dev, but from where I stood I couldn't see the titles.

The few small side tables were overwhelmed, their surfaces covered with books and papers, but a clunky, old electric typewriter sat forlorn on a big round oak dining table, not even a pad or pen to keep it company.

"My father used to write at a table like that," I said, my lips stiff as they formed the unaccustomed words, "but you couldn't even *see* the top of his table." Ordinarily I'd've kept such an observation to myself. Volunteering information about my family was something I never did, but this was a trivial scrap compared to what he already knew.

A flicker of something crossed his face, but I couldn't make it out. "Plays, I know. Any of them get produced?"

"Not many. Not anyplace important. Look, will you *tell* me what the hell it is you found out?"

"Not now," he said, tone clipped, face dismissively closed.

That did it. "You listen to me, mystery man! You've got no right to dangle me like you're doing. This *thing* killed Mike. I know he was your friend, but he was more than that to me. And I'm going to get even—with you or without you, so you may as well—"

"No. You listen to *me*, actress." His voice remained level, but it was iced with contempt. "I don't know that 'this thing' killed him, and you don't either. So we are starting from scratch here—*mutatis mutandis*. As your L.A. police recognize, Mike was not in a gentle business."

"You are one supercilious son of a bitch, aren't you? My boarding school Latin may be rusty, but I don't believe that all other things *are* equal. I don't buy this particular coincidence, do you—really?"

"Coincidences happen."

"Why don't you just admit it? You blame me for Mike's death. That's why you're so hostile. Well, I'll tell you something. I blame me too."

He shook his head slowly. "That's vanity speaking. It's self-indulgent. More important, it's a waste of time. We'll do this my way or not at all. So sit yourself down or leave." He hadn't raised his voice—not at the Morgan, not now. I wondered whether he ever did. Maybe he didn't have to, I thought enviously.

I took a deep breath and let it out slowly. He was holding all the cards, so I guessed we'd do it his way. I slipped off my coat, put myself on the sofa, and waited.

"You drink coffee?"

"Sure. Black, no sugar," I said. "Got anything to eat?" It came through to me all at once that I was ravenous. Possibly it was just nerves, but the last food I'd had was an oversweet, stone-cold Danish on the plane.

He constructed coffee in a Japanese electric drip and came up with a jar of chunky peanut butter and some crackers, which he served me with a "Sorry about that" and an almost smile. He took his own coffee and a large yellow pad and pen over to the Eames chair, where he sat, coffee mug perched on the stacked papers on the table beside him, pen uncapped and poised over the pad.

"I feel like I'm in a shrink's office. Am I supposed to say something momentous? You know everything I told Mike— the shots, the voice, how it came downstairs looking for me. You've seen the clippings. That's it. I was nine years old. I don't know anything else. Nothing relevant." I vented my frustration on a peanut butter cracker and washed it down with some coffee, which revealed the first thing about Dev I liked so far: he made good coffee.

"Nine-year-olds can't judge relevance," he pointed out mildly. "Why don't you stop parrying me, Emily? I know something about what a tough time you had. But you're going to have to dig some now—and it's going to hurt. You can holler ouch when you have to, but quit being a prima donna."

The reprimand hit its mark and stung, but I knew he wasn't wrong. "All right. Where do we start?"

"When you woke up in the hospital, Mike said a cop was there." I nodded. "Did he tell you his name?"

"No. But I remember what he looked like. Squashed kind of nose, freckles, thin, rusty hair. I suppose he'd be bald by now."

"If he's still alive. How old?"

That was a tough one. To a kid, a grown-up is a grown-up. Thirty-five and fifty look pretty much the same. "Maybe about my father's age, maybe a little younger."

"He the only one? Did you talk to any other cops?"

"Not then. Not right after. Not till I started making a pest of myself with the police a few years later. But I never saw that one again. I asked for him, described him, but they didn't seem to know who I meant."

"Uh-*huh*."

"What? Are you onto something connected with that?" My pulse began to race.

"Cool it. We're never going to get anywhere if you jump that way every time I ask you something. Tell me about your parents' friends. Did the two of them have the same friends? Different ones?"

"Some of them, some not," I said, swallowing the impatience bubbling in my throat. I figured I knew where he was going with this question. Two of the friends had talked to the papers: "FRIENDS DOUBT POLICE." Nick Kennoyer, composer, "Tuck was a great talent. I scored his last play, you know, *Falling Snow*. He was no killer, he was a lover. He radiated love. Sure he drank, but he couldn't have done this." Irene Cheyney, actress, "I'm devastated, simply devastated. Celia Silver was a fine actress, a wonderful wife and mother. I don't believe what the police say. Not at all." I knew the quotes by heart. I remembered equally well Lieutenant Edward Fitzsimmons's quote, "We understand that friends are shocked and upset, but we have to go with the evidence we've got."

"I tried to get to Irene and Nick," I said. I thought if they went with me, maybe the police would listen about the voice and start to do something. But her phone was disconnected. I went to where she lived, but the superintendent said she'd moved. I never found Nick. I had no idea where he lived and his number wasn't in the book. I called a couple of other friends—the few whose last names I even knew—but they didn't want to get involved, just gave me pious stuff about how we all have to go on with our lives." I held my hands out in futility.

"So I went to see Lieutenant Edward Fitzsimmons on my own. He patted me on the head and told me to be a good, brave girl and concentrate on my schoolwork. That was the first time. The second time, he said I'd be a lot smarter if I'd just put all this behind me. The third time, he called my grandmother, and she grounded me for a month."

"Yeah," Dev said, "well, Fitzsimmons is kind of beside the point now. He died of a heart attack two years ago." He reached over and took a healthy slug of his coffee. "The papers said the gun was in your father's hand and the wounds were consistent with the murder/suicide."

"I don't give a fuck what they said. *That's not the way it happened!* I'm sorry," I mumbled after a second. "I don't mean to be a prima donna."

For the first time, Dev's smile reached up as far as his eyes. "I told you it was okay to holler ouch." Then the smile was gone. "Let's talk about the voice. You heard it in the back of a movie house a couple of weeks ago. Why are you so sure it was the same voice? Twenty years is a long time, and as you point out yourself, you were only nine. An imaginative, terrified nine-year-old. Would you call yourself a reliable witness?"

"You sound like my grandmother, only she said *'fanciful* child.' I pleaded with her to believe me—to tell the police. 'You're a fanciful child, Emily. That is what I would have to tell them.' "

"Good imitation. But then, you are an actress."

"You know my grandmother?"

"No, but I heard her speak once at some benefit I got dragged to. Emily"—his voice turned gentler—"have you ever really considered, despite what you think of her, that your grandmother might be right?"

"She isn't right," I said, giving equal, flat weight to each word. I clenched my fists in my lap, restraining my impulse to jump into battle. I had to convince him that I wasn't a fanciful child, grown up. "I have a thing for voices," I said, speaking the truth but sounding shaky, nervous about what was at stake if he didn't believe me. "A special talent. I've always had it. When I first got to Hollywood, way before I ever met Mike, I supported myself for a while doing Bette, Marilyn, Joan, and the like at parties and little clubs." All at once, my forced composure left. "I'm not a nut! I *heard* that voice—that night and for twenty years of goddamned vivid dreams. It is not possible that I would forget it. Ever."

"Could you do it?"

"Could I do what?"

"Do the voice for me. Imitate it. Make me hear it."

I played it in my head—the foggy, velvet hoarseness of it. I had it there, but could I really reproduce it? I'd tried it only once—for my grandmother, years ago, when I was begging her to believe me. Before I'd gotten three words out, she whacked my face into silence. Now I felt the sweat break out on my scalp and neck. "I'll try."

He held his hand up. "Wait a second." He went over to the bookcase and got a tape recorder, which he put on the low table in front of me, next to my chilling coffee. He flipped it on. "Okay. Be the voice," he whispered. "Say what you heard it say."

I shut my eyes and drew the scene in my head. My heart seemed to expand and block my air passage. I didn't know whether any sound could come out of me. *"Oh Jesus, the kid!* Wait a minute, that's not right—too harsh. *Oh Jesus, the kid! Where's the kid? Emily. Emm-i-lyy!"* My hands shook, and my knees. I felt the burn of the peanut butter crackers at the back of my throat. I made myself open my eyes. Somehow, he knew not to touch me.

"Is that the way it was?" he asked after I had no idea how long.

"Yes." I concentrated on regular breathing.

"Good. You have any feeling at all whether it was a man or a woman?"

"No."

"Ready to go on?"

No. No, I wasn't. I needed . . . I didn't know what I needed.

"What are you?" I asked shakily. "A private detective or what? And how did you know where to find me?"

"I think 'or what' about covers me," he said. "Right now, I'm an investigator for a law firm. The work has its ebbs and flows, but then so do I. Mike got me the job, as a matter of fact." I saw the pain in his face as he said Mike's name. It reminded me we were on the same side. "I happened to be walking into the office when you called."

"Brighton, Davis? But the woman I spoke to said you didn't work there. No Dev anything or anything Devlin, she said. What *is* your name, anyway?"

"Paul Hannagan." He took in my puzzled look. "Paul *Eamon De Valera* Hannagan," he added with a mocking twist of that oddly expressive mouth.

"Eamon De Valera. Irish patriot, right?"

"Boarding school history? I'm impressed. He was called Dev by disciples—and would-be disciples in American bars."

"Your father one of those?"

"Yeah." I watched his mouth tighten. "Left me with two souvenirs. The name was one."

"What was the other?"

"Recess is over," he said, heading for the kitchen. "Want some hot coffee?"

"Sure."

After he settled himself back in his chair with fresh coffee and a fresh page turned over in his pad, he looked at me neutrally. "What did the voice say this time, at the movies?"

"I heard only snatches of the conversation. The other person must've said things too, but I didn't hear that at all. I was so knocked out, you see, hearing the voice again, not being prepared, I . . ."

He held up a hand. "Easy now. I know you're not a human tape recorder. Just tell me what you heard—what you remember."

"I remember exactly what it said." It came out irritated. Was he implying my memory might be faulty? Then maybe he didn't quite believe me about twenty years ago either. Now stop it, I told myself sternly. He's all you've got. Don't fuck it up! "The words I caught—I know they don't add up to anything, but—" I took a deep breath. "It said, '. . . old-fashioned, like Mother.' Then some loud stuff came on the screen for a couple of minutes. After it quieted down, the voice said, '. . . wouldn't alter . . . just plain chance . . . we'll see what happens next chapter.' That's it."

He scribbled on his pad. "We'll see what happens next chapter?"

"Uh-huh."

"Tell me about these friends, the ones you couldn't find."

"I remember Irene very well. She was my mother's best friend. She was very pale, ethereal-looking, with a clear bell kind of voice."

"What about Nick Kennoyer?"

"That's the weird thing—I really don't remember him at all. I was surprised that he was the one to speak out. He couldn't have been anything like as close as he sounded in those news stories."

"Maybe he wasn't. People in your business have been known to look for ways to get their names in the papers." I watched his face shift gears. "Tell me about your grandmother."

"You already know something about her. You saw her speak at a benefit. You read the papers. The hospital board, the library, the museum. The grande dame of New York philanthropy—makes everybody else seem lazy and inefficient. In a different time and place she'd've been president by now."

"That's it?"

"No." I dropped my eyes to my lap. "She terrifies me," I admitted. "Still does."

"In what way. She beat you?"

"No. Well, not really. Just twice she got furious and slapped me hard. Otherwise, just whack, whack, whack on the behind with a ruler, but that was kind of ceremonial, and I guess I earned it. I . . . I wasn't a very easy kid. No, it was the way she spoke, moved, looked at you. The absolute command. If you defied it, it was like defying God. You just waited for the lightning to strike you. The fateful lightning of the terrible swift sword. You know?"

He could have nodded a perfunctory uh-huh, but he didn't. Just looked at me as though making up his mind about something. "No," he said after a moment. "I don't know. I've never felt that way about anybody—not even about God. Especially not about God. But you *did* defy her, didn't you?"

"Oh yeah. I specialized in it. Short of becoming a junkie or a hooker, I did every rotten kid thing I could think of— almost got expelled from Chapin three times in five years. Would've except that I was her granddaughter. Snotting at teachers, cutting classes, smoking in the john. I liked it better at prep school—Fletcher. It got me away from her. My major accomplishments there included sneaking out to sleep with boys, getting mellow on grass, and organizing protests. I used to think that I did it all for the high of getting away with it, which happened occasionally, but now I'm not sure. Maybe it was really all about getting caught, punished."

He grinned. "And maybe you've been reading too many pop psych books." Not true, but I surprised myself by grinning back. "You said she didn't believe you about what you heard the night of the murder," he said, changing pace again, his eyes narrowing. "Why was she so eager to accept that her son was a killer? Most mothers would grab onto a third-person possibility."

"Right, but she's not most mothers. I threw that at her when I was pleading with her to make the police do something. Didn't move her half an inch. She just got white in the face. I thought she was going to slap me, but she didn't—not that time. 'My son killed your mother and himself. That is all there is to it.' Then she skewered me with those ice eyes. 'We shall *never* speak of this again.' We didn't. Even when Fitzsimmons called and complained that I was bothering the police, she just doled out the punishment and warned me to stop."

"The papers called him 'the estranged son of socialite Cordelia Tucker Otis.' Why were they estranged?"

"I don't know. Oh, I guess I do. Because he was an unsuccessful playwright who drank. Because he married a Jew. Because her only child—Samuel Tucker's grandson—wouldn't carry on the family tradition, go to law school, join the firm like he was supposed to. They weren't totally estranged. He'd go see Gem by himself from time to time. Maybe that's when she'd give him money. My mother never went there with him, and they'd always have fights when he came home."

"Gem?"

"That's what I started to call her after I came to live there. 'Grandmother' was a mouthful to keep saying, so I shortened it to 'G.M.' After a while, it sort of became 'Gem.' " The name sounded odd to my ears. I hadn't uttered it in a very long time.

"What happened to 'Gandma'?"

"She wasn't the 'Grandma' type."

"So you think she was an anti-Semite?"

"Maybe. I don't know. Oh, it was nothing obvious, but she acted as if my mother didn't exist. I noticed it even when I was a kid. On Christmas mornings, when my parents were still alive, I got sent by myself to visit her. I used to bring up my mother, purposely, just to see. And each time, Gem would get this funny look on her face. After I got a little older, I started to wonder whether . . ." I held my hands out to complete the sentence.

"*You're* half a Jew. The more important half, I understand. She took you in, brought you up."

"Believe me, she wishes she hadn't."

"Would it surprise you to know that your grandmother's contributed a couple of hundred thou to the UJA and fifty to the Holocaust memorial?" he asked casually.

It did, but I felt my barbed wire go up. "So? She gives

to lots of things. It's tax-deductible." I knew it was stupid as it came out of my mouth. I just couldn't help it.

"Uh-huh." He nodded noncommittally. "When was the last time you spoke to her?"

"June seventh, 1981," I said unhesitatingly. "Want to know the time? Three-seventeen p.m." I felt my chin rise in challenge.

"Forty years and a half after Pearl Harbor—give or take a few hours. What started *your* war?"

"Oh, we were well into our war, Cordelia Tucker Otis and I. This was the final battle. A group of teenaged activists captured the law offices of her precious father, the late, great Samuel Tucker, and occupied them."

"Ah, that was it! I remember reading about it. Seemed a bit out of joint with the times, I thought."

"Is that what you thought?" I felt the blood rise to my cheeks.

"Among other things."

"What? That it was pathetic and stupid in the 'gimme' eighties for a pack of eighteen-year-olds to object to this big, fat law firm fattening its bank account by helping murderers get away with it?" Eleven years evaporated for me, and the fury I'd felt back then surfaced, fresh and hot.

"No, that a bunch of prep school kids were more interested in having a collective tantrum than in reading the Constitution, which gives even automobile manufacturers the right to legal—"

"Those fucking cars were death traps! They—"

"—counsel when someone claims their cars malfunctioned," he overrode, not with volume but with the piercing insistence of a practiced trial lawyer. Noticing his technique brought me back to the present with a thump and cooled me down.

"But that was in another country, and besides, the wench is dead." I turned away, took a sip of coffee, and slathered a cracker with peanut butter.

"I doubt it." He smiled. "Want to know what else I thought?"

"I suspect I'm going to hear it whether I want to or not."

"I thought that Tucker's great-granddaughter, who, as the papers noted, 'organized and led the invasion,' piggy-backed a whole nother agenda onto this and probably ought to have her ass kicked pretty thoroughly."

"Who better than Tucker's great-granddaughter to stand up for the family honor? I'm not backing off the principle. I know there's a right to legal defense. There's *also* the right of people to protest. First Amendment."

"Why didn't you all take some cash from your little trust funds and fly to Detroit to protest?" he teased.

"We should have, but . . ." I broke off. "Look, you want me to say I was giving my grandmother the finger? Right. I was. But I also believed—"

"I know, I know—in the principle. So that episode sent you packing to Hollywood?"

"Yeah. I'd just graduated. I didn't really want to go to Vassar anyway. I certainly didn't want to become Miss Otis, debutante. And Gem and I—well, we couldn't stand the sight of each other. Can you believe she told the cops to go ahead and use tear gas, nightsticks, anything—just to get us out?"

"Talking of rights, that was hers, but I don't remember reading about the police using any force."

"You didn't. She gave that instruction over a bullhorn in her inimitable style, along with some other choice bits. By the time she was finished, my fellow protesters were ready to slink off and go home. She never said a word to me until everyone else had gone—kids, reporters, cops—then she walked over and just stared. She had a look on her face I'd never seen before. Just blank. 'You have not been worth it,' she said. Those were the last words she ever spoke to me. I happened to see the big wall clock—three-seventeen."

"Have you told her you're here in New York?"

"Not yet." Without warning, a serious yawn crept up on me. "Sorry, not the company," I mumbled. "I was on my way to see her when you turned up at the Morgan."

"Prodigal granddaughter seeks family reunion? Or do you think she has any information you don't?"

"The second—maybe. If she does, I thought the surprise might . . ." Another yawn.

". . . no doubt delight her into cooperating." He hauled himself out of his chair and repositioned the sofa cushion to do head pillow duty. "Why don't you lie down and cork off for a while?"

"But we have to—"

"Nothing's going to change in an hour or two." I was dubious. My eyelids weren't. "Come on." He patted the cushion as though coaxing a stubborn child.

I kicked off my shoes and lay down. I remember wishing I had a blanket and then feeling one float down and cover me. It was the last sensation I had before I fell off the edge into welcome oblivion.

CHAPTER
SIX

We sat facing each other, tucked into a dimly lit wooden booth in a bar that was neither chic nor amusingly funky. Just a bar that looked as though it'd always been there. No one else in booths, only the hard-core regulars drinking up front. It was after midnight.

I sipped my scotch and let myself enjoy the warmth as it went down. Dev took a long pull at his Guinness. His lips curled in a smile that said, "Well?"

I had slept a long time. When I finally woke up, he'd been ready to resume the interrogation, but I'd held out.

"I'm on strike, warden, but I'm offering you a deal. These are my conditions. Answer me a few questions and I'm yours to grill for the rest of the night. Also, I need food that isn't peanut butter."

He'd raised his straight, black brows and paused for a quick inner debate. "Come on, you get two questions and the best corned beef sandwich in Brooklyn."

So here we were at Castlebar on Pineapple Street. I got my mouth around the sandwich. Not easy, but well worth the trouble. Smoky, moist, mustard-slathered meat separated the slices of fresh rye bread by a good four inches.

I felt the pulse pound in my temples as I got ready to ask the question he'd evaded for the past twelve hours. "What did you find out?"

"It's what I *didn't* find out. The police records of the incident appear to be lost."

"Lost? You mean someone took them. Stole them?"

"Maybe. And maybe they're just lost."

"But that's—"

"Look, Emily. It's tempting to make assumptions, but your parents died before the place was computerized, and some clerk could've misfiled the sheet years later—under traffic accidents."

"Well, how about *people,* goddamn it! It was a pretty high-profile case. What about the cops who worked on it? I know you said Fitzsimmons was dead, but aren't some of the others still around?"

"Right. And that's what's ringing my chimes." The odd purple eyes gleamed brighter as the brows above them knit.

"What do you mean?" I leaned forward.

"Well, first person I went to see was Frank Strohmeyer. He's a lieutenant now, was a sergeant at the time—worked under Fitz. Figured I'd cut through a lot of red tape. I've dealt with Frank on a number of things for the law firm, and he's been a great help. No world-beater but a decent guy, bachelor, early fifties, almost thirty years in, getting ready to retire. We have a beer together from time to time.

"When I walked into his office, we talked hockey for a while. He's a big Rangers fan. He leaned back in his chair, had all the time in the world—until I got around to the reason I was there. All of a sudden, he's urgently busy and has to run. He did not look happy."

"How did he look?"

"Surprised. Shaken. So I backed off and tried it another way, through a sergeant I know—younger, wasn't around back then, but she's resourceful and determined, loves a challenge. She's helped me out before." He made a tent with his fingers. They were long, tapered, growing from blunt workman's hands—as odd together as his triangulated face and brashly squared chin. The man seemed built from incompatible pieces.

"And?" I prompted.

"At first, she was all gung ho to help out—said she'd work on it and get back to me the next day. I didn't hear from her. When I called a couple of days later: brush-off. She got very starchy about regulations and how busy she was. When I pressed her, she told me the file was missing. Now, normally, that would've just whetted her appetite to show me how smart she is. She'd have had two dozen ideas how to track the information. I asked her out to dinner. She's never refused before, but she did this time."

"Well, what are you trying to say? That a cop killed my parents and they're covering it up?"

"Did your parents know any cops?" he asked sharply.

"No. I don't think so. But we've all heard about rogue cops who go nuts, maybe break into places, hurt random people and . . ."

"And just happen to know that these random people have little girls named Emily sleeping downstairs."

I blew out a frustrated breath and took a sip of scotch. "Okay, Dev, what's your version?"

"I don't have a version yet, and neither do you. Anyway, I tried to take another crack at Strohmeyer, but he kept ducking me. Couldn't even get him on the phone. Finally, I went out to Little Neck where he lives and camped on his doorstep. He had to ask me in for a beer, but he obviously didn't want to. He warned me at the door, 'I'm not gonna discuss ancient history with you, so if that's all you're after we can save your time and my Heinekens.' "

"Well, what did you get him to tell you?"

"Not a thing. After about our fifth brew I gave it one more try. All I got was, 'Let it lay, Paul,' and I didn't much like the way he said it."

"So what next?"

He put his hands out, meaning nothing. "Before I pull any more tails at NYPD, I'd like to have some idea about why I'm pulling."

"What does he look like, Strohmeyer?"

"Not like the cop who questioned you in the hospital—

the baldish one with the freckles. No, Strohmeyer's got hair everyplace, head, hands, even ears. Little fireplug, strong as hell, neck about the size of most people's waists. Not the guy I'd choose to mess with. If I had a choice."

"You telling me you want out, Dev? Because if you do, that's fine. I'll just—"

"You'll just *nothing*." His face tensed, anger heating up his narrowed eyes. "You have no idea what to do or how to do it." He saw that I was readying to speak and cut me off before a sound came out. "Take a big bite of that sandwich, actress, and chew it while you listen. That'll give your mouth something more useful to do than blather when you don't know what you're saying."

"I don't get talked to like that."

"You just did. Mike Florio was not just my friend. He was a lot more. I owe him, and his death does not erase that marker. He asked me to do this. I started and I'm going to finish. And that has nothing to do with you. Understand? A lousy thing happened to you when you were nine. I'm sorry it did, but hot bulletin: Lots of kids have lousy things happen to them. They get beaten senseless and raped and killed—and they don't get the chance to almost be kicked out of Chapin and Fletcher." His voice was not loud, but it vibrated with a fury that I recognized very well. It reminded me of my own, and I sensed that, like mine, it had been in residence for a long time.

"You want to avenge Mom and Dad, avenge Mike, lay down your life, maybe—a Shakespearean gesture." His cartoon of the most important thing in my life flicked at the raw, but something in his eyes kept me from lashing back. "That's very dramatic and all, but from where I sit, it's just more vanity. You might very *well* lay down your life, but it would be for nothing—and it would fuck up what I'm trying to do." He paused and examined my face. "I said I wouldn't choose to mess with Strohmeyer, if I had a choice," he said quietly. "I don't have a choice."

My eyes locked into his. Without looking down, I picked

at half the sandwich, took the bite he'd told me to and chewed very slowly. I swallowed and waited another few seconds before speaking. I wasn't used to giving in, especially without a fight, but this was too important. "I need you, Dev," I said, "and you know that. But you need me, too. I knew my parents. You didn't. And I was *there*. I'll remember things, new things I don't remember now. I'll be able to put bits and pieces together. I can track down their friends. Some of them must still be around. Maybe I can even get something out of my grandmother. I'm not sure I can, but I'm sure you *can't*. Blood's not just thicker than water for her, it's the only thing that counts. Look, I won't fuck it up. I'll do what you tell me. Promise."

I felt the heat rush to my face as I looked at those purple eyes and willed them to believe me, to let me in. He kept calling it vanity, but it wasn't that. I'd vowed to see this through, and I wasn't going to turn it over to Dev or anyone else.

Finally, he stuck his hand across the table. I took it and we shook gravely without saying another word.

We finished food and drink in silence, each reluctant to tamper with the tenuous treaty we'd just negotiated.

"It's after two," he said at last, as he signaled for the check. "Should I put you in a cab, or do you want to sack out at my place?"

I didn't want to sack out anywhere. I wanted to ask questions, get answers, and that wasn't too likely to happen alone in my room at the Ramada. "Do you have a spare toothbrush?"

"And panty hose and bathrobe."

I raised my eyebrows in surprise. "What do you run, a women's shelter?"

"Something like that."

Our footsteps echoed on the pavement as we walked the five cemetery-silent blocks back to Pierrepont Terrace, where his house was. Brooklyn Heights was dead asleep. I liked the English village look and scale of it. So close to Manhattan, and yet foreign to me, about as foreign as the man walking beside me who lived here—the stranger I'd just promised to obey.

I was deep into my own thoughts while Dev unlocked the blue door and my feet followed his up the four flights. He turned his key in the lock, then hesitated.

"What's the matter?" I asked.

He fiddled with the key some more. "Sshh." He turned back to me and held a hand up, the instruction clear to stay put. He disappeared inside the apartment for a minute or two and then opened the door and motioned me inside. His face was puzzled. I glanced around. Everything looked the same to me as when we'd left.

"What's this about, Dev? You think someone's been here?"

"I know someone's been here," he said quietly. He walked over to his Eames chair and examined his notepads. Then he switched on the tape recorder, and I jumped as I heard, *"Oh, Jesus, the kid!"* I'd done a good job re-creating the voice—good enough to scare myself. He turned it off. "Sorry," he said absently.

"Did they . . . Did they take anything?" The back of my neck prickled with excitement. Action—I was ready for it.

"Don't think so."

"How do you know someone's been here?" Did you leave a piece of Scotch tape on the doorframe? A hair across the threshold?"

He laughed. "Nothing that esoteric, actress. I didn't double-lock the door when we left. Our guest did. He also rewound your tape for me."

"But—"

"Just sit down and don't talk for a minute or two while I have a look around. One thing about this place, not a lot of options if you want to hide a bug." I watched him search the apartment and dismantle and reassemble the phones with an efficiency born of experience. "Okay, unless it was the CIA or Feebs with really fancy equipment—which seems unlikely—I think we're clean," he pronounced after less than ten minutes.

"Has it occurred to you that they could come back and kill us, like they did Mike?"

He shrugged. "It's occurred to me that they could've done that last week, week before, if they wanted to. But they didn't."

"Then why did they kill Mike?"

He opened a cabinet door, took out a half-full bottle of Bushmill's, and poured himself a decent-sized shot in the bottom of a wide, squat glass. "Want some?" I nodded. He handed me a duplicate and we sat on opposite ends of the sofa. "I think Mike was doing some poking around of his own out there," he said, his tone casual, the sharpness in his eyes anything but.

I was shocked. The glass shook in my hand and I put it down on the table. "In California? Poking at *what?* Did Mike tell you that? Did he find something? Did—" *Why didn't he tell me?* Tears sprang unbidden to my eyes.

Dev's hand gripped my shoulder. "Easy," he said. "Don't do this to yourself. I don't know what track he was on, but he did think he had a lead."

I looked at him, amazed. "How could he have?" I asked, my voice reduced to an incredulous whisper.

"I hate to keep saying the same thing—I don't know. But we're going to have a shot at finding out. Here, take a sip of this stuff." He handed me the whiskey. "Now, here's what we're going to do. You'll call his secretary in the morning and tell her to Fed Ex you copies of his message slips starting the day after you heard the voice. Also, see if she remembers any calls, any meetings during that period that were out of the ordinary. I'll see about getting the phone company records. What about Mike's appointment book?"

"I don't know." It hadn't been among the things the police handed over to me. His watch—I felt it warm and solid on my own wrist where I'd strapped it the day after he died—wallet, pens, cash. "I guess he had it with him when . . ."

"Call LAPD tomorrow," he said tonelessly. "I doubt they'll have it though. Anyone who killed him would've taken the book—could've been something in it about the union, another trucker, you name it. Okay, make those calls. Ready for your next assignment?"

"Sure."

"Go see your grandmother, just like you planned. Maybe you *will* get something out of her, after all." His mouth stretched into a slow smile and the purple eyes went along for the ride. "Just remember to act like a lady. Now, drink up. We're going to bed."

He must've seen it in my face, the completely unexpected rush of pure desire that had sneaked up and blindsided me. "Separately," he said, looking a bit shaken himself—or was I just imagining that? He walked briefly over to a large closet near the bed and returned with a white terry robe. "Here. You get to use the bathroom first. You'll find a new toothbrush in the cabinet."

"Uh-huh." All at once I felt like giggling, and had to fight to keep a straight face. It was the first time I'd seen him really caught off base. It made him seem more human, just as his anger did. I wondered again where that smoldering anger had come from. "Where do I sleep?"

"The couch. I wouldn't want you to think I was chivalrous."

CHAPTER
SEVEN

MY ass edged out, exploring, questing for the warmth of a furry stomach to burrow into. Suddenly, I was falling, falling bewilderingly off the edge. I awoke with a cry as I hit the polished wood floor, sending the light coffee table skidding out in front of me. I lay there motionless for a long moment, listening to the sound of my own breath, sorting out where I was, letting it come through that I'd never again wake up nestled into Mike's warm maleness. Finally, I picked myself up and looked around. The bed under the eaves was empty and the bathroom door open. Dev was gone.

The note was lying on the coffee table.

I'll be back about five or six. Here are the keys, in case you get here first. Good luck with Cordelia Tucker Otis. Try to remember that no matter how big her eyes, ears, and teeth, she really is only your grandmother.

If you want to feel like a native, try the subway. The Lexington Ave. line, 4 or 5, will take you to the Upper East Side. You get the train at Court Street. These panty hose should fit.

I scratched my head, remembered last night, and felt ashamed of myself.

* * *

I'd lain on the blue sofa, unable to sleep, excitement juicing through me. I let my brain flea-hop from one thought to the next, hoping to distract my lower regions from their insistent throbbing. It didn't quite work. You're ridiculous, Emily, I told myself. Stop thinking with your cunt, goddamn it! The man you love is dead, remember? This one across the room is an angry, sarcastic stranger, who doesn't much like you. The only business you have with him is to track down the voice. Now *cut it out!* But I was disturbingly aware of his terry robe on my bare body, of the faint clean smell of shampoo and shaving lotion that clung to it.

I got up and padded over to his bed. He was fast asleep on his back, arms flung out on either side of him like a candidate for crucifixion. I touched the smooth, Indian-straight black hair that fell across his forehead. His deep, regular breathing continued undisturbed. I put my other hand inside the robe and pressed it against my crotch, which was beating like a wild heart. I shut my eyes and gave in to it for just a moment, before I forced my hand into a pocket and fled to the other side of the big room.

I snapped on a table lamp and knelt in front of the overstuffed bookshelves. Dickens, Thackeray, Eliot—George and T.S.—Joyce, James, Shakespeare, Shaw. I wasn't surprised to see Flaubert or Stendhal, but I was surprised that the editions were in French. So he liked to read good stuff and he spoke French. He'd also dropped a few words of Latin.

But I still didn't know anything about him, not really—except that I'd come uncomfortably close to crawling into his bed. I stared at the two-drawer file cabinet next to the shelves and wondered what its contents might tell me. I didn't let myself even touch the drawer handle though—not out of high-minded respect for his privacy but because he'd know. If the sound didn't wake him now, he'd discover it later, and he'd throw me out. I was sure of that.

Dev. Paul. I said the names softly to myself, trying them

out. Paul Eamon De Valera Hannagan, who revered Mike Florio, but not God. Whose mouth tightened when he mentioned his father.

I turned off the lamp and made myself go back to the sofa and lie down. Along about six, I finally fell asleep.

Now I glanced at my watch—Mike's watch, loose and heavy on my wrist. What would he think about his girl prowling his old friend's room like an alley cat in heat? A couple of years ago an actor I knew from class died in a motorcycle accident and his wife showed up at a party with her new lover less than a month later. I'd railed about it to Mike. "How could she? Shallow. *Disgusting!*" Mike had just shrugged, patted my ass, and said, "Dead is dead, Rocky, and alive's alive." Easy to say then, but how would he feel now? If he could feel. I bit my lip hard.

Quarter to one. I picked up the phone and dialed Mike's office. Instead of Lucy on the other end, I got Jerry Staleigh. Little Jerry, a joke for every occasion. At the funeral, he'd tried to smile at me, started some patter, and then, abruptly, his monkey face had shriveled into a sob.

"How's it going, Jerry?"

"How could it be going without the Mikester? Hank and me, well, he's a tough room to play."

Then stop trying to play him, I wanted to say. "Where's Lucy?" I asked.

"Doctor's appointment—be here in an hour or so. She's still in bad shape. Jumpy, got this rash on the side of her face. How you doing?"

"Not too bad. Look, Jerry, I need copies of Mike's phone message slips for the past three weeks. I wonder if you'd tell Lucy to xerox them and Fed Ex them to me. I'm at the Ramada—Seventh Avenue at Thirty-second Street, and—"

"What's going on with you, Emily?" He gave a nervous little laugh. "You joined the cops? Just the facts, ma'am."

I waited a beat, then decided it wouldn't hurt to try.

"Jerry, you and Mike were pretty close. Do you recall him mentioning anything . . . out of the ordinary the last two weeks before he died?"

"Out of the ordinary?" He took some thinking time. I listened to his breathing, and hoped. "Well, he *did* seem kind of keyed up—like his head was someplace else."

"Uh-huh," I encouraged.

"That's it. He never said anything. You know, I was pretty busy those last couple of weeks. Out of town a lot."

Shit! I'd thought I had something. "Tell Lucy I'll ring her later. And Jerry, if you think of anything, call me. Please."

The police had found no appointment book on Mike or in his truck. Stivic was noncommittal about the progress of his investigation, and asked how long I expected to be in New York. Not long, I told him.

I had a quick shower and shampoo, searching my brain the whole time for what Mike might've found out. He'd had no information except what I'd told him. So what could he have known that I didn't?

I got myself to the subway station with directions from a spry old woman on a racing bike. I bought five dollars' worth of tokens and bounded down the stairs to the platform. Dev was right, I felt like a New Yorker—like a Brooklyn Heights-er, which seemed to me better. As I stepped confidently into the almost empty number 5 express, I noticed how clean the car was. The bold graffiti I remembered seemed to be a thing of the past. The feisty drive to leave a rude mark, flaunt an insufficiently noticed existence in the face of power was gone. The times were too scary. Too many people had no jobs, no homes. Despair and feistiness didn't go together.

Once the train hit Manhattan, I knew the turf. I got off at Fifty-ninth Street. Bloomingdale's—big black temple of rightness. The right clothes, the right linens, the right kitchen machines. Macy's had some of the same stuff, but it couldn't confer the same stamp of self-approval. That's

what Lin and Courtney, my Fletcher roommates, had painstakingly explained again and again, as though to a border-
line retard. My grandmother, on the other hand, had always
thought Bloomingdale's "vulgar," but Gem's clothes were
made by a dressmaker, her linens handed down, and her
kitchen machines human.

I walked uptown on Lex. The weather was bleak, eastern
February. There'd been a trace of blue in the sky when I
left Dev's, but it had faded into total paper whiteness while
I was underground. Or maybe the sky was just bluer in
Brooklyn. As I turned west on Sixty-sixth, I felt my breath
quicken. Her street. The house was between Madison and
Fifth—less than three blocks to go.

She wouldn't be home. Of course she wouldn't. Two
o'clock on a Thursday. She'd be at a meeting or a luncheon
or the hairdresser's, reddening her springy curls. As I approached the house, I decided to take a chance anyway.
No, it wasn't a decision—that would imply choice, control,
reason. I stood in front of that elegant pile of nineteenth-
century limestone, my grandmother's castle, and at that
moment, nothing in the world could've kept me from running up those steps.

I rang the bell and waited, acutely aware of the blood
pounding its way to and from my heart. Finally, I heard a
heavy step approach the door.

"Is that D'Agostino?" a familiarly harsh voice called.

"No, it isn't," I answered, my throat almost blocked. "It's
Emily."

For a moment I thought that she wasn't going to open
the door—that she'd turn and walk stolidly back upstairs,
hoping I'd just go away. But I heard footsteps. At last, the
massive door swung open.

"Hello, Mackey." Another name it felt odd to say. My
grandmother called her Mackey, and her husband Mac. I'd
been instructed to do likewise. A matched set: Mac and
Mackey, jolly and smiling, taking the little orphan under
their wing. Only they didn't. Mac, broom-handle thin and

gloomy, found it hard to look me in the eye, let alone speak three words together in my direction. Mackey, round and flat of face as the oatmeal cookies she baked, was sharp-tongued and disapproving. Each time we came upon each other in the house, her look was one of unpleasant surprise. She'd never pretended to like me, and the feeling was quite mutual.

"Hello, Emily." She'd grown rounder and her face flatter, but her greeting was as chill as ever.

"How are you?" I asked, determined not to impersonate a sullen child no matter what she said or did.

"Very well."

Okaay. "I'd like to see my grandmother."

"I don't know . . ." The small, raisin eyes looked speculatively out of her doughy face. My stomach lurched. Good! She was home. "Just a moment." As Mackey turned, the heavy silver crucifix she wore around her neck caught the light and winked dully at me. Was it supposed to give her comfort? Fill her heart with love for the human race? If so, it didn't seem to be doing its job. That cross had bounced against her plump bosom ever since I'd known her, but she'd never seemed anything like comfortable—or loving.

As I waited there in the inlaid marble hall, I remembered my one illicit peek into the MacNiffs' private life.

I never figured out what it was that possessed me to sneak into their quarters that day. General devilishness, probably. I knew perfectly well that those downstairs rooms were off-limits. I wasn't even especially curious. But it was a rainy Saturday and I was a bored eleven-year-old. No one was around, except for Mackey, who was up in the living room busily dusting the endless whatnots.

With no conscious plan in mind, I darted downstairs and opened the door. At first glance, the rooms were disappointingly unremarkable. One small one was entirely empty. Another contained a worn brown sofa, a plaid armchair, and a couple of spindly tables. The bedroom captured me. Two narrow beds covered in much-washed chenille were guarded by a stern, wood crucifix—tougher big brother of the one on Mackey's neck—which hung dead center on the wall behind.

I'd had little experience with religion. My Jewish mother and Episcopalian father had adhered to only one: the theater, and my grandmother attended St. James's, me by the hand, twice a year—Christmas Eve and Easter Sunday. But this tormented figure, writhing on his cross, his sharply carved face accusing rather than forgiving, was no friendly, clubby Episcopal version of Jesus. This was a guy to watch out for! Could anyone actually sleep under that?

I stared at it, moving slowly at first to the left, then to the right to see if the carved eyes tracked me. Then I turned around. Behind me, under Jesus' full gaze, was a narrow table covered by a lace-trimmed white cloth, on which stood dozens of framed photos, all of the same girl at different ages. Her round, pan face smiled above the velvet collar of a winter coat. She lay on a fuzzy rug in a pale pink romper, proudly displaying a pair of new front teeth. She wore a white dress, like a miniature bride, and held a bouquet of roses. Watching over her, elevated on a fluted pedestal, was a painted plaster statue of Mary, as benevolent as her son was fearsome. The Virgin was flanked by two tall candles, burned down halfway.

A working shrine! I felt a shiver at the thrilling strangeness of it. So the MacNiffs had a daughter. Maybe she had died. No wonder they were so sad all the time. I picked up an oval silver-framed photo of her wearing a robin's-egg-blue suit, waving at the camera, round face smiling, eyes narrowed against the sun. Sixteen, maybe.

"What do you think you're doing!" Mackey's voice blasted hot with fury. The photo slipped from my hands and clattered to the floor.

"I . . . I'm sorry. I didn't . . . I didn't know you had a daughter." The words burbled out of my terrified mouth.

Suddenly Gem appeared, her face stark white, the coral rouge like spots painted on the cheeks of a doll. She didn't say a word, just walked toward me, drew back her hand, and cracked it hard against my face. It all seemed to happen in slow motion. I saw it coming, but I couldn't move out of the way. My head exploded with pain. I was too shocked to cry. I knew—knew by their faces even more than the blow—that I'd committed some unspeakable sin. I stood there, still unable to budge, waiting for them to kill me. Then I heard myself catch a long, ragged breath, and I ran for my life up the stairs to the safety of my room.

For about a year after that, I'd carried on a brief, secret love affair with the Catholic Church. Every day on my way home from school, I'd stop at St. Vincent Ferrer on Sixty-sixth, kneel before the altar, light a candle, cross myself, and pray fervently that the deliciously exotic rituals, the pastel statues, the smells, would transform me into a good person—a believer. It was the same year I was wreaking my damage on the Morgan Library. . . .

"Mrs. Otis will see you in the study." Mackey's dry voice brought me back to the here and now. She stood on the bottom step, searching my face for who knows what. Then she turned abruptly and went back upstairs.

Alone, I walked into the rotunda and scanned its paneled walls, which bore at least a family resemblance to those of the Morgan Library. I looked up at the large oil portrait of Samuel Tucker. The legendary lawyer's eyes met mine—in challenge, I thought. "Wish me luck, Great-grandpa," I said softly. "I'm going to need it."

CHAPTER
EIGHT

As I walked up the wide, curving stairway to the parlor floor, I mentally squared my shoulders the way I always used to when I was headed for the study. So many times. *"I'll see you in the study, Emily."* Never for anything good. The dressing-down, followed by the passing of the sentence.

I paused for a second, sucked in a deep breath and let it out slowly. You can do it. Do it! I turned the heavy brass knob and pushed the door open.

Eleven years had done double time on her face, and the determinedly red-gold curls were grayed down and wispy. The wiry body I remembered looked frail and shrunken in the tall, green velvet wing chair. "You look peaked, Emily, and your hair is still unkempt." Her tone was as imperious as ever.

"You don't look too terrific yourself, Gem," I said, chin high and girded for battle at the sound of her, a reflex that had nothing to do with will.

"I have reason. I am old and ill. You are neither." She tilted her head back, appraising me through the silver-rimmed glasses.

"I know I'm not exactly ready for the cameras," I said. "Can I sit down?" I did, without waiting for a "Please do," on the twin wing chair catty-corner to hers.

"May. If you'd gone on to Vassar, you'd—"

I felt my jaw tighten and then reverse abruptly into a grin. "Gem, you were lecturing me about 'may' and 'can' back when I was in fourth grade at Chapin. I'm going on thirty now, and I speak how I speak. Think of me as incorrigible."

"I have—for a very long time." A ghost of a smile tweaked one corner of her mouth and creased her thin cheek as though it were tissue paper.

"You really don't look well, Gem. You said you were ill. What is it?" I knew she'd prefer the straightforward question. My grandmother did not "hold with beating about the bush"—only one of a number of things she did not hold with.

"Cancer," she replied in kind, her eyes leveling at mine. She said it with the scorn of someone referring to a cockroach.

"I'm sorry." The sudden stab of tears at the back of my nose told me I meant it.

"Would you care for some tea? I told Mackey to prepare it."

"With oatmeal cookies?" The madeleines of my youth.

"They are a given in Mackey's kitchen. Toast as well, and muffins. She seems to believe that if she displays enough food before me, I shall be forced to eat some of it." She reached out and pushed the bell. Then she turned to me. "I imagine there is a reason for this visit, Emily."

"Yes." I felt the pound of my heart all the way from temples to gut. "I need to ask you some questions. Important ones. Important to me at least." She regarded me in silence. "About my parents."

"No." She shook her head slowly and decisively. "No, we will not rake up all that. *We will not!*"

I'd screwed it up already. "Not about their . . . death," I improvised. "About *them*. About things you know that I don't." I thought I could see her deliberating, making up her mind whether or not to throw me out.

"Please. I . . ."

The door swung open and Mackey set down the silver tea tray on the table between us. Her eyes avoided any contact with mine, but I thought I saw something I couldn't read pass between her and Gem.

This was never going to work. In the nine years I'd been under Gem's care, she'd mentioned my mother not at all and my father only once. I remembered that occasion very well. My tenth birthday. Two days before Christmas. We'd been at Orchards, her upstate house, the two of us alone in the big living room, eating fudge-topped birthday cake. I'd burst into tears, sobbing my parents' names over and over, unable to stop. My first birthday without them. Gem walked silently to the cavernous fireplace and threw on a fresh log. "Your grandfather crashed a car one night, not far from here. He died. So did the person with him," she said, her attention focused on positioning the massive piece of wood just so. "He was an alcoholic, as your father was. Some believe that such people are not responsible for the damage they cause—that they are simply ill. This is not true. They *are* responsible. You must not ever forget that." She'd spoken in the matter-of-fact tones of a radio announcer detailing a weather forecast. Afer a moment, she turned back to me. "Now finish your cake. You like chocolate."

Mackey made her exit and I beamed back, with some effort, to the present. "I'll pour," I said, thankful for the chance to busy my hands. "Little milk, no sugar?"
"Thank you."
I prepared hers and poured some black for myself.
"Muffin? Toast?" God, she was thin!
"No thank you."
"But you really should—"
"I don't care for any just now." The edge in her voice retired the subject. I looked at the oatmeal cookies, pictured Mackey's hands making them, and helped myself to

a piece of toast. I was conscious of Gem's eyes on me, watching, weighing. Finally, she spoke. "What is it that you believe I can tell you?" she asked carefully.

The chewed toast turned to sawdust in my suddenly dry mouth. I took a large sip of tea and got it down. *She was going to talk to me!* The surpise of success instantly blanked my mind. I didn't know what my next line was, and there were no other actors on stage to cover for me. "Tell me about what my father was like. What he was like when he was younger—in school? He went to Exeter, right? And Yale."

"Yes. Tucker was not an outstanding student. Certainly he was intelligent, things came easily to him. But he was just as easily bored, couldn't seem to sustain an effort." *Tucker.* Was this really the first time I'd ever heard her say his name? "Erratic. My father had hoped that someday he would join the firm—that Tucker, Stanley would become Tucker, Stanley and Otis. But we all realized fairly early that that would never be. It was . . . a disappointment."

I'll just bet it was! I felt my neck prickle and told myself to simmer down. I was not here to defend my father. I was here to learn. One thing I already knew very well was Cordelia Tucker Otis's reverence for her father. "Did my father always want to write for the theater?"

"No. Initially, he wanted to be Scott Fitzgerald. By the time he finished at Exeter, the single accomplishment of Fitzgerald's he'd been able to emulate was drinking." Her mouth turned down, as though tasting the acid of her words.

"How did he get into Yale?"

Her gray eyes were as expressionless as their glass shield. "The Tuckers and the Otises, too, have been most generous to Yale. All things considered, it would have been preferable if he'd been rejected." She was staring at the opposite wall, as though talking to herself. "The theater obsession began there, when he met Nick Kennoyer." My ears perked up. "Neither of them had sufficient strength of character. They were not good influences on one another."

Uh-*huh*. So Nick Kennoyer had been around since college days. "Did you hear . . ." I'd been about to ask whether Nick had contacted her after the murder. "Do you ever hear from Nick? I think I'd like to meet him."

"No." The tone warned me to let it alone.

"Gem, when did you actually break with . . ." For just a second, "my father" warred with "your son." ". . . my father?"

"I never broke with him. He broke with me. But he continued a relationship with my checkbook," she added with a touch of bitterness. "I did not approve of his—I believe you call it—lifestyle."

"Is there anything, *anything* good you have to say about him?" I heard the quaver in my voice and dug my nails into my palms. *Don't lose it, Emily!*

"Tucker was perhaps the most charming person I have ever met," she said tonelessly. "I do not . . ." She lowered her head and coughed dryly. "I do not," she began again, her eyes desolate, "however, necessarily consider that anything good."

"But—"

"Emily, I'm afraid I will not speak further of Tucker today." I didn't protest. I knew about "shall" and "will" as well as I did about "may" and "can."

"Will you say anything about my mother?" I asked quietly, feeling my eyes moisten with wanting.

"I barely knew your mother," she said, her voice as drained and colorless as her face. I'd spent twenty years frightened of this small woman, dwarfed by her elegant chair. I'd been furious with her. Now for the first time, I felt sorry for her. Not only because she was so sick, but because she'd lost a son—a charming son who'd disappointed her. I felt a sting in my eyes and I gave them a quick rub.

"What do the doctors say—about the cancer?" I forced myself to say the damned word. I knew she'd hate it if I weaseled out on that. "Where is it? Can they operate?"

"A bit late for that, I'm afraid," she said in the firm way she'd always had of reporting unpleasant facts. "It began in my left breast, which is now gone. It has progressed. They are attempting to poison it. Chemotherapy. Whether or not they will poison *me* first remains to be seen. For the moment, the only effect appears to be that my hair is falling out. I shall require a wig shortly." She gripped the chair arm and leaned forward toward me. "It does not seem likely that I shall live very long."

"Have the doctors said that?"

"Not in those words, but I'm not a fool. And I don't hold with pretending. I imagine that you must be wondering about my will."

"You imagine wrong!" I shot out. In that instant, cancer or not, I felt like hitting her. "I am not interested in your money. Give it to your charities. I have as much as I need. More." I did. Mike's estate amounted to $150,000 or so, besides the house, besides the buyout money I'd get for the business. It was a more than comfortable nest egg for someone not yet thirty, and it had been left to me with love. So much love.

"Emily, it is true you are not leading the life I had in mind for you, but . . ." She seemed to be searching for a way to tell me something. "I am not ashamed of you."

I didn't reply immediately. "What do you know about the life I am leading?" I asked with a sudden, uneasy suspicion. I watched her face closely, and could see discomfort harden into resolution.

"I have kept myself informed about you."

"*Informed?* Could we speak English here?" The hot blood of outrage flooded my face. "Have you had some detective tracking me, or what?" All this time, it hadn't been as I'd thought. I hadn't been free—just on a long leash!

"Not in the way you mean," she said. I noticed her hand, white and clawlike as it gripped the green velvet chair arm, and imagined it gripping me across three thousand miles. "You were eighteen when you left. A child. I needed to know that you were safe. No one follows you about, or peers into your windows."

She was explaining to me, something I'd never known her to do. Did she feel guilty, or was she trying to tell me she cared about me? Not loved me, my mind amended quickly; that would've been a lie, and she didn't tell lies. We didn't love each other—never had.

"I know about your acting career, and approve of the way you have conducted it." Was that the hint of a smile? Did she know about my dropkick to DeRenkin? The idea twitched the corners of my own mouth.

"I was concerned at first about the men you chose." I saw by her face that she must've learned a fair amount. I didn't fault her for the look of distaste. I'd done some pretty distasteful things those first two years. "But I gather that the one with whom you are now living, though not an educated man, is a good man."

She didn't know. "He is a dead man," I said quietly.

Her eyes widened and her face seemed to bleach even whiter. Her mouth began to open and then shut itself.

"He was murdered." I answered her unasked question in tones as matter-of-fact as her own.

"I am . . . I am very sorry," she said, her voice coming out almost a whisper.

"The police believe it was union thugs. I'm not so sure."

She looked at me, eyes bleak and somehow puzzled. Then she straightened her shoulders and stood up. The effort was visible and hard to watch. "I am afraid I must leave you now, Emily. I have a hairdresser's appointment and then a meeting."

"Don't you think it's crazy to keep going on at this pace when you're sick?"

"On the contrary. I think it would be crazy to stop. If I did, what would be the point of going on at all?" She turned and walked toward the door. "Stay as long as you like. Mackey will serve you something more substantial, if you're hungry."

I stood up. "No, I'll leave, too." I joined her at the door

and put my arm on her fragile shoulder. "I'm staying at the Ramada, right across from Penn Station." She turned toward me, her face looking up at mine. I thought, for a second, that she was going to suggest I stay with her. But she didn't speak. "I'm glad I came, Gem," I said.

"Yes," she said. The vertical lines between her eyes deepened. "Yes."

We left the house together. Mac was waiting, standing in front of the long black car, ready to help her in.

"Hello, Mac," I said. "How have you been?" The question was unnecessary. His body had grown stooped, his face more furrowed. A sad man who'd become sadder.

"Well enough, miss. And you?" His eyes examined the ground in front of him.

"Fine. Thank you." Thank you for making the effort to ask. I declined Gem's offer of a lift. Suddenly, unexpectedly, I wanted to kiss her, but I didn't make a move. And then the moment was gone.

I walked fast back toward Bloomingdale's and the subway, taking deep, grateful breaths of the frigid air. I felt strong and healthy—equal to anything. On the other hand, I realized after a few minutes that I was having trouble keeping back the tears. Dev was right. She wasn't the wolf, just my grandmother, over eighty and frail and sick. I'd disappointed her, as my father had, but she'd cared enough, no matter what, to keep tabs on me. At first I'd been furious. Now I wasn't at all sure how I felt about it. Loving gesture? Monstrous intrusion?

Nick Kennoyer: my father's oldest friend. I could hardly wait to talk to him.

I checked my watch. Almost four. I'd meant to stop by the hotel for a change of clothes, but did a quick calculation and figured it would be more efficient to buy one at Bloomingdale's.

Fifteen minutes later, I stood on the lower platform waiting for the 5 express to Brooklyn. On my arm was a Bloomie's bag containing two pairs of black panty hose, two new bras, and a short, dark green cashmere shift with a high turtleneck. Trip would've been proud of me. I was turning into a regular clotheshorse.

The crowd on the platform milled and paced with the impatient look of people who'd been waiting longer than they expected. I leaned over and peered at the tunnel for some sign of action. Nothing. When I turned back I saw his face.

Would I have recognized him if I hadn't spent the last twenty-four hours steeped in the events surrounding my parents' death? I'll never know that. But I *did* recognize him. He hadn't changed so much. The reddish hair was almost gone now from his freckled head, but that squashy nose looked exactly the same, and the kind, button eyes. As he watched the workings of my mind register on my face, our eyes engaged for an endless, paralyzed moment. He broke and turned, as if to speak to someone next to him. Then he disappeared into the crowd.

I darted frantically, this way and that, searching, turning. Dizzy with it. I *had* him. I couldn't lose him. Suddenly, a violent push at my back toppled my balance. A quick second shove sent me careening over the edge. "No!" I cried out as I fell, helpless as a rag doll, and landed breathless, sprawled on my stomach across the tracks. I lay there stunned, only dimly aware of an indistinguishable buzz of voices on the platform above. Not far above, not far at all, but I was in another world. Me, the cold metal track against my cheek, a distant hum in my ear.

The hum rose to a roar that demanded attention. I lifted my head just slightly and was blinded by yellow lights. My heart stalled. I was suffocating. Dark circles began to spiral in front of my eyes as the sound and the lights swelled and bore down. I am going to die, I thought slowly—each word forming itself in a cartoon balloon in my brain.

Then a voice. A man—loud, commanding. From the platform? From inside my head? *Mike?* "Roll. *Roll, goddamn it!* To the right. Under the platform. You'll be okay. Under the platform. Roll, Emily. *Now!"*

The train crept forward in slow motion. Twenty feet away. Ten. The slow motion burst into crazy speed. I rolled. I rolled for my life, and reached the sheltering overhang of the platform just as the hot breath of the oncoming train seared the side of my face. I huddled there, frozen, realizing all at once that the long scarf still circling my neck had come partly unwound and was lying stretched across the tracks. Slip it off, I told myself. But my body said, *Stay still. Very still. Don't move.* My body won.

Then the train shut off all light and thought. Nothing but deafening sound. A clutch around my neck, as the scarf jerked tighter and tighter and tighter. I heard a sickening scream rise above the encompassing shrieking roar. A flashbulb went off in my head. Then nothing.

"Jeez, you are one lucky lady!" The tall black transit cop threw me a grin as he helped me over to a molded plastic bench. My legs buckled, a sharp pain shooting up my right one. My neck ached like hell. My throat was sore. And my eyes felt as though sand had been sprinkled under the lids. All told, I agreed with him. I didn't recall how I'd gotten off the tracks. Had I passed out?

"Good thing you were wearing that coat," he said. "Wrapped you up like cotton wool. And good thing you were cool enough to roll like that." I scanned the thinned crowd on the platform for the squash-nosed cop, but he was nowhere in sight.

I answered the questions. I was a tourist here. Thought it would be fun to try the subway. In L.A. we're in our cars all the time. Ha ha. Not used to so many people. Got too close to the edge. Gosh, New York's a bit bewildering! I got testy only when they started to push about having me checked out at Lenox Hill Hospital. "I am fine," I insisted. "And I have an urgent appointment, so please just let me alone." I needed to get to Dev!

A small Hispanic woman handed me my Bloomie's bag. My purse, miraculously, had never left my shoulder. I unwound the striped scarf from my bruised neck and laid it on the bench. I never wanted to see it again.

Another 5 express barreled into the station. I rose and, ignoring the chorus of official and unofficial protesters, hobbled into the train.

Forty minutes later I unlocked Dev's door and found him sitting at his round table, staring intently at the typewriter. He jumped up quickly at the sound behind him. I saw surprise give way to alarm on his face as he took in my condition.

"I know," I said with a try at a worldly chuckle. "The people on the train thought I looked pretty bad too. I got a cab from the station, but the first two I flagged didn't stop for me. Must've thought I was a bag lady or something."

"Are you going to cut the social commentary and tell me what happened?" he snapped. I limped over to the sofa and shucked off my coat. And then, with no warning, burst into tears.

I felt them roll down my face, stinging as they hit the scraped places. I bent my head, eager to be curtained off behind the fall of heavy, tumbled hair. A Kleenex made its way under my tent. "Here. Blow," he said. "Sorry I barked at you. Now what the hell happened?"

I lifted my head and blew. "I wasn't crying about you," I said, "believe me." It seemed important somehow to declare that I was no trembling flower who dropped petals when some guy hollered, though I was sure Dev would consider that just another piece of vanity. Maybe he'd even be right. Then I told him what had happened.

As he took it in, his eyes seemed to darken, and his mouth thinned. He didn't say anything for a moment. "Baldish, freckled head, squashed nose. Your long-lost cop, huh? About how tall?"

"I don't know. A little taller than you. Maybe five eleven, six feet. Thin."

"How old?"

"Fiftyish."

"Was he alone?"

I shut my eyes, trying to see the platform, picture him at the moment I'd spotted him. "No," I said tentatively. "I'm not at all sure, but I have a vague idea he was with someone. Maybe something about the way he turned his head to the side and looked down. Doesn't do much good though. I haven't got a clue about the other person. But who *is* squash nose, Dev? If he's a cop, he can't just disappear, can he?" I shifted my position slightly and felt a sharp pain in my right knee. I winced and clutched at it with a protective hand.

"Let me have a look at that." He knelt at my feet and moved his fingers up and down my leg, as though he knew what he was doing. "Does this hurt?" He manipulated my kneecap.

I gasped slightly. "Not very much," I said stoically.

"Nothing's broken. You'd have gone through the roof." He stood up quickly and turned away. "I'm going to run a hot bath for you. Then I want to hear about your visit to Grandmother's house."

I wound my hair up in a towel and lowered myself gingerly into the tub, like an old lady. The steamy water felt therapeutic on my leg, not to mention my hip, which felt destined for a whopper bruise, but nothing worse. I lay back and immersed my aching neck. I felt, as I hadn't at Mike's funeral, glad to be alive. Enjoy it while you can, I thought, you're never going to make it through this.

I shut my eyes and saw Gem behind them. Sick, frail now—and not giving up an inch of ground to it. I felt the tears start again and didn't try to stop them. Why? Why was I crying for her? What difference did it make to me that she was going to die? I hated her. But . . . But what? I drew a deep, ragged breath. I didn't know what, and right then I didn't want to.

Gem dissolved to black and Mike appeared, smiling, his dark eyes flashing encouragement. Mike. *Mike. Goddamn you, why'd you have to go and get yourself killed?*

When I emerged from the tub a long time later, I was better. Not good, but better—back on track, determined to find Nick Kennoyer, convinced that Dev would find squash nose.

I pulled Dev's robe tight around me and made myself ignore the faint smell of him that clung stubbornly to the terry cloth. When I limped back into the room, he was just hanging up the phone. "A great pair of gimps, the two of us," he said. "A match for just about anything, I'd say." A smile lightened his eyes to violet. A shock of black hair fell across one side of his forehead. The effect was rakishly piratelike—appealingly foreign, but I couldn't exactly place the flavor.

I smiled back and sat in what I'd come in this very short time to regard as my place on the sofa. I started to tuck my legs under me, but my right one complained and I stretched it out across the coffee table. "What're you so chipper about? *You* may be next off the subway platform."

"Scotch or Irish whiskey? And don't tell me 'a little white wine,' because I don't have any."

"Irish."

He handed me my glass and carried his own over to the Eames chair—his place—took a healthy sip and leaned back. "You learn anything from your grandmother?"

"Uh-huh. That Nick Kennoyer was a very old friend of my father's. They went to Yale together. She wouldn't say much about him, just that as far as she was concerned, he was a bad influence."

"She have any idea where he is?"

"No. At least that's what she says, and she won't be pushed." I sipped my drink and welcomed the friendly burn of the whiskey as it passed down my throat. "She's dying," I said, staring past him at his typewriter. "She has cancer."

"I'm sorry," he said. A note in his voice drew my eyes quickly back to his face. Was he mocking me somehow?

"What do you mean?" I asked sharply.

"*Explication de texte:* I mean, I am sorry that your grand-mother may die before you have settled your very compli-cated hash with her. Is that clear now?"

"Yes," I said after a long minute. But I said it into my glass, hair shielding my face.

"That was Strohmeyer on the phone. I'm going to meet with him tomorrow morning out in Little Neck at his house."

"He called you?" The whiskey seemed to expand and vibrate in my gut.

"No, I called him. I told him about your mysterious sub-way friend. He didn't say anything—only way I knew he was still there was the breathing. Finally he said, 'Okay. Here, tomorrow, eleven.' I could hardly hear him."

"Can I come?"

"No, and that's a dumb question." I knew that—but it was worth a try. "While we're on the subject, you can't go anywhere."

"Now wait a minute. I have to find Kennoyer, and you can't tell me—"

"Yes I can. That was the deal, remember? I call the shots, and you are going nowhere alone till I find squash nose. Anyway, your best tool for finding Kennoyer is right here— the phone. And your dialing finger's in better shape than your leg at the moment. Understood?"

"Why was Mike so important to you, Dev? How did you know him? What's this 'marker' you owe him?" The volley of questions popped out like birdshot. He took another pull at his drink. "If you tell me it's none of my business, that you can march all over my life, but yours is off limits, *I* will march over that chair and—"

"And what? Kick my balls in, like you did to that asshole director?"

I laughed in sheer surprise. "Is there anything about me you *don't* know?"

"A lot, I'd say."

"But we're talking about you now, mystery man."

"Okay." His jaw tightened almost imperceptibly. "What was Mike to me? He was my savior, my big brother, the father I wanted. He was only seven years older, but in the ways that mattered, he got to be my father." Mine too, I thought. Oh God, mine too! "I met him when I was ten. He was not quite eighteen then—in Navy boot camp preparing to go to Vietnam. What I owe him is complicated. Maybe my life."

I waited a moment for him to say more, but he didn't. "Come on, Dev." My voice trembled a little with urgency. "Don't leave me hanging. I need to know who you are."

He topped up his drink. My glass still had plenty in it. Then he settled back in his chair. "Who I am. Well, I'd probably have to lead off with my father." His eyes looked at me gravely for a moment and then past me. He started to talk quietly, but not to me. "Liam Hannagan tended to be a violent man when he drank, which was most of the time, except when he was working—which naturally got to be less of the time. I think the illness he really suffered from was chronic disappointment. Everything he ever came across in his life disappointed him, ultimately—everything except his fantasies about the Great Irish Struggle. Funny thing was, he was second-generation Boston, had never been near Ireland, and I never heard him once express a desire to go. I guess, screwed up as he was, he knew that it would turn out to be just another disappointment, that the dream was only safe an ocean away.

"My mother was just the opposite—gentle. Even when he belted her, she never yelled. Never tried to get away. Never even complained, that I recall. She lived on some spiritual plane somewhere, my mother. Maybe that was her Indian side. Her mother was Algonquin, her father was Quebecois, Paul Duquesne. She named me for him. I think it was the only time she ever stood up to Liam and won. Well, maybe not. Maybe that dreamy, stoic withdrawal of hers was a victory of sorts. He'd be spoiling for a fight, and she'd just look at him, rosary in her hand, like he wasn't even there. Sometimes she looked at me the same way."

I looked at Dev and saw her genes—straight, slightly broad nose, thick, glossy black hair, golden skin. But I knew that his mouth, so often thinned in anger, was his father's, and that those disturbing purple eyes must be his own.

"What was her name, your mother?" I asked.

"Miriam. Mim, everybody called her Mim—even I did."

"Liam, Mim, and Paul. Hard for me to think of you as Paul."

"Yeah." His slight smile spoke of memories—not happy ones. "Hard for me, too—even after all this time. Liam succeeded in getting his precious De Valera's hooks into me, one way or another. He had himself a son he could call Dev."

"And that disappointed him too?"

"Oh yeah. We lived in Kittery, Maine—major industry, the U.S. Navy. Lots of Canadians down there trying to make a buck one way or the other. My mother had some clerk job at the naval base. He drifted north from Boston looking for work too. He'd been in the Korean War. They let him paint submarines or some such. The two of them found each other—my earliest piece of evidence against the existence of God."

"You said that yesterday, that you'd never believed." I felt a pang of envy at his sureness.

"Not in God. On my tenth birthday the world changed. God had nothing to do with it.

"My father was going to take us out to a movie and dinner to celebrate—he did that sometimes. Out of the blue, he'd take me somewhere and we'd have a good time. Mim used to go too sometimes, but only if she thought he'd stay dry. She didn't always guess right though, so she stopped going along at all. That morning I caught him in a good mood—sunny, summer day, maybe the weather perked him up. Anyway, he promised me he'd stay dry. And she promised she'd come along for my birthday.

"So we got dressed up, Mim and I did, and we waited for him to get home from work. And waited. And her face got that faraway look I couldn't stand. Finally, I told her I was going out to play, but I didn't. There was a bar down near the base where he always hung out with his buddies, and I knew that was where he'd be. I walked in and grabbed his arm. He was holding a drink. It spilled all over the bar.

"He picked me up by my shirt and pants like a sack of wash and hustled me out onto the street. My feet never touched the ground. Not that he was all that powerful, but I was a scrawny kid and he was wild—not just the drink, but I'd shamed him in front of his pals. He let me go and then he knocked me down. Picked me up and knocked me down again. I heard something crack—heard it before I felt it. Then when I did feel it, I almost passed out with the pain. My hip.

"Some young sailors happened to be passing by. But one of them didn't pass by, he took over. Mike. He got me to the hospital, saw that I got attended to, stayed with me the whole time they set the hip—not perfectly, as it turned out. After I was settled in a room with a shot of something to make me sleep, he paid a visit to my parents. Later, Mike told me that he'd spoken to Mim alone and asked her what she wanted—*really* wanted. Did she want Liam to stay or go? She looked at him with that gentle, opaque face of hers and told him she never wanted to see Liam Hannagan again—that she'd work day and night, whatever it took to support herself and her boy, but she wanted Liam gone. Mike asked her if she was sure. She nodded yes. And Mike made it happen. I still don't know how, he'd never say, but when I got home from the hospital, Liam was gone."

"What if Mike had asked you the question instead of Mim? What would your answer have been?"

"I don't know," he said softly. "That day, I didn't just want him gone, I wanted him dead. Later, I kind of missed him, from time to time. He was dangerous, but he was *there*. Living with Mim was like living with a gentle holy ghost. Mike was the one who pulled me through. He kind of adopted Mim and me. Kept an eye on us, sent money, booted my ass into college, when all I wanted to do was travel. You're crying again, actress. Don't tell me it's for me this time."

I hadn't been aware of the tears streaming down my face till he mentioned them. If they burned the raw spots, as they had earlier, I wasn't feeling it.

"Yes. For you—and for Mim."

"Mim's dead. TB. She seemed to just fade away. I think she welcomed it." He walked slowly over to where I sat. I watched the slight, rolling limp and thought of the beaten child. He wiped at my tears, not with a Kleenex but with his fingers, his two palms cupping my face.

My arms reached out and wrapped around his neck. I didn't think, didn't try to stop, just gave over to a feeling different from any I'd ever had.

CHAPTER
NINE

I was half awake, the other half not wanting to come along. The early morning sun streaming in the windows lit the view behind my closed eyes to a pearly rose. I felt as though I were nestled safely inside a seashell. I breathed deeply and imagined I smelled the beach. "Mmmmm." I heard the low, purring groan with no consciousness that it was coming from me.

A finger traced a perfect circle around one nipple. And the other one. A tongue licked at my ear, my neck, found my lips and then moved down. Eyes still closed, I savored the unfamiliar feel and taste of him. The roughness of his cheek surprised the inside of my thigh in a shock wave. His tongue darted into me and I shuddered, breath suspended. He moved upward slowly and entered. I came at once—a hard, rhythmic pounding, my own cry drowned out by his as he joined me.

We lay there holding each other, the only sound our staggered breathing. I didn't want to move or to talk. That would give substance to the ecstatic dream that had begun last night.

I knew that words would come from one or the other of us now, and when they did, responsibility would have to follow. Gem had drummed that into me, at least. *"You are responsible for what you do, Emily."* But I didn't want to be.

"Hello," he said finally, his voice morning-hoarse. "How do you feel?"

At the question, the throb in my knee reasserted itself, followed quickly by the aches in my neck and hip, reproachful reminders of the real world, which had, along with my bodily pains, gone on hold.

"I don't know," I answered. It came out a husky whisper. I rose on one elbow and looked at him. The eyes that had been dark as royal velvet last night were now narrowed against the sunlight, translucent as tinted crystal. I bit my lower lip hard. "Look, I—"

He cupped a hand over my mouth. "We're not going to have that conversation. Not now. I'm going to take a shower and get to work, and you're going to stay here and get to work." He kissed my forehead solemnly and jumped off the bed.

By the time he emerged from the bathroom, I was over in the kitchen, robe primly wrapped, standing in front of the coffeemaker, staring as though hypnotized at the stream of fragrant brown liquid dripping into the glass canister. Details of domesticity. He takes his shower, she makes the coffee—or the other way around. Somebody brings in the papers, pours the orange juice. "What does your day look like, honey?" God, how easy to fall back into the comfortable, soothing rituals. How easy! So what difference does a little shift in personnel make? So Mike is dead and Dev happens to be alive. Take it where you find it, right?

A wave of nauseous self-loathing almost overpowered me. You are a fucking alley cat, Emily. About as deep as a mud puddle. I concentrated on the last trickle coming out of the coffeemaker, resolutely refusing to notice the lean, naked body passing three feet in front of me on its way to the clothes closet.

I took my coffee into the bathroom, along with my Bloomie's bag of fresh clothing. When I came back out, I was fully dressed. So was he.

"I have to stop by the office," he said neutrally. "Then

I'm headed out to Little Neck." He glanced at his wrist. The curved rectangular watch was old, pleasingly dull gold, the strap weathered. His father's? I gritted my teeth. *Will you just stop it, you moron? It's none of your business!* "Nine-thirty now. Strohmeyer warned me not before eleven. It's his day off and he won't be happy if I get in the way of his sack time. I should be back by two or so. Need I tell you, lock the door behind me, put the chain on, and don't let anyone in?"

"No, you needn't." Why didn't he just *go?* I felt he was lingering, teasing me.

"Anyone!"

"I heard you. Okay? I'm going to have to take my coat to the cleaners, though, and go back to the hotel. All my stuff is there and I'm expecting a Fed Ex there from Mike's office—the message slips."

"I'll take the coat. Give me the hotel key and I'll get your things and the Fed Ex," he said patiently.

"Leave some stuff in the room. I don't want to check out." What I should do was move back in.

"Okay. Any other instructions?"

I hesitated for a moment, a burst of angry words trapped behind my closed lips. Then I got the coat and key and handed them to him without comment.

"Thank you," he said formally. He took his last gulp of coffee, slipped on his Burberry, grabbed a fat briefcase, and headed for the door. "Yale alumni office might be a good place to start searching for Kennoyer."

"I know. Contrary to what you may think, I'm not an idiot."

He turned and gave me a dazzling smile. "That's a nice dress. I like dark green." Then he was gone.

I locked the door as instructed and stood looking at it, feeling trapped, foolish, and mad. What did he think this was, some sitcom? Meet cute over the murdered boyfriend and hop into bed. Even as it flashed into my head, I knew how unfair I was being. But . . . I paced the apartment like some zoo critter. On my second round past the kitchen counter, I grabbed a slice of cold pizza left over from the pie he'd ordered sometime last night. I munched it hungrily as I walked, not tasting, just chewing and swallowing, trying to fill the sick emptiness in my gut.

The ring of the phone made me jump. I stood frozen for a second, deliberating whether to answer it. On ring four, I pounced. "Hello?" I waited. *"Hello?"*

"Oh Jesus, the kid!"

The sharp intake of breath burned my dry throat. "No," I gasped, and stood frozen, the phone at my ear. *"Where's the kid? Emily. Emm-i-lyy!"* Then nothing. I felt the sweat break out all over. I wanted to hang up the phone, but my arm wouldn't move. Then I heard a click, followed by a dial tone. That broke the spell and I hung up, just in time to dash at top speed to the bathroom, where I bent over the toilet and retched up everything in my churning gut, except for the impotent fury at what had just been done to me.

After I'd cleaned myself up, I sat on the sofa and sipped a glass of cold water. The tape. Whoever had broken in here the other night had made a dupe of my imitation of the voice, knowing what effect it would have on me to pick up the phone and hear it with no warning, knowing it would have me gibbering in terror. That was the purpose. I ran my hand over my still-damp face. No more, I promised myself. No matter what happens, they're not going to get you like that again. Now shape up, you've got work to do. I checked Mike's watch. Nine-thirty. Too early for California, but the Yale alumni office should be up and operating.

I settled myself in Dev's Eames chair, phone on the table next to me, yellow pad and pen at the ready for notes, but the number I found myself dialing was not Connecticut information, it was my grandmother's. Unexpectedly, and to my great relief, she answered it herself.

"Hello."

"Gem." Suddenly I realized I had no idea what to say. "Gem, it's Emily. I . . . I wanted to give you the number

where I am, just, uh, in case. I'm not at the Ramada anymore. I'm staying with a friend of Mike's. In Brooklyn
Heights," I added.

"Yes," she said noncommittally. Coldly? I read Dev's
number off the phone. "Thank you, Emily."

"I had an accident yesterday," I blurted. "I was pushed . . .
I fell off a subway platform."

Silence at the other end. I thought I heard her breath
quicken. "Are you all right?" she asked sharply, as though
angry.

"Yes. Yes, I'm fine." Beat, beat, beat. "Gem, it was good
to see you. Can I come again? I mean, may I?" I added,
feeling a smile stretch my dry lips. I hadn't planned any of
what I was saying, any more than I'd planned to call her
just then. It all just seemed to come from somewhere in
me that I didn't know about or begin to understand.

"Yes, you may." Dead air, but I felt her in the room with
me, close enough to touch. "You must be careful." Her
tone was urgent. It felt odd to hear her worrying about me,
just like someone's normal grandmother. "You—" She
broke off abruptly. I guessed it felt odd to her, too. "I have
to leave now, or I shall be late for my meeting."

"Well . . . goodbye, Gem. I'll call you soon."

"Goodbye, Emily." I waited for the click. "It was good
to see you, too," she said softly before it came.

I chanced a bigger sip of water, and it sat all right on my
stomach. Hearing Gem had strengthened me somehow; as
constrained as the conversation had been, it felt like a cool
maternal palm on my forehead. You'll be calling her
"Grandma" next, if you don't watch out.

I checked New York, Brooklyn, Long Island, and Westchester information. No Nick Kennoyer. No anything Kennoyer. I dialed Connecticut information and got the number
for Yale.

"Alumni Affairs." My heart sank at the sound of her. It
was a nasal, letter-of-the-law voice—one that rang with
crisply crossed *t*'s and precisely dotted *i*'s. I doubted seriously whether it would simply give Nick's address to some

unauthorized petitioner. I shut my eyes tight for a second, the way I do just before I go on stage, and then took what I figured was my best shot.

"Good morning," I said briskly, with my best British accent, "please hold for Ms. Onassis." I took two beats, then switched to the Jackie voice, the one I could always rely on to break Trip up when we were rehearsing even the most serious scene. "Oh, thank you so much, we're trying to reach a Mr. Kennoyer—about his manuscript. I believe he was class of '54."

"His manuscript?"

"Yes, he's submitted it to us, and we're very interested." A rush of panic as I realized I hadn't an idea in the world what publisher Jackie was with. If the woman questioned me, I was sunk. I speeded up. "The only thing is, one of the secretaries—not mine, of course—stupidly threw away the envelope, and we haven't a clue where to reach him, you see. In the memoir, he speaks very fondly of his years at Yale, so I had the idea that you might know where I could reach him." A long pause. I held my breath. "It would be *such* a help," I coaxed, and then made myself shut up and leave it to the potent persuasive powers of celebrity.

"Well, we don't really . . ." Oh God, don't say you'll take my number and pass it along to him, I pleaded silently, forcing my jaws to stay shut. My agent, Bernie Clegg, had told me once that at the make-or-break point in a negotiation, the first one to talk loses. "But I'm certain Mr. Kennoyer will be eager to hear from you, Ms. Onassis." She gave me an address in Key West. I thanked her and got off stage before I could find a way to screw it up.

The Florida operator provided a phone number. I punched it in, misdialing twice in my nervousness. After nine rings, just as I was about to hang up, I heard a muffled, sleepy hello. My heart skidded just slightly. I quickly put the phone back in its cradle. So he was there! Almost ten in the morning. He didn't have a regular nine-to-five job, that was for sure. I started to pace again.

I'd actually *found* him! I knew his address, his phone number. And it hadn't even been hard. Optimism swept through me like a cleansing rain. Maybe I could leave for Key West tomorrow. Hell, maybe tonight. I could hardly wait for Dev to get back, so I could tell him. And he'd have things to tell me, too, after his meeting with Strohmeyer.

I picked up the phone and called the Ramada. Message from Mike's secretary, Lucy. I dialed into my home machine and heard Bernie Clegg bark, "Where the hell are you? When you coming back?" and add that I gave him more trouble for less money than any client in the house. Then I heard Trip. "This isn't right, buddy. Not right at all." His voice was dead serious, nothing like the bantering tone we usually used on each other's machines. "I know you're hurting and I know you're up to something, but you can't shut down on me this way. It's not fair."

My throat lumped. Maybe there was someone in the world more self-centered than Emily Silver, but at the moment I couldn't think who it might be. I punched in Trip's number. He picked up, sounding as sleepy as Nick Kennoyer.

"Hi, it's the Wicked Bitch of the East. Why aren't you over at Warner's in a makeup chair."

"Because our shoot took most of last night and I'm sleeping."

"Well, if you can't get your line readings right, what do you expect?"

"Line readings, my ass! Amie and I had to do every one of those damned kissy-face close-ups eight times before Brian got one he could print. She kept hollering how she could smell hamburger on my breath and it broke her concentration. Do you love it? She's got the concentration of a fucking mosquito."

"I hope you at least had onion on the burger."

"No, that's what *you'd* do—'cause you are evil and I'm a nice midwestern boy." He gave a characteristic snorty laugh. No one but Trip laughed quite that way. Then he broke it off abruptly. We'd both jumped into the accustomed give-and-take of our relationship—maybe to find out whether it was still there for us. "You got my message," he said after a moment.

"Yeah. What can I say, Trip? You *are* my friend. My best one, but I guess I do a good imitation of a selfish asshole, huh?"

"Sometimes. I know about your turning down the Spielberg thing. Your best friend had to hear about it from Amie the Vegetarian Moron. I don't know if I'm madder at you for turning down a chance like that or for not telling me about it—not even calling to let me know where you are."

"I'm sorry."

"If we *are* friends, tell me what the hell is going on here."

Silence on both ends. I couldn't lie and I didn't want to risk telling him the truth. "There's some information I need to find out. About Mike's death."

"And when did the LAPD hand you a badge? Are you nuts? What do you think you're doing messing around with people who kill people? This isn't some movie."

"I know, I know, I know," I said impatiently. "I'm not messing around, just . . . clearing up things."

"Right," he said in a reading heavy with irony.

"Trip Walter Grody Colby, I care about you and I don't want to pile stuff on you that isn't good for you to know, okay?"

"Not okay."

"Well, it'll have to do," I snapped, and felt my eyes sting with tears. During the last day, I'd cried more than in the past ten years. This time it was the sheer frustration of being tethered by feeling—connected to him at a time when I shouldn't be connected to anyone.

"I'm sorry," I said quietly. "Look, Trip, I'm here doing something important enough to me that I gave up a chance to be in a Spielberg movie for it. I hope it's going to turn out the way I want it to, but if it doesn't, I've got to do it anyway. I told Mike and it got him killed. And that's why I won't tell you."

"What about the police. Isn't that how they earn their living?"

"They earn their living by working with evidence, and I don't have any. I have a professional detective helping me here—an old friend of Mike's. It'll be all right," I added with a confidence far from real. "And I'll keep in touch. I promise."

I could almost hear him mulling. "I love you, you crazy bitch," he said finally.

"Me too, Walter." My voice broke just a little. I hoped he didn't catch it, but figured he probably had. "Next time, order the onion."

I put down the phone and chewed on my finger while I tried to hold back the tears and take control of my own strings again. My stomach rumbled the message that I was hungry, but I didn't dare risk the cold, plasticky pizza again. By default, I settled for peanut butter and crackers and the lone withering apple I found in the fridge. I sat back down in the Eames chair and had a hard time finding a comfortable position. I dialed Mike's office. Lucy answered my questions before I had a chance to ask them.

"I Fed Exed the copies of the message slips to your hotel, Emily. Really nothing unusual. Clients, drivers, people looking for donations. And the union, of course. But check it out yourself. That cop, Stivic, keeps coming back. He's here almost every day. The same damned questions over and over. I can't believe . . ." She let it trail away.

"Um," I said, wanting to cut off this line of conversation with her. "How're you bearing up?"

"Oh, all right, I guess. Not too bad. Well, terrible, if you want to know the truth. Every morning I come in here. I unlock the door, start the coffee, and would you believe it? I still make enough for both of us—can't seem to get it through my dumb head that—" She cut herself off abruptly. "Listen to me, bending your ear with *my* troubles."

"Thanks for getting the messages off to me, Lucy, and . . . I know what you mean about the coffee."

My hand was still on the phone when it shrilled, sending

a shiver through my whole body. I let it ring again, scared to pick it up, scared not to. I took a deep breath. *They can't do it to you again.* Let them play anything they want in your ear. It's only a phone. Third ring. It might even be Dev.

"Hello," I said carefully, steeling myself. Silence. "Hello," I repeated testily.

"Hello." The voice was pleasant, female, and sounded caught off base, upset. "Is . . . Is Paul there?"

I let out a shuddering breath and almost giggled in nervous relief. A girlfriend, wondering who the hell I might be. "No, he isn't just now, but I expect him back about two. Who is this?"

"Who is *this?*"

We could work it into a stand-up routine. "This is Emily Silver," I said. "Can I give him a message?"

A pause. "Just tell him Ronnie. He knows where to get me." She hung up.

I'd walked the length and width of the room twice before I identified the sour irritation I was feeling. Unfounded, senseless, but undeniable—in the middle of life-and-death matters, I was fuming like some dopey, overage debutante, some road company Scarlett O'Hara, being *jealous.*

The scratch of a key in the lock took me by surprise. My eyes darted to my wrist. Ten of twelve—much too early for Dev. For an instant I felt only panic. They'd already broken in here once. What would I do if I was trapped? I bolted for the kitchen and grabbed an almost empty bottle of wine. I could break it and—

"Slip the chain. It's me." I ran to the door, my breath irregular as it tried to adjust from terror to relief. He stood there, hair wet, snowflakes clinging to his shoulders, my canvas suitcase in his hand. Then I noticed the drained grimness in his face.

"What's the matter?"

"Strohmeyer's dead."

CHAPTER
TEN

I felt the breath go out of me, as though I'd been punched in the stomach. They were everywhere, a step ahead. No one could escape. You got anywhere close, they just reached out and annihilated you. I swallowed hard.

"How?"

"Ate his gun."

"What?"

"He put his gun in his mouth and blew the back of his head off," he explained tonelessly.

"Are you telling me he killed *himself?*"

"Looks that way." Dev double-locked the door and hooked the chain back on. "Come on, let's sit down." He strode quickly to the sofa. I followed. His mouth was compressed, lips whitened. He drew a folded piece of lined yellow paper from the inside pocket of his tweed sports coat and handed it to me.

Paul:

It is not what you think. Leave it alone. Please. I am committing a mortal sin, and I know I will go to Hell for it. But I am there already. I only hope God will understand that I never meant to hurt anyone.

Frank

"Couldn't someone have forced him to write this? You know, held a gun on him and then shot him anyway?"

He shook his head slowly. "I don't think so."

"Why not?"

"You'd have to have known Frank Strohmeyer. He was a simple guy, not so much brave as stubborn. It was his main quality as a cop. He was famous for it. They tell the story about one time when some yo-yo shooter he went after got him trapped looking down the wrong end of a forty-five, and demanded that Frank walk him out of the building into a getaway car. Frank lunged at him. Took a bullet in the thigh, but he got hold of the gun. Look, I'm not saying that they couldn't have faked the suicide—one guy holding him while the other stuck the gun in his mouth—but nobody could have made him write that note. And I think he did write it. I'll be completely sure after I have it checked against some samples in my files." He dropped his head and pressed his palms against his temples for a moment. Then he looked at me. "Frank was a good Catholic. That's an understatement. He attended Mass every day. When he had to miss it occasionally, it shook him. He really believed in heaven and hell." His brow furrowed, almost closing the purple eyes. "It's hard to imagine what would've pushed him to a mortal sin like suicide."

"Fear of getting caught? Fear of being disgraced? Maybe he was involved in a cover-up and knew you were closing in. Maybe he just couldn't face it."

"Maybe," he said miserably. "And maybe my inept bumbling helped kill a lonely, superstitious man for no good reason."

"Look," I shot back, "Mike was killed for no good reason, and so were my parents. If this Strohmeyer had anything to do with any of it, he deserved to die. The only thing I'm sorry about is that you didn't make him talk to you first."

He studied my face. His eyes said that they didn't like what they saw. I watched him get up and walk to the front windows. My furious words echoed back at me in the silence. Did I mean them? A man tormented enough to doom himself to Catholic hell—and all that mattered was that he'd failed to provide the information I needed before he blew his brains out. I dipped my head and hid behind my hair. I didn't like me much either.

When I finally looked up, Dev was still at the window gazing out at the thickening fall of snow.

"How come you have the suicide note?" I asked. "How come the police let you go?"

"I didn't stick around for the police. If I had, I'd be tied for hours, days."

"So they still don't know about him?"

"They do. I called nine-one-one from a phone booth. Didn't give my name."

"And you took the note."

"Right. Removing evidence. Probably good for a few years. Maybe I can work it off in community service."

"What do you suppose he meant in his note, 'It's not what you think'?"

"I don't know. I'm not yet sure what I do think."

"I've found Nick Kennoyer," I said, the excitement of the discovery blunted now. "He's in Key West." Dev, still at the window, didn't answer me.

"I want to go there, Dev. I want to go right away."

"Good idea," he said after a long pause, surprising me. I'd expected an argument, one of his you'll-stay-right-here-and-do-what-I-tell-you's. "You're going to go right now," he said, running suddenly for the phone.

"Bet I got you out of the darkroom," he said to whoever was on the other end, in a tone that made me sure he wasn't talking to a man. "Sorry. I need a favor." Small chuckle, flavored with innuendo. "No, but it would be nice." Another chuckle. I wanted to hit him. "Call the garage and tell them you want your car in half an hour. No, it can't really wait—the snow's starting to get heavy. Okay. I'll be down in a few minutes and fill you in. *Danke schön.*" He hung up and turned to me, his eyes doing a quick professional once-over, like a director setting up a scene. "Come here," he said over his shoulder, beckoning me to follow him into the bathroom.

I hesitated. "What . . . do you want?"

"Not to seduce you into the shower," he said impatiently. He flipped the toilet lid shut and grabbed a bath towel off the hook. "Sit down. Monsieur Paul is going to give you a new coiffure."

"Is Monsieur Paul going to let me know what the hell is going on here?" I asked, not moving.

"Sit down," he repeated, tapping the toilet lid. "We don't have lots of time. That mop of hair is like a flag planted on your head, which is just what we don't need."

I sat. He draped the towel around my shoulders. "Don't move. I'll be right back," he said, holding up a restraining hand. He disappeared from view and returned a moment later brandishing a large pair of scissors. He stepped around to the side of me, lifted a handful of dense, curly hair and snipped decisively. I gasped inadvertently as I saw it fall, lifeless, on the white tiles. My hair: treasured by my father, his "Wild Princess's crown"; portable hiding place where, at the drop of my head, I could bring the curtains down around me. The scissors bit into my mane again, and again, and again. I felt the air cool and unfamiliar on my newly bare neck. I was having a hard time breathing. In some strange way, I was thrilled—as though I were being reborn.

The click of scissors continued. I blinked in the bright bathroom light and saw bull's-eyes form and erase themselves in front of my eyes. Suddenly, the towel was whipped off my neck. "*Voilà,*" Dev said with a flourish. "Go have a look."

I peered at myself in the medicine cabinet mirror. There, on a neck that seemed to have lengthened several inches, was my face, an ear visible at each side, topped by a street urchin crop from an antique Italian movie. My face, but not quite mine, without its baroque curlicued frame.

Mostly we'd led separate lives, the face and I. I knew it had given me a boost in Hollywood, and for that I was grateful. But in my head, the face I still saw was the one I'd had till I hit fifteen—an odd-looking assemblage of angles, crowded with eyes, nose, and mouth, all too large for it. Eyes still riveted to the mirror, I took a deep breath and felt, suddenly and inexplicably, wonderful. I grinned a greeting at the face in the mirror, as though meeting it for the first time.

"Okay, no more time for primping," Dev said behind me. "Put on jeans and sneakers, and stick some clean clothes and a toothbrush in your purse. I'll be back in a couple of minutes."

The door slammed and he was gone. I followed instructions and was just sweeping the last of my fallen hair into a garbage bag when he returned. He went to the closet, pulled out a herringbone tweed overcoat and handed it to me. "Here, this should do it."

"Do what? I know you're allergic to questions, but could you give me some clue, please?"

"I want to get you to the airport without being tailed. Marcie is a good friend and she's going to help."

"Marcie? I thought it was Ronnie," I zinged.

"What about Ronnie?" he asked abruptly.

"She called."

"Why didn't you *tell* me?" Tense. Angry.

"Because I forgot about it." I laughed. Maybe this new chop-haired Emily didn't flare up as easily as her predecessor. "Somewhere between the suicide and the haircut, it slipped my mind."

The radiant smile of this morning lit his face for a split second and then clouded over. "Sorry for jumping. It could be important."

"To both of us, or just to you?"

"I'll tell you later. Here, put the coat on, and this cap." The cap was a flat-topped, green-checked job with a peak.

If I were doing costumes, I'd've put it on an Irish navvy. "Skip the sunglasses," he said as he saw me fish them out of my bag—a California reflex even when it was raining. "We're halfway to a blizzard, you won't need them. Besides, they'll make you easier to spot. Now here's the way it's going to work."

CHAPTER
ELEVEN

MARCIE Bottstein was round and blond, with lively brown eyes that focused and snapped like expert scouts for the cameras that earned her living. Marcie lived two flights down from Dev in an apartment that occupied the same space, but couldn't have been more different from his open loft. Hers retained all its original walls and period details—carved oak mantels, paneling, stained glass—which formed an odd but pleasing backdrop for the welter of complicated-looking photographic equipment that perched on antique chairs, tables, and settees like little robots who'd just landed in a Victorian time warp.

"I'd love to shoot you sometime." She gave me a professional scan. "I'm starting a series of humans with their natural animal relatives, but I can't quite decide if you're a fawn or a cheetah. Great face. I'm going to go get the car now, Emily," she said on her way to the door. "If you want a cup of coffee or something, it's in the bedroom over there. But don't, repeat *don't,* open the door to the kitchen—I mean what *should* be the kitchen. It's my darkroom." She laughed and patted her generous hips. "That's why the big ass and thunder thighs. I keep the fridge and the microwave in the bedroom, so Häagen-Dazs keeps me company under the covers."

"Chocolate chocolate chip?"

"You're my kind of woman. Except you're skinny, damn

you. You Paul's new lady?" Her voice altered just slightly with the question. Was it over between them? Knock it off—it's none of your business.

"No," I said, after pausing longer than I wanted to. "No," I repeated for no good reason.

The keen brown eyes snapped a quick candid of me. Then she turned and left. I roamed the living room, staying away, as Dev had instructed me to do, from the windows. Black-and-white studies of animals lined the far wall—lion cubs frolicking with their mother, monkeys reaching out to paw the lens eye trained on them, llamas parading like a corps de ballet. I smiled as my eye flitted from one to another. The playful exuberance of the photos was infectious.

"Okay," Marcie called as she opened the door, "let's do it." I slipped into Dev's herringbone coat and pulled the checkered cap on over my cropped head as far as it would go. I grabbed a large gray canvas camera bag stuffed with my own purse and some clean clothes and toiletries and joined her at the door. "Here, can you manage the tripod and these two cameras?"

I nodded and took them. We walked down the stairs and out the door to her waiting car. An observer, if there was one, saw a photographer rushing into her car to get to an assignment, accompanied by her tall young male assistant schlepping the equipment.

I fought the temptation to turn around and check whether we were being followed. "See anybody in your rearview, Marcie?"

"Don't think so," she said tensely. "Paul said to watch for a blue Celica. I don't see it, but let's make sure." She cut out and changed lanes with a graceful efficiency I envied, then made an abrupt left turn just as the light was changing and followed it with another left and then a right. She handled the car so smoothly that the manuevers felt quite safe, despite the snow. "Now I'm sure," she announced in triumph.

"Love those moves! You're one great driver."

"That's what Paul says, specially when he's enlisting me for one of his errands."

"I guess it was pretty inconvenient for you this time—dragged out of your darkroom. Why didn't you just tell him no?"

We were approaching the bridge to Manhattan. She leaned forward and peered closely through the windshield. "I hope you can get a flight out. The whole goddamn airport could be closed down by the time we get there." I figured she was going to skip answering my question. It had probably been presumptuous anyway. "Why didn't I just tell him no?" she recited after a few silent minutes, as though it were a spelling bee word she was about to attempt but doubted she'd get right. "Because he makes me feel special, important. Marcie Bottstein counts! Because the stuff he asks me to do is exciting, like being in some book." She paused but I sensed she wasn't finished. "Because I feel bad for him. Because each time, I think I'll get to understand better why I *don't* say no to him. But I never do—understand, I mean. So I just go on saying yes." She let out a deep breath. "Probably not a very helpful answer," she said with a little, apologetic laugh.

"Oh, I think I get it. But what do you mean about feeling bad for him? The limp?"

"No. But that's kind of fatally attractive, isn't it? Small, touching weakness in this strong, brilliant, impossible man." I felt my face flush. The two lovers comparing notes. Two of how many? I wondered. Part of me didn't want to hear any more—but only part of me. "What I actually meant was, I feel bad about his writing."

"His writing?"

"You don't know about that yet, huh? Paul published this great book of short stories thirteen years ago. He got these smash reviews."

A writer. A surprise, but somehow not. The typewriter sitting on the round table, just as my father's had. A quick montage of Tuck Otis freeze-frames cut through my mind:

his slender hands ripping a half-typed page from the roller and tearing it contemptuously to bits; his head tipping back as he took a swig of scotch from his stubby glass before feeding a fresh white sheet into the machine; his arms tight around me, their red-gold fuzz of hair glinting in the stingy sunlight that made its way through the apartment's small windows. "You bring me luck, my little Wild Princess." The memory burned too painfully hot to hang on to.

"Just the one book?" I asked. I saw Dev's typewriter, forlorn, naked on its table, and knew the answer before Marcie gave it. I tried to imagine how I'd feel if I stopped being able to act—if I opened the pages of a script and saw only words on paper.

"Uh-huh, but he won't talk about it, I'm warning you. And if you push him, he bites." So do I. "Are you in love with him?" she asked mildly, as she made a wide turn into LaGuardia Airport.

"Are *you*?" I countered.

"Maybe still a little," she said with a cheerfulness that sounded real. "We've been friends a long time, and for a while after Julia left we had a lot of fun. But I think that was just because he was so relieved to be free again. Ah! Here we are. They won't let me stand. Good luck, Emily, in whatever it is you're up to."

"Thanks, Marcie—for everything. By the way, I think your animal pictures are extraordinary."

She grinned. "They're my real love. Unfortunately, it's still the weddings and Bar Mitzvahs that keep me in Häagen-Dazs."

I opened the car door and slid out. "I'll return your camera bag as soon as I get back."

"No problem. Oh, in case you don't know it yet, he's hell on wheels when the black Irish mood hits."

No kidding! The door gave a satisfying thunk as I swung it shut. I gave her a farewell wave and headed into the terminal.

CHAPTER
TWELVE

I bought tickets for the 3:00 flight to Chicago, the 3:10 to Atlanta, and the 3:15 to Miami, as Dev had instructed, and settled myself in the seating area at the Chicago gate while I waited for him. I fidgeted through the pages of *New York* magazine, impatient for him to arrive, though from the look of the accumulating crowd, it didn't much matter whether he got here by 3:15 or not. There'd been no announcement, but nobody was taking off for anywhere anytime soon.

I kept the cap on my head and the coat wrapped around me, just in case. Marcie's skill behind the wheel had almost certainly broke us free of followers, if there were any. Still, my own superstition about the voice's omniscience was powerful enough to keep me in my seat despite a restless desire to pace, a sudden impulse to call Gem again, and a growing need to find a ladies' room.

At 3:30 I started to get nervous. Was the middle-aged man in the black leather jacket looking at me peculiarly? How long had he been sitting there anyway? My hair was sweating under the cap and the urge to pee was becoming more assertive. I cursed myself for not hitting the ladies' room when I'd first arrived an hour ago. Now I didn't dare leave my seat. Dev could show up any minute.

I chewed my finger and tried to concentrate on an article psyching out who the front-runners were for this year's

Academy Awards. Two of the people interviewed bet on Trip to win Best Supporting. I felt a shiver of pride that for a moment made me forget where I was and why. Awards night was only a little over a month away. I saw us sitting there—Anthony, Nadia, and me—flanking Trip, feeling with him the agonizingly delicious suspense. "And the winner is . . ."

The sound of a loudspeaker announcement snapped me out of my daydream. A female voice was telling us at last that no flights would be taking off or landing at the airport until the following morning. Her cheerful lilt seemed to be trying to make this sound like good news. A wave of groans and exchanged looks of resigned discontent united the would-be passengers. Everybody but me got up and started improvising contingency plans. I remained glued to my green plastic contour seat, having no idea what else to do.

At 4:15 I imposed a game. If I looked at my watch more often than every ten minutes, I lost. By 5:20 I'd won only one round, and I felt in my gut that Dev must be dead. I dropped my head and felt newly surprised when no fall of hair came along.

"Took a little longer than I expected."

At the sound of him, the mounting fear that had filled the past two hours vanished as instantly as seasickness on dry land, leaving me trapped in an emotional vacuum. "I need a ladies' room," I announced, and made a beeline for it before he could say a word.

When I got back, I found him sitting, hands behind his head, face upturned, mind apparently a million miles away. With his battered brown leather jacket unzipped to reveal a black turtleneck, he might've been one of the wilder Irish poets composing a song of revolution. His father would have been pleased. I stood there for a moment, just looking at him, thinking about his one book and the typewriter on his table. An incentive or a punishment?

"What now, chief?" I asked finally, bringing him back from wherever his mind had been wandering. "I'm not going back to Brooklyn and—"

"We're spending the night at the local Sheraton. I checked in on the way." The purple eyes were clear and neutral as they read the suspicion on my face. "Get off it, Emily. Change the tape." He stood up and started to walk with no backward glance.

I followed him silently out of the airport.

Dev unlocked the door of a room that was first cousin to mine at the Ramada—a poorer relation who'd decided to spice up the drab beigeness of its decor with touches of glaring turquoise Formica.

I slipped off the coat and cap, ran my fingers through my cropped hair, and stretched my arms up high. My whole body felt stiff and achy, thanks to yesterday's fall, compounded by today's hours of sitting around. But not just today's—I'd been mostly sedentary, cooped up with grief and anger and plan hatching ever since Mike died. Suddenly, I longed to run on the beach, to feel my legs and arms work as the fresh salt air tingled my skin—to come back and throw myself, spent but invigorated, on the sofa, my tongue tasting salt as I ran it over my lips, thirsting for the tall glass of fresh orange juice Mike would squeeze and bring me when he came in from his swim.

"I'm hungry," I said, to break the wave of sadness that was beginning to crest.

"Me too." He picked up the phone. "What do you want?"

"Club sandwich. Rye toast, if they have it. Extra mayonnaise."

"And?"

"Oh, I don't know. Perrier or something." He made a face and placed the order. I bent over to see if I could touch my toes without too much complaint from my knee. I could. Just to make sure, I did it again. Dev opened the little bar-fridge and took out a small bottle of scotch, twisted the cap open, downed a belt.

"Want one?"

"No," I answered impatiently. "I want to know who was

watching the house when I slipped out with Marcie and whether you're planning to come to Florida with me to-morrow and—"

"Whoa. Let's start with those two. I don't know, except that it was a blue Celica. Plates were mudded up—pur--posely. And no. As long as I'm convinced nobody's tailing you to Florida, I think you can handle Kennoyer better yourself."

I stretched out on one of the beds, lying on my side, hand propping up my head, and began to do leg lifts, which didn't get more than thirty degrees high. Dev sat in one of the turquoise plastic armchairs watching me, looking slightly amused. I turned to the other side and did a few more feeble leg lifts. I was restless, irritated—my skin felt buffed just slightly raw. Goddamned snow! I should've been half-way to Key West by now.

"I don't understand," I snapped, impatience flicking the words. "Why all this cat-and-mouse? As you said, they could've efficiently killed both of us a dozen times. Why haven't they?"

"Good question," he said slowly, separating the words. "Maybe we're not close enough yet to be dangerous."

"Then why did squash nose try to push me under a train?"

"I'd guess that was an impulse. He didn't figure you'd recognize him after twenty years, or he'd've tailed you more carefully—especially if he's a cop. You spotted him, and he panicked and pushed."

I told him about the phone call, the one where they'd played my taped imitation of the voice at me.

His mouth twisted in disgust. "Horror film stuff. But pretty effective, huh?"

"Had me gibbering for a few minutes," I said. "More than a few," I admitted.

A knock. Dev opened the bureau drawer and pulled out a very businesslike gun. He cracked the door and peered out, gun hand upraised. I saw his back relax as he quickly shut it again and called out, "Just a second." He returned

the gun to its drawer and then ran back to the door and
opened it wide to a slightly confused-looking room service
waiter wheeling a tray of sandwiches and a bottle of red
wine and one of club soda.

That snippet of pantomime—the gun, ready for use in
his hand—seemed, at the same time, both more and less
real than anything that had happened since I'd arrived in
New York.

"I didn't mean to scare you," he said after the waiter
had gone. "Just being careful."

"I'm not scared. Should *I* have a gun?"

"Do you know how to use one?"

"Sort of."

"Sort of isn't enough. You should stay away from situa-
tions where you might need one."

"That why you're so eager to get me out of town?"

"Partly. But I also think it's useful for you to talk to
Kennoyer." He leveled a gaze at me. "No, I'm not conning
you."

"No? You seem to be an expert." How about Marcie? I
thought. And Ronnie? And Julia? I suppose you weren't
conning *them* either. I realized almost at once, by the look
he gave me, that an actress worth her salt ought to have
better control over her face.

"Okay, Emily," he said wearily, sitting down on the other
bed, his face tense. "If you're going to keep worrying it
like some loose tooth, we'll talk about it. Nobody conned
anybody. You and I made love to each other. And I feel
only good about that. Now, you can beat your breasts and
rend your garments and howl about what crass, selfish animals we were. I can't tell you how to feel. But don't ask
me to join in some hair shirt come-all-ye, because I won't."
His eyes flashed anger at me and then broke away.

He got up and strode over to the table in front of the
long, unopenable windows. "I thought you were hungry,"
he said, pulling a blue-frilled toothpick out of a sandwich
quarter and taking a decisive bite.

I joined him at the table and went to work on my own

sandwich. I skipped the club soda in favor of the wine. Nobody spoke until all the food and half the drink was gone.

"I should be able to find squash nose while you're away," he said.

"Do you have any idea where to look?"

"No, but I will tomorrow. Ronnie'll help now."

"What's Ronnie got to do with it?"

"She's my policewoman friend—the one I told you shut down on me when I tried to push her about records of your parents' case. She called because she'd just heard about Strohmeyer. It shook her up. I'm seeing her tomorrow morning. If squash nose works anywhere in NYPD, Ronnie will nail him for me. Also, I don't know who might turn up at the wake and funeral, but I'm going to be there to find out."

I reached for the wine bottle and refilled our glasses. I was feeling decidedly better and not inclined to look a gift horse in the mouth by analyzing how much of the upturn was due to what.

"You're smiling," he said.

"So are you."

"I like looking at you. I think I give a thumbs-up to the hair chop."

"You know, in a funny way, I agree with you. I feel different in some way I'm not sure of. My mother had long hair, only hers wasn't quite as curly. She used to jerk her head and toss it back when she got mad. Like this." I demonstrated the gesture, surprised I remembered it. I remembered so little about her. "I got used to hiding behind my hair."

"Everybody hides behind something."

"What do you hide behind, Dev?"

His eyes narrowed as he considered the question. "My work," he said. "It keeps me in other people's stories— and out of my own." I watched his thoughts dip back into private territory. A moment later, when I saw he was about

to speak, I sensed he was going to tell me about his writing.
I was wrong. "Your father's always there, top of your mind,
isn't he?"

"Yes. I guess he is."

"What about your mother? You say your grandmother
never mentioned her. You don't either."

"I . . ." I felt my face get hot. My mind seemed to stall,
leaving me with a vague guilty feeling. "She was a very
good actress, I think." I coughed. Why was my throat so
tense? "She had other jobs, too. She worked very hard.
She had a lot of energy. She seemed always to be moving."
It was coming out in constricted little bursts. "She looked
like me," I added finally. "Well, maybe a little less after
my haircut."

"Umhm," he murmured. "But how did you feel about
her?"

"I loved her," I said quickly. His eyes stayed focused on
me, but not in any challenging way. I ran my tongue over
my lips and took a swallow of wine. "The truth is, I don't
really know," I admitted, looking into my empty glass.

He reached over and lifted my chin. "I'm not wanting to
hurt you, Emily."

"I know. And I . . . I'm trying to trust you. Mike did."

For a second, his mouth softened and looked as vulnerable as his eyes. "I hope I deserve it."

"He didn't make many mistakes about things like that."

"Did Mike keep any ties to the church?" he asked, face
and voice back to business.

"The church? He never went. He used to say that the
last place you'd go to look for God would be in a church—
that you should try a mountaintop or a beach or a bed, if
you really wanted to find him. Why?"

"I just wondered."

*Running. I was running for my life, clutching a doll by
the hand. Her large glass eyes widened with fear as her shiny
brown wig flew off into space, leaving her head bald and vul-*

nerable. Suddenly, the ground under my feet gave way and I was falling. I looked down at the doll, but all that remained was her hand, still clutched in mine. "Nooooo . . ."

"Sshhh, easy, easy, darling." A hand, warm and firm on my shoulder. Another gently massaging my neck. I opened my eyes and turned my head. Dev stood at the side of the bed, still dressed in his jeans and turtleneck. His hair was rumpled and his gaze worried. He continued his soothing work on my neck.

"Ummmm," I heard myself grunt. Then, with no warning, I started to shudder.

He sat down on the bed and put both arms around me. I still had my jeans and sweater on. After watching the late news, from which we learned nothing we didn't already know about Strohmeyer's suicide, we had chastely and without discussion put ourselves onto separate beds and gone to sleep.

The shaking subsided. "There was a doll," I said almost to myself, as though saying it would minimize the unreasoning fear I still felt. "I was holding her hand and running, and then her hair fell off." I laughed shakily. "Reaction to my haircut, wouldn't you say, Dr. Freud?"

"Vould you zay more about dat?"

"No more to say." I had a feeling there was, but it kept getting away from me—and I wasn't sure I wanted to go after it. "What time is it?"

"Six thirty-five. I was going to wake you anyway. Time to go."

"Airport's open?"

He nodded. "I just checked. I called and rearranged your reservations yesterday, so you're all set. Now here's what you're going to do when we get there."

I walked quickly into the terminal, cap in place on my head and on my nose a pair of small round sunglasses, which couldn't have been more different from the large black ones I usually wore. I knew Dev was somewhere behind me, but

I didn't look around to check where; he'd warned me not to. If I saw squash nose, I was to signal by scratching the back of my neck. Otherwise, I was to wait in the seating area for the 7:15 Atlanta flight, get on line to board, and, at the last minute, slip over to the next gate and join the boarding line for the 7:25 to Miami.

No sign of squash nose. I breathed a sigh of relief as I cut out of the Atlanta line and walked in a pace as relaxed-looking as I could manage to make the switch to Miami. In my head I was practically on that plane—which is why I almost failed to stifle a gasp of astonishment when I spotted, out of the corner of my eye, a long, grizzled head on a tall, thin, stoop-shouldered frame, turning slowly back and forth, searching.

I stood frozen for an endless second of agonizing indecision. Then I stepped up my pace and joined the Miami boarding line, inserting myself in front of a tall, bulky man carrying a fat suitpack. I felt my heart pound chokingly in the base of my throat. What was my grandmother's chauffeur doing here?

CHAPTER
THIRTEEN

"THE captain has turned on the seat belt sign in preparation for our landing in Key West . . ." I looked out the window as the plane circled over shimmering turquoise water and felt my excitement renew itself. Nick Kennoyer had casually filed away in his memory so much I needed to know. My head was all at once a corn-popper of questions, new ones making their tiny explosions each second. To my surprise, they weren't the big questions—the ones I'd searched him out for—but rather, Was my father the wonderful playwright he'd wanted to be? Or just good? Or terrible? Why did he become an alcoholic? Did he love my mother when they married? When did it start to go bad? Was I an accident, or had they planned me? If I had never been born, do you think . . . ?

I'd spent most of the flight to Miami focused on another question: What was Mac doing at LaGuardia Airport, stationed between the Atlanta and Miami gates at seven a.m.? I tried to come up with an answer I liked, but the only one that rang true was that Gem was tracking me, just as she had in L.A. And I didn't like that one a bit. But how could she have known about my plans? And why use Mac instead of a professional? That thought made me feel queasy. If she *had* used a professional, I'd never have known. It could've been the man next to me, or the woman across the aisle. The anger I felt was vintage—the rich, thick,

head-pounding kind that harked back to the time I was nine
and powerless.

You're not powerless now. And you're not nine. So stop
acting like it, I told myself. Cool down. I knew Mac hadn't
seen me, and even if he was able to find out from the airline
which plane I'd boarded, it would be hours after the fact.
Just to play it safe, I'd wandered around the Miami airport
for an hour or so, and struck up a conversation with a
streetwise-looking woman about my own age on her way
to visit her folks in Puerto Rico. I paid her fifty dollars and
she bought a round-trip open-return ticket to Key West that
allowed me to travel as Mercedes Ruiz. She shook my hand
firmly and wished me well—and, to my relief, didn't push
for a life story to go with the fifty.

I walked out of the Key West airport into balmy, jasmine-
scented air, with Dev's heavy wool coat slung over my arm
like a drab, shed snake skin. I almost yielded to an impulse
to shove it in the nearest trash can, and wondered fleetingly
why anyone who had a choice would ever leave this island.
Once, when I was sixteen, I'd sneaked away and run off
for an illicit weekend here with Stan Beecherson, a Yale
sophomore who'd briefly seemed fascinating because he
liked both Thoreau and BMWs. I remembered the trip
fondly, more for the island than for Stan, but most of all
for getting away with it—one of the few outlaw escapades
Gem never found out about.

At least, that's what I'd always thought. Now I wondered
whether there was anything at all about me that had escaped
the floodlight of her extended eye.

"Cab?" I turned around to face a very slender, handsome
guy, maybe twenty-three, with a delectable caramel tan,
set off perfectly by his pale blue T-shirt.

"Sure." I smiled to myself as I climbed into his slightly
rattly red car, paint dulled by the sea breezes but still jaunty-
looking. He reminded me of Trip—the Trip of eleven years
ago, who'd just stopped being Walter Grody and started

on his way to becoming a movie star. He'd driven a cab then too, sometimes. He and Evan had shared it, as they'd shared everything, until Evan got sick . . .

"Where to, pretty lady?" My driver swiveled his head around and gave me a grin that almost bisected his thin face.

"I'm not sure," I said. "Someplace on Duval Street, I guess." I figured a central location made the most sense. "By the way, where's Caroline Street?"

"In Old Town, off Duval," he answered, starting the car. "Block or a coupla, three, depending on the address. You looking for anyone special?"

A tingle of warning went off. Key West was a small place. The last thing I wanted to do was send up an alarm, but maybe . . . "A friend of mine said to be sure and say hi to Nick Kennoyer when I came down." I felt my pulse quicken as I said his name.

He laughed. "Another member of the Kennoyer fan club."

"What do you mean?" I asked sharply. Suddenly my guard was up. Was it possible that they'd beaten me down here? That . . .

"Hey, relax." He gave me a fast over-the-shoulder glance. "I just meant that Nick's act is pretty popular."

"Oh, of course," I covered. "Excuse me if I jumped. It was hell on wheels getting out of New York. The airport was closed for snow and—"

"Yeah, I heard about your storm. That's New York for you. God, I hate that place."

"Are you from there?"

"No, but I lived there a couple of years before I saw the light and came down here."

"Where is it that Nick, uh, performs?" I chanced.

"Pier House."

"A hotel is it, or a club? I have a head like a sieve these days, and I forgot what my friend said," I added quickly.

"Hotel—bottom of Duval, smack on the gulf. Carriage

trade. And Nick keeps that piano bar packed." Bingo! "Hey, something's been bothering me about you." Oh my God, how have I screwed this up? "Didn't I see you on *Northern Exposure*?"

"Yes." My relief made it a breathless whisper.

"Way to go! I'm jealous."

"You an actor?"

"I was." Something about the note of finality in his tone struck me. "I'm not strong for long enough now." He served up the fact ungarnished by even a trace of self-pity.

"I'm sorry," I said.

"Yeah, me too."

I wanted to say something, but there was nothing I knew to say that might make a handsome twenty-three-year-old stranger feel better about watching death stroll deliberately in his direction. I thought again how much he reminded me of a younger Trip, and felt the sweat cold on the back of my neck.

"Hey, we're not at my funeral yet," he said, catching my eye in his mirror. "My problem right now is where to take you. There's a great little B-and-B on Duval. How about that?"

I realized the last thing I wanted was the intimacy of a bed-and-breakfast—and I needed a private phone. "What about the Pier House."

"It'll cost you."

"I'll treat myself."

"Way to go!" He made a sharp turn. "Another *Northern Exposure* ought to take care of it."

I signed for two nights in a room bigger and fancier than I needed, because it was the only one available. Last-minute cancellation, the smiling desk clerk told me. Otherwise, he assured me, I'd have been out of luck: "You snow bunnies love us to death this time of year."

On my way to the elevator, Nick's name jumped out at me from a standing promotional display for the piano bar.

I walked over and stood examining the glossy photo, wanting it to tell me something that would help me approach him without messing up. It was standard stuff—Charlie Gracious Star seated at his piano, hands on keys, head turned to greet the camera. The jolt was that he looked so old. Silly as it seems, it took a long few seconds to get through to me that Nick Kennoyer looked sixty because he *was* sixty—or close to it. My father had been thirty-eight when he died. So, of course, he'd be thirty-eight forever.

Nick's face was roundish and a little pouchy, dominated by a black mustache and prominent, hooded dark eyes. Straight, shiny black hair formed a W high up on his domed forehead. His smile said that he loved a good double entendre. He reminded me of William Powell—a hopeful sign. I liked William Powell.

My oversized room was all tropical pastels and rattan. I could see the small, man-made gulf beach out the window, still dotted with people at almost five. I opened the window and watched a tall, silver-haired woman incline her elegant bronze neck toward the shoulder of a sleek, portly man with a George Washington ponytail, so that he could light her cigarette along with his own. Next to them, a pair of identically trim male butts in matching black bikinis lay side by side, their prone owners holding hands. The casual intimacies pierced through to my heart like an icicle.

I plunked down flat on one of the queen-sized beds and rang Dev's office. He wasn't in. I hadn't expected that he would be. I left the message that I'd arrived safely, along with my phone number, backward minus an area code, as we'd arranged. I'd thought the procedure overcautious, but seeing Mac at LaGuardia had changed my mind.

I stripped off my clothes and lay there naked, letting the fragrant sea breeze brush my body while I did the deep breathing that we used in Nadia's class to head-clear and prepare for a scene. I floated, as though through warm water, and saw my father slowly rubbing the bridge of his nose between thumb and forefinger. He held his glasses loosely in his other hand and smiled ruefully, sharing the joke of how useless his blurred gray eyes were on their own. He . . . With a start, I snapped out of the drift and sat up. Dev was right—it was always my father, never my mother. Why had I gotten so clutched when he asked about her? Because she was mostly a blank. Where are you, Celia Silver? I loved you. I *did.* So why aren't you there in my flashbacks? Why have I blanked you out?

I leapt up, needing suddenly to be in motion. I pulled my jeans, T-shirt, and sneakers back on, stuck my room key in my pocket, and bolted out the door.

I ran along the back streets of Key West for more than an hour, forcing from my brain everything but sensation— the rhythmic moving of my limbs and the feel of the lowering sun on my back. I ran till I was hot-faced and exhausted. Then I walked back to the hotel, winding in and out of the white-and-pastel-gingerbread-lined streets, taking in the delicious details of another time. Down Southard and up Fleming past the library, its pale pink paint peeling, as though by design; down Eaton and up—I realized with a shock of recognition—Caroline. I paused in front of 178, a pale blue cottage with wedding-cake white trim. Nick lived no more than a couple of blocks from the hotel. For a second my body tensed, ready to spring through his front gate and hammer on the door. But reason prevailed and I kept walking. I'd have a better chance at the piano bar, where he couldn't shut the door on me.

Back in the room, after a long, cool shower, I fell deeply, dreamlessly asleep.

CHAPTER
FOURTEEN

THE ringing felt like a siren inside my head. I woke in the dark, my stomach swooping with apprehension. I sat up fast and groped for the light before grabbing the phone.

"Hello," I croaked, heart pounding.

"Hi. What's the matter?"

"Nothing, Dev. I was . . . I guess I was pretty fast asleep."

"Another nightmare?"

"No." I was getting my bearings back. "Look, can I, uh, talk?"

"Yeah. I'm in a phone booth at the Castlebar, so proceed *en clair,* as the spooks say."

I told him about MacNiff at the airport.

"You're sure he didn't spot you?"

"Just about a hundred percent sure," I said. "But if he knew I was at the airport, I figured he could find out what flight I was on, so when I got to Miami, I paid somebody to buy my Key West ticket under her name."

"Brava!" My face flushed, either with pleasure at his approval or embarrassment at knowing I'd fished for it—I didn't want to think about which.

"Dev, I don't understand this part of it at all," I said, the glow extinguished almost at once by troubling questions. "Why did my grandmother send Mac to the airport?

How could she know I'd be there? It was better between us when I went to see her—better than it's ever been. I almost thought . . . Why would she *do* this?"

"I don't know," he said slowly, his voice telling me that he was as troubled by it as I was. "I seem to say an awful lot of I-don't-know's for a detective. I think I may've found squash nose, though," he added, almost as a throwaway.

"You *have?* Who is he? Can you have him arrested? Can you—"

"Sorry, that's not how it works. All I know now is that he matches your description and that he was a close buddy of Strohmeyer's. Even after you ID'd him, it would be your word against his that he pushed you off that subway platform, or even that he questioned you twenty years ago. And his word's better. He's a cop. His name's Andy Logan."

"Well, how come you didn't come across him when you were first poking around?"

"That's the strange part. What I don't get at all is what he was doing in your hospital room back then. The guy's a vice cop—always has been."

"A vice cop? Are you sure?"

"I'm sure. Ronnie just gave me the word. Strohmeyer's funeral's tomorrow. I figure Logan'll show up. I'll have to play it by ear. How are things on your end?"

"I'll know in a couple of hours. Nick plays piano at the Pier House, which is why I'm staying here. Soon as I get off the phone, I thought I'd go down and listen to some Cole Porter."

"I'll call you at nine tomorrow morning."

"Okay."

"Good luck with Nick, actress."

My mouth went dry and my hands slightly numb. I felt a chain of prickles run up my spine. These were symptoms I was well acquainted with. The actress was having a case of stage fright.

CHAPTER
FIFTEEN

I strode into the piano bar, head resolutely high in keeping with my role: young woman with mission, confident of success. I wore a white shirt, unfolded fresh from its laundry pack, a short black cotton-knit skirt, and black mules on bare feet—not exactly the costume of choice, but the only choice available other than jeans.

Nick Kennoyer, dark and debonair—the hair had to be dyed—in a spandy white suit, white shirt, and ascot, sat at a white grand piano, having fun with " 'S Wonderful." Within about ten seconds I knew he was good—hands sure, voice a true, slightly gravelly tenor that did nice things for the Gershwin. For no good reason, I felt a surge of personal pride in him. All seats around the piano were taken. Probably just as well. No rush, there was plenty of time. According to the lobby poster, he played Saturday nights till one a.m.

A short crew-cut kid in beach whites showed me to a small table in the back part of the room and told me a waiter would be over to take my drink order. I scanned the room and locked into eye contact with the silver-haired woman I'd seen on the beach. The reason our eyes met was that hers were trained on me, an unmistakable half-smile of recognition on her mouth. Before I could decide whether this might be good news or bad, she stood up, leaned over, and said something into her ponytailed companion's ear. He put his hand on her arm and said something back. Then she shook her head no and started toward my table.

"Excuse me," she began, her cigarette-throaty voice as gracefully assured as the way she carried her deeply tanned model's body. "Aren't you Emily Silver?"

My heart gave a small upward skid. "Yes?" I said, my reply more of a question than an answer.

Her brown face broke into a warm smile. "I'm Sondra Hersh. We saw you in a film called *Running Fast*—in New York when we were back for the holidays. And I said to Howard, 'That has *got* to be Celia's daughter!'"

My breath caught in my throat. Anything resembling composure deserted me. I felt my knees begin to shake, and I gripped the table hard to keep my hands from doing likewise.

She put a long, pearl-nailed hand on my shoulder and squeezed. Her face looked stricken. "Oh my God, stupid me, coming at you like that out of nowhere. I am so sorry. The last thing I meant to do was upset you."

"No, no," I said quickly. "I'm not upset, just . . . surprised out of my mind." I felt myself start to smile, and went with it. "You knew my mother?" As I asked it, a powerful wave of longing broke over me, but not for my mother. I looked at this appealing stranger—this woman whose name I'd never even heard—and caught myself wishing that *she* were my mother.

"Yes. Yes, I did." Her face grew serious, recalling, I guessed, that she was talking about a murder victim.

"And my father?" I asked it almost defiantly.

"I knew Tuck, too," she said gently. "He was my brother's friend."

"Your brother?"

She gestured toward the piano. "Nicky. He'll be excited to meet you—though I shouldn't say 'meet,' should I? You must have known him when you were a child."

"I . . . ." My head was buzzing with enough messages and

countermessages to make it short-circuit. "Won't you sit down?" I asked.

"No, but you must come join us," she insisted, taking my hand between her long, cool ones. I got up and let her lead me to their table. The husband, Howard, eyes wary behind tinted aviator glasses, wrapped a welcoming brown arm around my shoulder, while his other hand reached over to the next table and commandeered an empty chair.

I had an instant fantasy about how cherished their daughter would be. "This is . . . quite a coincidence," I said, treading water. Part of me wanted to plunge in and make a grab for every single scrap of information, every impression, every thought either of them possessed about my parents, as though they had, stored in their heads, my confiscated property. But another part hollered no, and I obeyed. "Do you spend much time in Key West?" I asked cautiously.

"We live here now," Sondra said, lighting a fresh cigarette, "most of the year. When we retired from—"

"No life histories till we get this girl a drink. You like rum and tonic?" Howard asked, indicating a tall, almost empty glass in front of him.

"Yes, thank you." I'd rather've had a steadying scotch, but didn't say so. He waved for a waiter and ordered a round for the three of us. "You were saying you'd retired. From what?"

"The shmatte business," Howard said, "but the genteel end of it. Accessories—only two seasons a year instead of six, like in women's wear. Sondra designed. I sold. We had all of them—the best specialty shops in the country. Even so, when Sondra turned fifty, that was *it*. We cashed in our chips, decided to enjoy life."

"When you're in the fashion business there *is* no life," Sondra chimed in, "just the business—except for the occasional weekend getaway. It's all Burdine's didn't get this and how fast can we fill the reorder for Nan Duskin and on and on and on."

The waiter set down three tall, frosted glasses. I squeezed the lemon into my drink and took a long, thirsty sip. "This is wonderful," I said. "There's something different about the taste. I can't really place it."

"The key lime," Howard said.

"It's like nothing else," Sondra continued. "They say it's a cross between a lemon and a lime, but it isn't really. It has a flavor all its own." I wondered what it might be like to have a kind of unity with someone that let you seamlessly complete each other's thoughts—and felt sure that I'd never find out. I looked over at Nick, who was crooning with tantalizing suggestion about how birds and bees do it. He wasn't just good. He was *very* good.

"Did you move here because of Nick?" I asked.

"In spite of," Howard answered, sharing a private joke with his wife.

"Oh, don't listen to him, Emily. He's very fond of Nicky." She drew a deep drag that made me want a cigarette. "I'll tell you, we loved Rio, until we were robbed at knife point. We loved Haiti, until we got caught in a coup."

"And then *I* said," Howard cut in, "if we buy someplace, it's going to be in the U.S. of A."

"So we came down here to visit Nicky and we fell head over heels for this asylum without walls!" She studied my face for a moment, her head cocked slightly to the side. "It *is* amazing how much you look like your mother," she said softly, "even with the short hair. In the movie it was long, very much the way Celia wore it."

"Yes," I said. "I recently got it cut. Did you . . ." I began without reviewing it in my head. "Did you know my mother well?" The question hung there for a second.

"I wouldn't say well," Sondra answered, her voice careful—different. "She worked for us for a short time."

One of her job jobs. "What did she do?"

"Everything in the showroom, helped out with buyers, handled the phones," Sondra said, blowing out a lungful of smoke. "She was a dynamo," she added. "Nobody

ever did so much so well as Celia. Isn't that right, Howard?"
"Right."

They were holding something back. Or maybe I was just hearing the normal reticence of nice people discussing someone who'd died violently. "Could I have one of your cigarettes?" I asked, throwing away without a second of deliberation eight years of abstinence. Howard contributed a Marlboro and a light for it. The deep drag tasted as good as I remembered. It gave me a shot of courage to ask, "Did you like her? Did you like my mother?"

Instead of an answer I heard another question, behind me. "Didn't anybody bother to order the hardworking piano player a drink?" I whirled around in my chair and found myself face-to-face with Nick Kennoyer.

His dark, heavy-lidded eyes widened and the tan on his suddenly drained face looked as lifeless as scuffed luggage. A round white scar about the size of a dime stood out, smooth and glossy, on the dulled skin.

"I had the same reaction when I saw Emily's movie, Nicky." Sondra jumped in to smooth the moment. "Remember? I told you."

"I think Christine Lahti might object if she heard you calling it Emily's movie," I said, making my own effort at lightness. "I'm glad to meet you, Nick. I enjoyed listening to you." I held out my hand. After a moment he took it with a tapering, well-manicured hand, which felt unnaturally cold.

"Thank you," he said, summoning up a performer's smile. He pulled over a chair and the waiter arrived, unbidden, with a squat glass of something brown on ice. Nick tipped back his head and drank. The motion reminded me of my father. "So you're an actress, Emily," he said in a fairly good imitation of party small talk. It occurred to me that by now Sondra was probably well into being sorry she'd started the whole thing.

"I guess it's in the genes. It certainly wasn't what my grandmother would've wanted." I took a pull at my cigarette while I waited to see what he'd do with that.

"No, probably not."

"You knew my grandmother, right?" I heard my voice rise and crack slightly the way it does sometimes when I'm tense.

"Yes," he said, "but that was in another country, and besides—" He stopped abruptly, realizing how the rest of the line went.

"The wench is dead," I finished, remembering how recently I'd quoted those words to Dev about myself. "She isn't, though." The three of them looked at me, not knowing what to say. I took a long sip of my drink, more grateful for the cool of the citrus and quinine water than for the alcohol. Sondra reached her hand across the table and gave mine a pat. I pulled my hand away in a jerky reflex.

"Look," I said with a nervous intensity that took me, as well as them, by surprise, "if you all feel you have to walk on eggs because my parents were murdered twenty years ago, please don't. I'm used to that fact. I grew up with it." Embarrassment was clear on their faces. "And yes, I said murdered." I knew, not in the back of my mind but right there in front, that it was too fast, that I was jumping the gun. I just couldn't stop myself. "I agree with you, Nick. My father never killed my mother or anybody else. Wasn't that what you said in the paper—that he was a lover, not a killer?"

It hung there for a second. Then Nick mumbled, "I don't remember what I said." His face was stiff, eyes down. "It was a long time ago. I was shocked. People . . . People say things." He stood up and turned away. Neither Sondra nor Howard spoke a word.

"Nick, talk to me. I need—"

"I have to get back to work," he said.

I stood and held his arm. "Please, please talk to me. This is very important."

He lifted my hand off his arm. "Emily, understand me. There is nothing I can say to you that's going to help your life." He began to walk. I darted in front of him and blocked him like a basketball guard.

"Nick," I whispered urgently, "I know you're working now, but can we talk when you're done?"

He shook his head wearily. "I'm not done until one in the morning. And by then I'm beat." He stepped around me. I followed at his side.

"I won't leave you alone. I know where you live." That stopped him in his tracks. He turned slowly and faced me.

"This is no coincidence, is it, you being here?"

"No. Please. Just an hour. Then I'll never bother you again. I promise."

His long index finger absently massaged the small scar on his cheek as he looked for something in my eyes.

And I saw something unmistakable in his. Fear. "Why are you so scared?" I asked softly. He didn't answer. "Look, no one knows I'm here," I said, "and it'll stay that way, if you give me an hour." A quick flicker of hesitation. He was wavering, and I was playing blindman's buff. "Otherwise, I will make your life miserable, Nick," I said, hoping my words would strike some target.

"Celia's daughter," he said with a bitter twist to his mouth. "I'll see you at one." Then he turned and approached the piano, his step abruptly taking on the spring common to entertainers making an entrance. I watched him bestow a hug here, a kiss there to new arrivals around the piano before he sat down, flipped up the piano lid, and began to noodle some Noel Coward.

CHAPTER
SIXTEEN

I walked reluctantly back toward the table, feeling not a trace of the elation I'd expected at having nailed Nick. *Celia's daughter.* I had her face. I had her voice. I'd chosen to take her name. Why did the label disturb me? I had no idea what Sondra and Howard might be speculating about my strange behavior, and wasn't eager to fabricate an explanation. I'd have retreated to my room for a couple of hours, except that I didn't quite trust Nick not to disappear.

Sondra rose and walked quickly to meet me. "Come on, Emily. I'm headed for the ladies' room. Why don't you join me?"

A strategy to give her brother the chance to bolt? I bet not and followed her. Wordlessly, we peed in adjoining booths. Then I washed my overheated face, while she applied fresh, melon-colored lipstick and fluffed her silver hair.

"Want to step outside for a few minutes and get some air?" she asked.

"Yes, but . . . I don't think I can," I finished in a rush.

"What do you mean? Of *course* you can."

I bit my lip, wondering whether to try to lie to her. There didn't seem any point. "I need to make sure that Nick doesn't slip out sick or something before I can talk to him."

"Oh." She reached out and placed her cool hand on my

still-warm cheek. "Did he agree to talk to you?" she asked, her tone puzzled but kind.

"Yes, at one, after he gets off. But he didn't want to."

"I don't know exactly what's going on here, Emily, and you certainly don't have to tell me, but if Nicky promised he'd talk to you, I think he will."

I started for the door, reminding myself that Nick could've bolted already while I was in here. Sondra caught my arm. "How would it be if I speak a word in his ear. I think he'd honor a promise to you. I'd stake my life on his honoring one to me."

"You'd do that?" I asked, unbelieving. "Why would you do that for me? You don't even know me."

She smiled, but just slightly, and not happily. "Let's just say I owe your mother a favor."

I stood near the back of the room and watched Sondra lean over her brother's shoulder as he played "Send in the Clowns," and deliver a message. I saw him nod and say a few words without looking up. Sondra kissed the top of his broad forehead, returned to me, and took my arm. "Don't be afraid, he's not going anywhere. This is his world—and it's a very small one."

We walked over to the hotel's small gulf beach and perched on a short, fat stone wall. The breeze was a shade stronger than gentle.

"Sondra," I said, aware of my sweaty fists clenching and unclenching in my lap. "Tell me about my mother. You were so—I don't know—guarded when you mentioned her. And Nick . . ." I paused, not wanting to say what was on my tongue, that Nick had said her name as though she was someone he hated.

Sondra shook a cigarette out of her pack of Ultras, offered me one, and lit us both. "Perhaps it wasn't the wisest thing I've ever done, approaching you tonight. Howard thought I should let it alone, and Howard, God love him, is the most sensible person I've ever met. But I couldn't. I needed somehow to . . . know you."

"Why?"

"Because you're Tuck's daughter," she said finally, her eyes gazing out at the water. "As much as you look like Celia, you're his, too. And I don't know whether any woman ever fully gets over the first man she loved."

"You and my father?"

She smiled. "Very ancient history. Nicky used to bring Tuck home from Yale on vacations sometimes. We lived in Douglaston—good old respectable Queens. We were far from poor, but a long way from the kind of money he came from, and a long way from his kind of world altogether.

"It wasn't only me, our whole family fell in love with Tuck. Here was this golden Martian who seemed to find us as exotic and exciting as we found him. He'd harmonize with Nicky at the piano and they'd write funny, risqué songs together. He'd put old records on and let my mother teach him the Charleston. He'd roar at Daddy's salesman's jokes and tell him new ones. And he'd talk with me for hours about paintings. Van Gogh's, Picasso's, and mine—as though it weren't at all ridiculous to discuss the three in the same conversation."

"I remember him like that," I said, my heart lifting in excitement at discussing my father with someone else who'd actually known him, loved him. "He made you feel like you were the most important person in the world." The memory flashed through my head and made me smile. "He'd teach me old songs—maybe some of the same ones he sang with Nick at your piano in Queens. We couldn't afford to have a piano, but we had lots of records. He had these two Cole Porter records, one with vocals, one just instrumental. He taught me the songs from the first one and we'd sing duets with the second. My favorite was 'You're the Top.' I loved shouting out, 'You're Mickey Mouse!'"

Sondra looked straight out at the water. "I daydreamed my way through half my senior year in high school—a hundred and one scenarios where I'd leave everything and run away with Tuck." She stubbed out her cigarette and turned to me. "That Christmas vacation, I got pregnant."

"So he conned you into bed. Is that what you're saying?" I asked flatly, needing to get a jump on my disappointment.

"No, it wasn't that way, Emily. Not at all. I was seventeen. Tuck wasn't even twenty. Sure, he should've used a condom. I should've . . . well, who knows what I should've done? Maybe I *wanted* to become pregnant—make my fantasy come true."

"And?" All at once, my heart was thumping hard. Was she going to tell me I had a brother or sister?

"I had an abortion, of course. Nicky saw me through it. My parents never knew."

"What about my father? Wasn't it *his* place to see you through?"

"That wasn't Tuck's long suit," she said, lighting a fresh cigarette. I declined one. We sat silently, like fishing companions alone in a boat, each intent on the action at the end of her own line. The sour feeling in my stomach wasn't triggered by surprise but by the confirmation of what I'd always known—that my father was no one to depend on.

"Your father was who he was, Emily," Sondra said. "If you're looking for blame to assign, you'd have to go back to his parents and then *their* parents. So what's the point? Besides, if I'd run off with Tuck, I'd never have met Howard. And you'd never have been born." She laughed.

"I know. I just don't think I agree, completely—about blame, I mean. People are responsible for what they do." I felt a twinge of something I couldn't identify, hearing my grandmother's words come priggishly out of my mouth. "How could Nick have stayed my father's friend after that?"

"Things aren't always that black and white. Nicky loved your father very much."

"Can we get back to my mother? We started talking about her and then got off onto him immediately—as usual. It even happens in my own head. I think of my parents and it's all him. I just can't seem to find my mother." I wasn't sure about the look I caught in Sondra's eyes, but I thought it was one of pity.

"Your mother was talented and beautiful. She was a person of extremes. Intense. She loved. She hated. She didn't have the insulation or the inner thermostat that protects most of us when the elements get too rough. As a result, she was very . . . vulnerable. I'm glad to see that you're a lot tougher."

I thought of my shaking fits, my nightmares. I hoped she was right. "Why do you owe her a favor?"

"Because I didn't do her one when I let her meet Tuck. She would've been better off with someone like her friend Irene's boyfriend—a nice, gemütlich Jewish doctor. 'Good old Herb Roston.' The two of them used to giggle about him when Irene would come up to meet Celia after work. But he's precisely the kind of nurturing husband Celia should have had—and I guess Irene finally recognized a good thing. I think I heard that she actually did marry him shortly after Celia died."

"You introduced my parents?"

"Not by choice. But still, I should have known. I should never have sat back and let it happen. They met at our showroom. Tuck had dropped up to take me to lunch and—"

"Take you to lunch? You mean you went on with him, just as though nothing had happened?"

"Not as though nothing had happened, no. But you didn't deal with Tuck according to the usual rules. Nobody did. Maybe that was the trouble. We had lunch sometimes. This particular time, he spotted Celia. She'd recently started working for us and Tuck was just knocked out by the way she looked. I imagine you get the same reaction from men, though Celia played to it in a different way. She dressed, made up."

A quick flash of dark red lips, lace blouse, spike heels. "She did, yes. I guess she found all that more fun than I do."

"I don't know that it was about fun. Anyway, after we

left the restaurant, Tuck insisted on coming back to the showroom with me to meet 'fair Celia,' as he was already calling her. He'd had a good few drinks by then. I should've said no. I did at first, but then I gave in. If I had it to do again, I'd have moved mountains to keep those two people apart." Sondra stood and turned toward the hotel. "Let's go back, Emily. There's really nothing more to say."

"There is!" My voice rang loud in the silence.

She turned, her strong face strained and tired in the bluish moonlight. She shook her head slowly. "I wish I could give you what you're looking for, but I can't."

"After they got married, what then?"

"I don't know. I didn't see them anymore."

"But why?"

"It seemed better—all around. I don't think your father did it, Emily. I don't think he killed Celia or himself. I . . . just wanted you to know that." She began to walk.

"My mother," I said, falling into step at her side. My voice shook and I felt tears stab at the back of my nose. "Did you like her?"

She touched my arm with a hand that had become ice-cold. "It's hard to like someone you feel afraid for."

CHAPTER
SEVENTEEN

"For I believe in doing what I like, crying when I must, laughing when I choose . . ."

Nick Kennoyer's voice, singing the Coward lyric, had the plaintive throb of a weary clarinet—subtly different from the way he'd handled any other of the evening's songs. We were sitting around the piano, Howard, Sondra, and I. Nick's face had a faraway look, as though he were off living in the words he was singing. At one point our eyes caught inadvertently, and we broke contact at once.

More than two hours had passed since Sondra and I had come back inside. When we first got back to the table, Howard had looked anxious. Sondra leaned over to plant a kiss on his cheek, took my hand, and said, as though speaking for both of us, "We're going to keep Emily company while she waits for Nicky. Emily will tell us about making movies and we'll tell her about making belts. Maybe we'll sit at the piano and sing a few songs. And that's all." She squeezed my hand just slightly. She didn't need to do any more. Those were the ground rules.

I obeyed them. Sondra called the shots.

The hours of waiting, which I'd dreaded, drifted by surprisingly fast on the seductive notes of show tunes, wrapped in a cloud of rum and tonics and cigarette smoke.

". . . that since my life began, the most I've had is just a talent to amuse. Heigh ho, if love were *aaalll*!"

He stood, blew a kiss to the left, one to the right, and extended a hand in a farewell wave. "Goodnight, boys and girls. Sleep tight."

Nick bid a few of the regulars personal goodnights and stood at my side, tight-lipped and resigned, the curtain decisively down on any vestige of performer's charm. "I'm here, Celia's daughter. All yours for an hour."

"My name is Emily," I snapped before I could edit myself. The last thing I needed to do was alienate him any further. "We could go to your house or—"

"Not my house," he cut in sharply.

"Fine. We'll go up to my room." I turned to Howard and Sondra behind me and hugged each of them hard in silent goodbye. My ideal parents. I knew I wouldn't be seeing them again.

Nick and I settled ourselves stiffly in the pair of upholstered chairs, low table between, which are standard equipment in any hotel room above the fleabag level. By all rights, I should've been revved up, pulses going like a crazy clock. Instead, I felt icy and stiff.

"Coffee," I said. "I'll call for some coffee. Want a drink or something?"

"Plenty of booze in that fridge." He gestured toward the far corner. "But for special occasions, I carry my own." He reached into his jacket pocket and pulled out a slim silver flask. He unscrewed the cap, took a long swig, and gave me a how-are-you-going-to-handle-it? look.

"Very Scott Fitzgerald," I said. "Goes with the white suit." I walked to the phone and ordered two pots of coffee from room service.

"How did you find me?" he asked when I came back. Not why, just how. I wondered what he might already know about the why.

"Yale alumni office. I said I was Jackie Onassis."

He threw back his head and laughed loud and deep. I saw a flash of the glamorous boy he must have been at Yale.

He ran a hand across his eyes to wipe them, and when he put it back down, his face had settled again into its tense, hostile lines.

"So, was he a good writer, Nick? Could my father really write plays?"

"You tracked me down here to find out whether Tuck could write *plays*?"

"Could he?"

"You really want to know? He could write *pieces* of plays. He'd get it. Then he'd lose it. Your father was not a long-distance runner, Miss Emily."

Miss Emily. Hearing it after all these years put me midway between a smile and tears. "He also used to call me 'Wild Princess' and 'Goose Girl.' "

"You remember that?" Nick's tone softened a little.

"Uh-huh. And he'd call my mother 'Mad Duchess.' " I leaned toward him across the low table. "Why do you hate her, Nick?"

"Why did *you* hate it when I called you 'Celia's daughter'?" he countered.

Room service's knock saved me from having to answer the troubling question immediately. I sensed that if I wanted truth from Nick, I would have to give it to get it. And the truth was, I didn't know why I hated his labeling me Celia's daughter.

I poured two cups of coffee and handed him one. Instantly, I wanted a cigarette. I was out of luck—Nick didn't smoke. I gritted my teeth and tried to forget about it.

"I don't remember a lot about my mother, Nick," I said. A sudden lump in my throat made it hard to swallow the sip of steaming coffee I'd just taken.

"How much do you remember about her?" His eyebrows lifted. I couldn't tell whether he was surprised or alarmed at my obvious discomfort.

"I came here to ask *you* questions," I hedged.

He wasn't having any. "Come on." He made a beckoning motion with his graceful pianist's hand.

I took a deep breath. "She was a very good actress, I

think. I saw her work a few times, and even though I was a kid, I could tell." He nodded and waited. "I was never relaxed with her," I mumbled, looking into my coffee cup.

"Why?" he asked, as though he were a teacher pursuing a point of logic with a slow student.

"Because . . ." I hesitated. My mother had never hit me. Neither of my parents had. But the way she'd grip my arm sometimes, the set of her jaw, the glint in her eye, shook me, made my stomach lurch and my legs tremble with fear at what she might do. Leave us, my father and me, to flounder helplessly without her? Swoop me up and take me away, so I'd never see him again? Lock me in a closet and never let me out? That last broke my forehead out in sweat, recalling a nightmare I hadn't had in twenty years. "Because I didn't trust her," I said, forcing myself to say the words—forcing my eyes to meet his as I said them.

"What are you doing here, Emily?" His eyes hardened with suspicion as he asked it, and I thought I heard a trace of fear return to his voice.

"I'm trying to find out who really killed my parents." He rose, ready to cut out. "Sit down, Nick. I told you before, if you help me, I'll never mention your name—not to anyone. But if you don't, I'll mention it all over the place. I promise you that. Everything I find out, no matter where I really find it out, I'll say I found out from you." It was a rotten thing I was doing. I knew that. And the trapped-animal look on his face underscored it. He sat looking at me silently, running a long, pianist's finger around the shiny, dime-sized scar on his cheek.

"The man I was living with was killed two weeks ago," I began. And I told Nick all of it—about the strange voice I'd heard the night my parents were murdered and then again in a Westwood theater; about no one believing me back then; about the case records somehow disappearing; and about Strohmeyer's suicide. He asked no questions, just listened, taking an occasional pull at his flask.

"Mike Florio was my family, just as much as my parents

were—more, maybe. Somebody's taken my family away twice, Nick. And this time I'm not some nine-year-old kid who can't do anything about it."

"No, you're not nine. But I'm fifty-nine—and I want no part of this. I live my life in a box, Emily. I go back and forth from my house to here to the party circuit. I have sex with someone from time to time. I drink a little. I let my sister mother me. And that's it. I'm a piano player. I was going to be Cole Porter. It was going to be *my* songs piano players would play. Tuck and I . . . Ah, what the hell's the difference? It's not much of a life, not what I planned for. But it's what I have and I'm not going to lose it for you."

"Who killed them, Nick?" I grabbed his arm hard across the table, unable to stop myself.

He didn't shake it off. "I don't know," he said simply, "and I don't want to."

I let go of his arm and sat back. I took a sip of coffee while the disappointment washed over me. I believed he was telling the truth. He didn't know. But he knew *something*—something powerful enough to frighten him still, twenty years later.

"You've heard that voice though, haven't you, Nick? You know who it belongs to."

"No!" He shouted through clenched teeth. "I don't. I heard that goddamned voice exactly once in my life," he ground out, "on the phone." My eyes widened in expectation. "End of story," he said, trying hard to compose himself. "Finito. Six words: 'May I speak to Tuck, please?' That's it. Tuck grabbed the phone and sent me downstairs— threatened to cut my balls off if I tried to listen."

"What . . ." My head spun. "Was it a lover, do you think?"

"Yes," he said bitterly, "I do think."

I swallowed hard, my throat almost too dry to make it. "Have you any idea who she was?"

He laughed. The sound was not pleasant. "She? Well, maybe it was."

"Was *who*?"

"A she." The hurt on his face was keen enough to have been newly inflicted.

And I got it, finally.

"He was your lover, wasn't he?"

"You want to know this, Miss Emily? You sure?" He tipped his head back and took some more painkiller.

The thing was, I wasn't shocked. Each new piece of my father's puzzle was clicking in with a certain inevitability. He'd abandoned the sister, broken the brother's heart, and both continued to love him—accept every enormity with the disclaimer that Tuck wasn't like other people. What was it about Tuck Otis anyway? I thought angrily, realizing after no more than half a beat that the anger was at myself, because I continued to love him too.

"Yes, Nick," I said. "I want to know."

CHAPTER
EIGHTEEN

So he told me. And as he talked, his face freshened with the excitement of reliving what was clearly the best time of his life—going triumphantly off to Yale, confident of becoming a new Cole Porter; meeting the shimmering charmer who wrote plays, or pieces of plays. Falling in love.

"I can sing you two dozen lyrics about life being a dream when you're in love. I found it was just the opposite. For me everything suddenly became intensely real for the first time. I noticed everything. Orange juice in the morning had a complex, blossomy taste that was completely new. The air smelled like apples in the fall, and then changed to pine in the winter. People had distinctly different textures to their skin, small birthmarks, freckles." He leaned back in his chair and gazed up at the ceiling, back there at Yale maybe, checking it out to see whether it really had been quite the way he thought.

"Most gays know it—at least by the time they're fourteen or so. Not me. There was a girlfriend back in Douglaston— Linda Shapiro—and that was pretty good. We never went what we used to coyly call 'all the way,' of course. People didn't then. Most people. But all of a sudden there was Tuck. My God! He was . . . radiant." Nick's eyes came back to mine, working to bolster his words—to make me understand. I *did* understand. I just didn't like what I understood.

"If you're thinking he seduced me, you're wrong," he said, reading my face accurately. "It just happened. For both of us. It was October. We'd been at Yale hardly a month, and I got this idea to put on a Halloween revue. Nothing formal, just a few friends. I wrote some songs. Tuck put together a couple of skits around them. We were rehearsing one Friday night, got back to our room late—after three—exhausted and manic. Couldn't stop laughing. Tuck decided he had to have a shower and went off down the hall to the john. I walked in a couple of minutes later to have a pee. He was soaping himself up. I looked at him and saw that he was glowing, a kind of golden haze all around his body. Probably just the light working on my tired eyes," he added with an ironic twist to his lips. "He smiled at me. Just smiled. Instantly, I got hard. I began to sweat. I could feel the ending of every nerve in my body tingle. All the clichés, but to me they were brand-new. I'd never felt anything like that with Linda Shapiro.

"Nothing would have kept me from climbing into that shower with Tuck. Nothing. I'd have walked barefoot over a mile of broken glass to get to him. Through fire. And I'd have knocked him down and raped him if he'd tried to resist."

Nick may have believed that of himself, but I didn't. I had enough violence in me to recognize its absence in him. "But he didn't resist, did he?" I asked.

"No."

"Was it his first time too?"

"Oh no. His first time was when he was fourteen. Some maid in his mother's house." Mackey? Unthinkable. And of course, it *was* unthinkable. The MacNiffs hadn't been with Gem when my father was fourteen.

"His first gay time?"

"Not that either. But you miss the point. It wasn't about gay and straight. It was about communion. Tuck Otis's favorite word." I combed my memory and tried to hear my father saying it. The bell didn't exactly ring, but there was an echo of something—something not pleasant. "You could almost see him vibrate when he got onto communion. He'd grab me sometimes, shake me to try and make me see how it was for him. 'It's not just one person connecting with another person, Nicko. Don't you understand? You make communion with the gleam in a person's eye, or with a powerful idea that you share, or a body part you need to stroke. And it's for the moment. Nicko, my dark angel, don't you get it? There are zillions of people. Why have communion with only one? And why build some kind of exclusionary fence around it? That would be *crazy!*' "

"Terrific," I said bitterly. No wonder Nick lent such authenticity to song lyrics. This stuff he was spouting sounded to me like a mush-minded rationalization for wanting all the candy and scooping it up. "Probably if he hadn't had the luck to be murdered, he'd've died of AIDS—maybe taken my mother with him. And who knows? Maybe he'd have decided he wanted 'communion' with me. Some body part he needed to stroke."

I felt the quick, sharp sting of fingers flicking my mouth before I even noticed his hand shoot out. We looked at each other for a mutually surprised split second. I was the one who'd stepped out of line, and I knew it. "I'm sorry," I said, swallowing the lump in my throat. "I said I wanted to hear it. And I do. You're telling me you had to share him. Was that okay with you?"

"No. It was not okay. But it was far more okay than losing him." He took a small, almost dainty sip from the flask. "You ever feel like that about anyone, Miss Emily?"

I thought about it before answering. "No," I said truthfully. And I never wanted to. "Did . . . Did my mother know about you—you and him—when she married him?"

"Ah, now that's a question, isn't it? To know and not to know. 'She who knows and knows not she knows. She is asleep, wake her.' " He smiled, looking suddenly bleary, as though the booze had finally gotten to him.

"So you woke her, right?" I heard my voice, hard, ac-

cusing. If he tried slapping me this time, I'd belt his teeth
out.

"It wasn't like that."

"Oh, quit telling me how it wasn't like that! You and your
sister both. I'm tired of hearing it. It *was* like that." Suddenly I felt an unaccustomed bond with my mother. I was
sickened by the three of them—my spoiled monster of a
father and his pair of romantic apologists.

"Tuck broke it off with me when he married Celia," Nick
said tonelessly. "He tried. We both tried. For six years we
saw each other only at the occasional big party. 'Hello.
Hello.' Manly slap on the back. Old Yale buddies. 'Aren't
you looking lovely, Celia.' I'd stay as long as I could stand
it, just to be in the same room with him. When I couldn't
bear another minute, I'd leave—go home and throw my
guts up. Then one morning my phone rang—early, before
ten. I was playing piano at the Waldorf then, working on
my own stuff during the day. 'I want you.' That was all he
said, but it was there burning through the phone lines, as
much passion and longing as I've ever heard outside my
own head. I was over there in fifteen minutes."

"So she was at work. Where was I? Locked downstairs?"

"At school," he said. I sifted his voice for grains of embarrassment, but came up empty.

"Why did he marry her, Nick? Why did he marry anyone?
Why not just keep running around fucking anything that
moved? That's what really turned him on, right?"

"Don't be vulgar. It doesn't suit you. But I'll answer your
question. He married her because she was pregnant and
threatened to kill herself if he didn't."

"Why didn't she follow your sister's example and have
an abortion? She wasn't Catholic. She wasn't any kind of
religious."

"True. The secular Jew. Me, Sondra, Celia. Lord knows
who else." He smiled, this time a real grin. "Oh, how Tuck
loved us! He used to say that being with Jews was like
standing with his back to a roaring fire. We warmed his

cold WASP ass." The smile vanished. "Turned out that
Celia burned it. He was scared stiff she really would carry
out the suicide threat. Apparently his father had once killed
someone in a car crash. His mother never let Tuck forget
about that—kept at him about his drinking, about how
much like his father he was. A real piece of work, your
grandmother."

"She was right. His father was a drunk too. Maybe even
a charming one." It was the first time in my life I'd ever
allied myself with Gem.

"There was another reason Tuck married Celia, Emily.
He made communion with the idea of being a father."

Was Nick saying that for effect? Did he know what an
unfair below-the-belt punch he was delivering? I searched
his face but found no answer. I blinked back tears and
cursed myself for being as sentimental a fool as he. "Did
it live up to his expectations?" I tried for wryness, but the
question came out sounding pleadingly real.

"Yes, Miss Emily, it did."

It felt suddenly as though a cigarette was the only remedy
in the world to keep me from crying. "Why the hell don't
you smoke, Nick?"

"Voilà!" He whipped out a thin silver case with the same
flash of pride he'd shown about the flask. I let him light
the long, slim, slightly stale whatever it was and took a deep
grateful drag. "I've never smoked myself, but I always carried them for Tuck. As you can see, it got to be a habit."
He put four more cigarettes on the table, screwed the top
on his flask, and stood up. "Your hour's about up. I'm going
home now." I heard the relief in his voice. It hadn't been
so bad after all.

"No you're not." He looked at me, eyebrows raised.
"You moved to Key West twenty years ago, right after the
murder. Why?"

"Why not? Tuck was dead. My life was over. I needed
to get away." The words rang true enough. It was the way
he said them that didn't.

"You're lying to me, Nick."

Indignant mouth set, but forced. "I'm not. I—"

"Yes you are. You were terrified of me earlier. What was it you said about how you don't have much of a life but you want to hang on to it? I made you stay here by threatening you. You claim not to know who killed my parents. If that's true, what the hell are you so scared of?" He looked at me, his heavy eyelids seeming to take on an extra weight of despair, his finger absently playing again over the smooth little white scar on his cheek. "You'd better sit down, Nick, because you're going to tell me."

"I was wrong," he said sullenly as he lowered himself back into the chair. "You're not Celia's daughter. You're Cordelia Otis's granddaughter." At the moment, given that the other known hereditary choices were my suicidal mother and my faithless father, taking after Gem seemed the least of three evils.

"You know that I went to the police after . . . after it happened." He spoke in a monotone, staring down at the small table between us. "And then I went to the papers, to the TV stations, hoping someone would get the message that Tuck Otis was no killer, and do something." Here was the grown-up ally I'd prayed for back then, and it didn't look as though he'd been able to accomplish a bit more than I had. "Then I did an interview on Channel Two, I think it was. The reporter got very interested. She called me the next day—wanted to work with me on getting the police to reopen the case. Said she'd already made a few calls. I was elated. Five months after Tuck's death, finally I'd made a dent. And then he came." I watched the long fingers on the table begin to tremble.

"What is it, Nick?" My own voice was unsteady. "Who came?"

"I never found out who he was. And I don't want to. I got home from work about two in the morning, same day the reporter called me—I was playing at the Carlyle then—and there he was, sitting on my couch waiting. I still don't know how he got in. True, I didn't have a doorman, but I had two locks and they weren't broken. When I saw him there, I tried to run back out the door, but he grabbed me before I could get there—hand on my arm like a vise. I started to scream, but he backhanded me across the face before I got much sound out. 'We can do this easy or we can do it hard, Mr. Kennoyer,' he said—very respectful, concerned, like a doctor telling a patient about possible treatments.

"I was scared, of course, but also mad. And I tried to twist loose—told him to get his fucking hands off me. He slapped me again, open-handed still, but hard enough to knock me down. Before I knew what was happening, he'd handcuffed my wrists behind me and thrown me into a chair.

" 'Now, Mr. Kennoyer, we are going to talk about your boyfriend.' I knew I must be looking at Tuck's murderer. Sitting there helpless, looking at him. And I knew he was going to kill me, too. I had no idea what any of it was about. 'Why?' I shouted, at least I thought I shouted, the way you do in a dream. I remember being surprised that it came out a squeaky whisper.

" 'That cocksucker killed his wife,' he said. He didn't raise his voice, but he was furious. His face went white and I could see his jaw working. I shouted no, no, Tuck hadn't done that. His arm moved back and I thought he was going to hit me again. I braced for it. But he didn't hit me."

Something in Nick's voice changed here. The bottom seemed to drop out of it and the breath supporting it became quick and shallow. "He just took out a cigarette, lit it—cooling himself down, I thought. Then he walked over close to me and I had the idea he was going to put it in my mouth, maybe to calm me down. I started to tell him I didn't smoke. And that's when he . . . hurt me." His finger went again to the scar on his cheek. I noticed that the size and shape was really a little smaller than a dime, more like the end of a cigarette.

"He burned your face with a cigarette?" I felt my skin crawl.

"That's when it changed. It wasn't even the pain of the

burn itself, it was the power. He'd branded me like some cow. He owned me. Up till that moment, I thought he was going to pull out a gun and shoot me the way he did Tuck. Sure I was scared. I won't lie about it. But I felt exhilarated, in a funny way, that there was something poetic about my dying by the same hand that killed the person I loved most." I saw a fine beading of sweat break out on his forehead. His face suddenly flushed. "Stupid me. Stupid, romantic me." He shook his head almost imperceptibly.

"After he . . . did that, he continued talking to me as though nothing had happened. 'Your asshole buddy killed himself,' he said. 'You remember that. And it was an easier death than he deserved. He couldn't keep it in his pants. Somebody should have cut it off. Would you like someone to cut yours off, Mr. Kennoyer? Or would you rather have your fingers broken, one by one, like dry sticks? Be hard to play the piano, I guess.' All the while, this respectful-doctor voice—Would you prefer aspirin or Tylenol? And while he was talking, he lit a new cigarette. As he walked toward me with it, everything became a blur of terror. He held it close to my other cheek, not quite touching me.

"I used to hear my parents talk about the camps when I was growing up. We lost some relatives in Auschwitz. I'd wonder sometimes at what point you stop being a person and just lose it all. As he kept on talking, telling me what 'somebody' could do to me, I felt the heat of that cigarette on my face. And I wet my pants. That was my point. I was a terrified animal. I'd have renounced anyone, done anything he told me to do." Nick was now speaking so softly that, close as we were, it was difficult to hear him. "And what did he tell you to do?" I asked, knowing the answer.

"To drop any effort to reopen the case, never to say a word about what had just happened, and to disappear. Get out of town. Move. He gave me twenty-four hours. Where better for a gay piano player than Key West? I told my sister and my friends that I was too broken up about Tuck to stay in New York. If they thought the suddenness was bizarre,

they never said. I guess they just assumed I was a bit out
of my mind right then."

"So you've never told anyone?"

"Until now. I welshed on what I owed Tuck. Terror won
out over love. That's what I've had to live with, Miss Emily."
His eyes, red and haunted, met mine for the first time since
he'd begun his story. "It might have been better to go down
fighting, whatever happened."

"I'll do it for you, Nick," I said, as carefully as if I were
placing a compress on a fresh burn, knowing that any words
I uttered would hurt. "I'll go down fighting. And I'll never
bring you into it. I promise. You'll be safe."

"You know a funny thing? Right this minute, I don't care.
If he walked in here now, he could do whatever he wanted
to me and I'd hardly feel it. I'd spit in his face." I didn't
believe that for a second, but I hoped hard that he did—
and that it was a comfort.

"What did he look like?" I asked.

"Ordinary. Rather kind, ironically. Thin, reddish hair.
Freckles." Nick saw my shocked face, heard me gasp. "You
know who he is." His voice choked with fresh fear.

"Yes." My heart was beating so wildly that I found it
difficult to speak. "But you're never going to have to." I
looked at him and saw that his eyes were streaming tears.

"Would you do me a favor?" he asked, his voice soft but
steady now. "There's a song that Tuck and I liked to do
together. Would you sing it with me?"

For a moment, I wasn't able to answer. "If I know the
words," I said finally, feeling suddenly shy.

"At words poetic, I'm so pathetic . . ." he began to sing
softly in his appealing, smoky tenor. I listened with chills
prickling the back of my neck. By the time he got to the
end of the verse, ". . . at least it will tell you how great you
are," and I chimed in with a quavering "You're the top,"
my face was as wet as his.

CHAPTER
NINETEEN

THE plane circled like a drugged fly over Kennedy. It would never land! Almost six o'clock already—nothing but delays. We'd been late taking off from Key West and again from Miami. I wasn't nervous about being followed this time. Even the menacing Andy Logan couldn't trace me to or from Key West. Dev's precautions and my Mercedes Ruiz tickets had taken care of that. No, my nerves were now those of the hunter, not the hunted. I wanted that man face-to-face. I could cheerfully watch him die for what he'd done to Nick Kennoyer. But if he was one of the men who had killed Mike, I'd do more than watch. I'd kill him myself. I didn't yet know exactly how, but I would. Right after I made him tell me the name of the voice that murdered my parents.

Alone in the hotel room after Nick left, I had watched the sun come up and rummaged through what I knew—that Logan was a cop and somehow had been able to control the investigation of my parents' death, probably through Strohmeyer, who'd killed himself as he saw Dev closing in on him. I knew that the murderous voice belonged to one of my father's army of lovers. What I didn't know was how he fit in with Logan and Strohmeyer. Maybe he was a cop too, and the whole thing was a case of the brotherhood closing ranks to protect its own. But I still had no idea of what Mike could've turned up in L.A. that had gotten him killed.

After a while, I'd flung myself on the bed, tense but exhausted, and slept. Well, not really slept—it was more like a delicate, hypnotic state, from which I kept awakening with a startled sense of having forgotten something important.

Nick and I had made no false promises about keeping in touch, and yet by the time he'd left my room at a little before five, I felt a bond with him. Not that I had any illusions about him. He had none left about himself, except for a few fleeting action fantasies. No, Nick's romantic illusions were all about the past: Tuck Otis and the golden years. Maybe that was our bond. Despite all evidence to the contrary, I couldn't let go of Tuck Otis either.

My father, Mike, Trip. All my close attachments had been men. Through the years, Trip, who knew very little about my past, had tried three dozen times to get me to see his shrink, citing not only my spiky temper but the fact that I had no close women friends. I'd greeted the suggestion each time by pointing out that I could come up with the answer as well as a shrink could. "I was brought up by Genghis Grandmother, Triplet. It wasn't an experience calculated to make me feel great about females." Then he'd call me an asshole ostrich and try to pin me to the wall with all the good things therapy had done for him. Fine, I'd counter, but quit playing missionary to heathens who are perfectly happy the way they are. "But you're *not* perfectly happy, E.S.," he'd point out. And to that one I never had an answer, so I'd just tell him to shove it.

I knew in my gut that he wasn't wrong, but as far as I was concerned, my unconscious was no skittish pussycat to be courted and coaxed into coming out and sitting in my lap—rather, a slavering tiger to be kept at bay with whip and chair.

But my session with Nick had provided a disturbing peek at the beast. For my father, I felt a growing dull throb of anger. I'd been betrayed—made a fool of. Nick had let me know, whether or not he'd meant to, that I'd been a side issue to the "radiant" Tuck Otis. Despite his so-called communion with the idea of being a father, I'd had very little effect on him. He'd just barreled along taking what pleased him when it pleased him, and all I'd seen was the glow. What stuck in my craw now was that I'd thought the glow had been especially for me.

My mother was another story, one I'd known little of, and still knew little of. But the picture Sondra and Nick had drawn—the emotionally naked neurotic—stimulated in me, I had to admit, a faint shock of guilty recognition. I reached for it and . . .

I shut my eyes and made myself cut this emotional umbilical cord abruptly. The job at hand was not to hold a posthumous family therapy session, I reminded myself, it was to track down a killer. But I looked down at the clenched fists in my lap and wondered how entirely true that was.

CHAPTER
TWENTY

I turned the key in Dev's front door lock as though it were my own, not bothering to ring the bell first and announce myself. It was almost seven o'clock. I'd spent the whole damned day in transit. I bounded up the flights, impatient to begin the endgame. Dev had called me as promised at nine that morning, and I'd told him what I'd learned from Nick—the factual parts, about the voice and about Logan. The rest, the personal parts, were not phone conversation. Strohmeyer's funeral had been at noon, so by now Dev would have things to tell me, too. As I inserted the key in his apartment door, a wave of delicious anticipation swept away anything in its path.

The apartment was empty. I had an instant flash that this was somehow the story of my life.

I peeled off Dev's tweed coat, nudged off my sneakers, and hunted up the Irish whiskey bottle. I poured myself a moderately healthy tot and shook a cigarette out of the pack I'd bought during the endless delay changing planes in Miami. As I lit up, I pictured Mike standing next to me— how he'd grab the thing from my hand the way he did the first time he broke me of smoking. But you're not here, I thought, and took a deep, self-punishing drag.

I looked around the place to see whether there might be a note. There wasn't. I was filled with restless energy and had no place to put it. I picked up the phone and dialed my grandmother's number. It rang seventeen times with no answer. Gem had not succumbed to the answering machine. She'd thought they were vulgar when they first came out, and I guessed she'd go to her grave without changing her mind. Odd, though, that Mackey wasn't home. It was dinnertime.

Well, the hell with it. I'd just go there tomorrow and let Gem know I'd spotted Mac at the airport. I'd tell her it had to stop, that I simply would not put up with being shadowed around.

I curled up on the sofa, legs under me, for a while and sipped and smoked. Then I got up and paced. I found a Beethoven CD and popped it into the player. The *Eroica*. Just as I was telling myself how well I was coping with frustration, my mother descended, with no warning, into my head. She wouldn't go away. She hovered there in the perpetual motion that I remembered as her keynote. I saw her whipping our small apartment into shape—running a vacuum, dusting, polishing. I watched her throwing her arms around my father's neck, hugging tight enough to make him groan an exaggerated "Aaargh, you're strangling me, Celia." I recalled once when she'd hugged me extra hard, I'd responded the same way, mimicking my idol. "Aaargh, you're strangling me, Mommy." She'd flung me away from her with enough energy to topple me on my rear end. Our eyes had locked in mutual shocked fury. After what seemed like a long time, she'd knelt by my side, taken my arm gently and pulled me up. "Oh, Emily," she'd murmured into my neck. "Mine. Mine. No. I see me in your face, but you're his. All his."

When had that happened? Not too long before they were killed, I thought, but I couldn't say for sure.

On impulse, I ran over to the bookshelves and pulled out the Manhattan phone book. Roston, Sondra had said. Irene Cheyney had married a Herbert Roston—a doctor. Nothing. Well, it was a long shot. They could live in Scarsdale, Great Neck, anywhere. My disappointed eye scanned the column randomly. And, miraculously, there it was! Spelled with an *e*: Herbert Rosten, M.D.—an office maybe, but it would get me to her. I stared at the name for a moment, profoundly grateful Irene's "good old Herb" hadn't been a Greenberg or a Cohen. Then I reached for the phone and dialed. She picked up on the second ring.

"Hello." The optimistic bell clarity I remembered.

I ran my tongue around my lips and took a deep breath. "Hello, Irene," I said, and then paused to clear the frog that had taken possession of my throat.

"Who is this, please?" The optimism dimmed slightly behind a thin cloud of doubt.

"It's Emily, Irene. Celia's daughter." I felt my scalp prickle as I described myself in the words I'd hated hearing Nick use.

"Emily. What a wonderful surprise!" For a moment I was speechless—caught off base. Whatever I'd expected, it hadn't been an enthusiastic welcome from someone out of my parents' past. I hunched my shoulder up to grip the phone while I used my hands to activate another cigarette. "But how in the world did you find me?"

"Uh   someone happened to mention your married name, and I . . . I would like very much to see you."

"That would be wonderful. Are you here in New York? Do you live here?"

"I live in California, but I'm in New York for a while. I'm an actress too." I added, maybe to forge a bond between us.

Dead air for a long moment. "Yes," she said, her voice a bit distracted. "Of course you would be. Like Celia."

"And you."

"Oh, not me, I'm afraid." A small, wistful chuckle. "Not for many years now." The clear, upbeat tone elbowed the sad note to the side. "So, California. Do you work in pictures?"

"Just one so far. It opened two months ago. *Running Fast.* Have you seen it?" It took me only a split second to register that that was a dumb question. If she'd seen it, she'd've said, first thing. "Mostly I've worked in rep companies and television."

"Wonderful!" Warmth colored her voice and gave the word a beguiling lilt. "I don't get to the movies, or watch the machine much either." The machine—what my mother used to call TV, and with the same deprecating tone. "But Celia would have been so proud that you wound up on the stage. What parts have you played?"

"Oh, Nina, in *The Seagull* and Miss Julie and Rosalind and—" I heard Irene clap her hand over the receiver and say something I couldn't make out to someone in the room with her. I stopped abruptly, embarrassed by my burbling. "I'm sorry,' I said sheepishly. "Ask an actress her credits and you'd better be prepared to be a captive audience for the next hour."

"No, I want to hear. That was just Herb. He's always fussing over me."

"Some people would give their eyeteeth for that," I said, more polite than sincere, since I'd never been one of them. "Look, Irene, could I . . . I mean, are you, by any chance, free sometime tomorrow? Maybe I could meet you for lunch or whatever's convenient."

"Can you come here? It's Eleven-eleven Park. That's Ninetieth Street."

"Fine." My heart gave a little leap of anticipation. "What time?"

"The morning is best for me. Would ten be all right? Coffee?"

The sound from behind of a key turning in the lock startled me into a tense jump. I spun around to see an elongated, angular figure framed in the doorway. Backlit by the hall light, it looked like a huge, black, Halloween cardboard cutout. I must have gasped. Suddenly, my lungs choked with smoke and erupted in a paroxysm of coughing.

"Emily? Emily, are you all right?" Irene's voice in my ear.

The figure limped into the room and the world snapped back into focus—almost. "Yes. Yes, I am," I said into the phone, my strangled voice echoing in my ears as though I were hearing it from the other end of a tunnel. "I'll see you tomorrow at ten. I'm looking forward to it," I added, trying to sound normal and feeling anything but.

Dev was at my side now. I stared into the purple eyes as though I'd never seen them before. They looked quizzical and more than a little worried. He took the phone from my hand and hung it up, the burned-down cigarette from between my fingers and stubbed it out. Then he took my arm firmly, steered me to the sofa, and eased me down into a sitting position.

"You surprised me," I said weakly. Free-form spots paraded past my burning, teary eyes. "I think I could use a drink. I put one down over near the phone."

He went to the table and picked up my glass, which I could see from where I was sitting was empty. Then he turned his attention back to me and gave me a quick once-over. "I think you could use a cup of tea, and maybe something to eat. Put your feet up and lie back," he ordered over his shoulder on his way to the kitchen. "And don't even think of lighting another butt. Turn my back on you for twenty-four hours and you pick up bad habits."

A giggle bubbled up from somewhere and, once started, wouldn't stop. My head felt light enough to float off on its own. The next thing I knew, arms were around me, holding firmly, one strong hand cradling my skull. "Easy. Easy now. Easy." He said it over and over, till it got through and decompressed my air-inflated brain.

"I'm sorry," I gasped with a small hiccup. "It was just so funny. You fussing over me, when I was just thinking I wouldn't like that, but, surprise, I did." I laughed again, but the fever was gone from it now.

The long, even strokes of his hand on my back. "Okay. It's okay. I've got you"—a soothing whisper in my ear. A kettle whistled. "Tea in just half a second. Sugar, milk?" He asked me no question more complicated, and for that I was profoundly thankful.

"Just plain." Suddenly, I heard the murderous voice in

my head. *"Just plain chance."* That's what it had said in the darkened theater. A shiver ran through me, though the room was far from cold. "Tell me about Strohmeyer's funeral," I said. The effort of focusing my scattered thoughts sharpened the tone of my request into an order. "Was squash nose there?"

"Not yet," he responded, walking toward me with a steaming mug.

"Thanks," I said shortly, taking it and placing it on the low table in front of me. "What do you mean, not yet?"

"Come on. Sit up and drink this now, while I scramble some eggs."

I sat up, irritated. Another one of those I'll-tell-you-when-I'm-good-and-ready go-rounds. "I am not hungry. I don't want eggs, I want answers. Besides, you don't have eggs. You don't have *anything* to eat in this goddamned place!"

"Wrong," he sang over his shoulder on his way back to the kitchen. "Larder's all stocked. Ronnie brought stuff in yesterday."

"How fucking cozy," I shot at him, wishing the instant the words were out that I could inhale them back.

He laughed. "I'm flattered you care." Before I could respond, he switched gears. "I want you to drink that tea while it's hot, and eat the eggs as soon as I cook them. Then we'll talk. This is not because I have turned uxorious, but because you are perched somewhere on the edge between exhaustion and hysteria, and you're not going to be much good to either of us till you even out."

I picked up the mug and took a long, warming sip. "You are such a verbal show-off. What's 'uxorious'?"

"Husbandly," he answered without looking up. The unmistakable smell of browning toast wafted in my direction. A moment later, I heard the sizzle of eggs poured into hot butter.

CHAPTER
TWENTY-ONE

D EV'S nutrition program did what it was supposed to. As I ate and drank, an inner trembling, of which I'd been only half conscious, stilled. I swallowed my last mouthful of toast and leaned back.

"I think I'm *compos mentis* now," I said. "At least as much as I ever was. Tell me about the funeral."

He did. His report was brief and, for the most part, not satisfying. The pastor of Our Lady of Perpetual Help had officiated at the rather bare-bones send-off given to Catholic suicides—those lucky enough to get buried in the church at all. Strohmeyer's police buddies had turned out for the Mass, along with a few church friends from the neighborhood. Dev had positioned himself between his policewoman friend Ronnie and Marcie, a small, unobtrusive camera in her hand, ready to shoot Andy Logan. But he didn't show.

Then Dev got to the nugget. "Just as the Mass was winding up, Ronnie nudged me in the ribs and whispered, 'Don't turn around, but he's standing in the back.' I had Marcie sitting on the aisle. I passed her a note to get moving as soon as Father Whatsit finished intoning the last blessing, and to stay with him until she could snap a few without his noticing."

"And?"

"He made a quick getaway, but Marcie tailed him around

the block to his car. The big surprise was, so did one of the old ladies. Marcie caught a few shots of them talking. Pretty heated stuff by the body language, though she couldn't get close enough to hear any of it. Then the two of them got into the car and he drove off. Marcie ought to be here with proofs for you to look at anytime now. Nothing's engraved in stone until you tell me he's our man."

"Of *course* he's the right man! He looks right. He was Strohmeyer's best friend. Then he sneaks into the funeral. You mean you didn't try to find him at his house or anything?"

"I hope you never sit on my jury, actress. But, as it happens, I *did* go to his house. Lives in an apartment right near the Little Neck train station—no more than ten minutes from where Frank Strohmeyer lived. Super said he'd left with a suitcase day before yesterday—out of town for three weeks. His lieutenant backs that up. Logan's taking a vacation."

"Shit! He got away. You let him get away!" It slipped out. I didn't mean it to. It just did.

"If you're happier blaming, go to it. If you want to hear the rest, shut up."

"Consider me shut up," I said. "I'm sorry." I added, meaning it.

"I think it's a lie. He hasn't gone away."

"Why? Disappearing for a few weeks—maybe permanently—would be the smartest thing he could do."

"Mostly a hunch. But, as you point out, he *did* show up at the funeral. Also, I've done some poking around about him—about the kind of guy he is."

"Oh, I know the kind of guy he is: a murdering sadist."

"Not the feedback I get."

"Oh really? He tried to push me under a subway train, and the job he did on Nick was worthy of a Nazi camp guard. What the hell more do you need?"

"His co-workers describe Andy as a dedicated vice cop. Quiet, a bit puritanical. Unusual in the vice squad, actually. Many of them become a lot like the sludge they deal with.

But not Andy Logan. Andy believes in the system—black
hats and white hats. Attends to details—dots all his *i*'s.
Devout Catholic, just like Strohmeyer. Logan didn't have
any close friends besides Frank, and the suicide really
wrecked him. Ronnie spoke to a guy she knows who was
right there when Andy heard about it. Says he fell apart.
Dropped to his knees and then just lay there sobbing his
heart out. In the end, he couldn't stay away from Frank's
funeral, even though it was a risk. And I believe, whatever
his role in all this, he hasn't taken off for the Bahamas or
somewhere. He's just making sure not to be anyplace I can
get hold of him."

"If you expect me to be moved, forget it."

"I don't expect you to be anything. I just wish you'd quit
declaring yourself every three minutes and listen to what
is with something that resembles objectivity."

"Objectivity? Who's objective? You? You're no more a
mental-health poster child than I am. By the way, if you
agree I'm down off the hysteria edge, I'd like a cigarette."

"Not a chance," he said evenly. "How long has it been
since you stopped smoking?"

"Eight years."

"Then start again on your own time, after all this is over—
if you still want to. Meantime, your vascular system doesn't
need any unaccustomed abuse, and I need you in good
shape."

"Give me a break!" I laughed. "What the hell do you
know about vascular systems?"

He shrugged. "Woman I used to live with was a car-
diologist." He looked straight at me while he said it, his
eyes clear and apparently guileless.

"Julia?"

"Right, Julia." If he was surprised, it didn't show. I
wanted to ask him to name a profession he hadn't laid at
least once, but didn't give myself the luxury.

He glanced down at his watch. "I wonder if Marcie got
sidetracked by a dish of ice cream. She should've been up
here by now." He got up and headed for the phone.

After a short conversation that ended with "Great!" on his end, he walked slowly back to the sofa and sat a good three feet away from me. "We've been bumped by the Goldblatt Bar Mitzvah—a rush set of extra prints," he deadpanned. "But she'll be up here with the Logan shots in a couple of hours. Think you can stay awake that long?"

"Are you kidding?" I turned in his direction and had a surprising urge to move closer. But I didn't.

"Who was that you were on the phone with when I came in?"

"My mother's friend, Irene. Nick's sister told me her married name, and I found her husband in the phone book. I'm seeing her tomorrow morning."

"I know. I heard you make the date. That what pushed you to the edge," he asked quietly, "the prospect of learning more about your mother?"

"No. Maybe. I don't know." The three answers—each of them partly true—tripped over one another on their way out of my mouth. "Nick told me things about both my parents that I'd probably rather not know." I put the words together awkwardly, one at a time, like a random handful of sharp pebbles.

"It's going to get worse, Emily," he said, his eyes shading to almost black, the way I'd learned they did when he was worried. "Sure you wouldn't rather walk away from it?"

"Could *you*?"

"No."

"You know the thing that gets me? My father turns out to have been a narcissistic, bisexual satyr, and it doesn't seem to make the difference it should." My throat felt all at once coated with sand. "I ought to . . . I ought to—"

"Cordelia Tucker Otis's granddaughter, and she's not oughting the way she ought to, huh?" He moved closer, cupped my face in his two hands and turned it toward his. We stayed like that, everything perfectly still, except for the warm, even jets of our breath, which after a while turned irregular.

We never got around to getting completely undressed, nor did we make it to the bed.

Afterward, we lay on the sofa like a pair of tossed rag dolls. "I want to tell you," Dev said into my hair, "that I have no warranties, and maybe there should be a warning stamped on my backside. It's been suggested more than once."

"I'll bet it has," I murmured, not turning to face him. "Are you like my father? Do you fuck anything that moves? Of course, he never used that crude term. Too honest. According to Nick, Tuck Otis had 'communion' with everything that moved."

"That what turns you on? That I might be like your father?"

"I hope not." We remained nested there, my back to him. Talking was probably easier that way. "I definitely don't approve of my father. What I wish is that I didn't still love him, but I do. You called me Cordelia Otis's granddaughter. Nick did too. A month ago, I'd've laughed you out of the room, or punched you in the mouth. But now, I have to admit there's some truth in it. And I find I don't even mind."

"Well, rest assured about one thing. I'm no way like your father. For one thing, believe it or not, I'm highly selective about the people I make love with. For another, the word 'communion' is anything but sexy to a Catholic boy. Stale crackers, bad wine—and a lot of hocus-pocus." He paused, but I felt there was more coming. "And for a third"—the voice in my ear turned dry with self-disgust—"your father did something I cannot do. He wrote."

"I think I understand how you feel," I said quietly, turning finally to face him.

"Maybe you do," he said. I couldn't tell if the slight curl of his lip was the beginning of a smile. "Fifteen years. I'm a contender for the longest writer's block in history." It *was* a smile. The bitter smile of someone who feels honor-bound to appreciate a cruel joke on himself. "I wrote a book of stories once—'highly promising,' they called it. I'll be thirty-nine in July. Finis, I think, to the statute of limitations on highly promising."

"Stop beating yourself about it," I said, reaching out to touch his cheek. "I've seen the way you look at that type-writer, circle around it. Why don't you put it away for a while—see what happens? Maybe you'll get a fresh burst of creativity and run out and buy yourself a computer, like every other writer."

"Now there's proof positive you'll never make a Catholic," he said, jumping suddenly off the sofa and away from my hand and pulling his pants back on. "You don't have quite the right sustained instinct for the refinements of self-abuse—all puns intended."

I forced a laugh as I lay there on my side, head propped on my raised hand, looking at him. "Don't be too sure. For a while when I was a kid I was very taken with what you call hocus-pocus. And I'm great at guilt. Mike used to say I'd make an excellent Catholic."

"Ah, what did Mike know? An Italian. The only serious Catholics are Irish. By the way, you sure Mike didn't take up again with the church?"

"Take up again? No. He said all that was over by the time he was sixteen."

"That's what I thought," he mumbled. He frowned, lost in some musing of his own.

"What is it?"

"Maybe nothing."

I stood up and zipped myself back into my jeans. "Whenever you say that, it means probably something. Tell me what it is."

"Those phone messages that you had the secretary send. I got around to looking them over this morning. A few from a Mother Saint Sebastian."

"Oh, Lucy did say something about a bunch of charity calls. Mike tended to contribute to everything. He figured if you spread it around enough, you were bound to do some good." I ran my fingers through my hair, still unused to the new crop.

The knock at the door went *bum-bitty-bum-bum.* Dev stamped his foot twice to finish the phrase before he went to open it. I wondered with a twinge if I was witnessing some remaining vestige of intimate ritual. Did I imagine a flicker of stocktaking in Marcie's brown eyes as they moved from Dev to me and back? It occurred to me that it was one thing for her to tell me it was over between them, with jaunty tips on his moods, but it might be quite another for her to walk in on the two of us obviously just out of the sack.

"Forty-two shots of Seth Goldblatt becoming a man just made the last Fed Ex to Grandma in Miami. Let's hear it for *Marcie,*" she responded with the appealingly weary smile of a wilted cherub. Dev and I collaborated in a round of applause, to which she bowed acknowledgment. "No autographs, please," she said, plunking herself into the Eames chair. "I have your proofs." She held up the brown envelope in her hand and waved it triumphantly. "God, I'm starved!" After a split second, she added, "Why am I bothering? You never have anything to eat in this place." I told myself to stop analyzing every word out of her mouth for ulterior motive.

"Oh, but he *does,* Marcie," I said, eyes wide in purposeful innocence. "Ronnie has the fridge stocked to its little gills."

"Aha!" Marcie joined me in the impromptu round of Gotcha.

"Okay, you two." Dev grinned. "Carve me up any way you want. But not before we take a look at those photos."

Marcie got out of the chair, opened up her envelope, and laid four eight-by-tens out across the phone table. I walked over and looked down.

Andy Logan was certainly the right man. That was the easy part. It wasn't his face that dropped my jaw into a gape. It was the flat pan face of the woman he was talking to: my grandmother's housekeeper, Mackey.

CHAPTER
TWENTY-TWO

"TELL me about Mackey," Dev said. Marcie had been dispatched downstairs with a quick kiss on the forehead, and he and I sat facing each other tensely on the sofa.

I didn't respond at once. I didn't have much to respond with. We'd been part of the same household for nine years and yet, I realized, I knew close to nothing about her. The rich and their invisible servants, I could hear Dev jeer in my head. I beat him to the punch.

"You're going to give me the spoiled-rich-girl routine, but I know nothing at all about Mackey. That isn't because she was the housekeeper and I was the highborn miss, it's because we've always hated each other."

"Not true."

"What do you mean?" I heard the truculence in my voice and was instantly angry with myself.

"At ease," he snapped. "I accept that you hated each other. But you know more about Mackey than you think. For starters, what's her name?"

"Catherine MacNiff."

"Okay. She's worked for your grandmother how long?"

"Thirty years, I think. Maybe a little less. She and her husband both. His first name is Gordon."

"Scottish. Born here or there?"

"Here, I suppose." I called up Mac's soft monotone. Was there a slight burr to it? "Well, maybe not him. He may've been born in Scotland, but Mackey's American—Chicago, by the sound of her."

"How long have they been married?"

"I have no idea." I thought of the shrine I'd seen long ago. "They have a daughter, I think. I sneaked into their room once and saw maybe twenty pictures of a girl, all grouped around a statue of Mary. There was this huge crucifix on the wall too. Scary. I guess there *is* something I can tell you about them. They're religious Catholics. At least Mackey is. She wears this heavy silver crucifix around her neck—goes around looking like she'd like to bash somebody in the head with it, though."

"How old would she be, the girl?"

"I don't know. I'd just started to look at the pictures, got as far as her first Communion, and then Mackey marched in with my grandmother. They were both furious. It was one of the times Gem really hit me—whacked me across the face. I was terrified. As a matter of fact, I couldn't even swear that the girl *was* their daughter. I asked Gem once, years later, and she told me that the MacNiffs' private affairs were none of my business."

"And you never asked them?"

"You don't get it. We had no relationship. I lived with them for four years. Then I went off to boarding school and saw them only on vacations. We never talked. Mackey hated me from the moment I moved in, and Mac always seemed embarrassed in front of me. Maybe that's just his way. I think he's a very shy man. Timid."

"But not too timid to try and trail you at the airport."

"No," I said, rubbing a hand over my eyes, which had begun to ache with fatigue. "What *is* this, Dev? Are you saying the MacNiffs are at the root of everything—that they had my parents murdered? Mike?" But that couldn't be right. I'd heard the voice that killed my parents. Nick Kennoyer had, too.

"I'm not saying that," Dev said wearily. "I'm not saying anything—just asking. How old are the MacNiffs?"

"Seventy, I'd say. About. Gem is eighty. They'd be ten years younger."

"So—" The shrill of the downstairs bell surprised us like an electric shock. Dev rose from the sofa and glanced at his watch. It was a few minutes short of midnight. We looked at each other for a moment in silent speculation. Then he turned and walked to the intercom. "Yes?"

The response was, to my ears, garbled, but Dev seemed to understand it. The tension in his shoulders seemed to relax—but not completely. I saw him take a deep breath. The buzzer sounded again. This time he pushed the release button. He turned to me and said, "You're in for a bit of comic relief." But the purple eyes were dark and his mouth did not look ready to laugh. He went to the door, opened it a crack, and waited. I heard the footfalls on the stairs coming closer.

The man who appeared was sixty-something, ruddy, silver-haired, handsome in a distinctly Irish way. His tweed coat was unbuttoned. Under it, he wore a neat blue serge suit, white shirt, red-striped tie, shiny black oxfords—all carefully preserved, but old, painstakingly cared for, and closeted between outings, left waiting for the next special occasion. The man was drunk. He didn't stagger, just the opposite. He held his compact body very straight and moved it very carefully. As I looked at him more closely, I noticed on his face the glazy glow of the steady drinker.

He placed a hand on Dev's shoulder and looked into his face intensely for a full minute without saying a word. Then he walked precisely into the room and reviewed me with glistening blue eyes.

"Pretty, Dev." The lilt of a brogue. But Dev had said his father was from Boston. "She's very pretty, this one."

"Emily," Dev said, his voice sharply edged in tamped-down tension, "may I present my father."

"How do you do," I mumbled, making myself meet the

man's eyes. I remembered the look on Dev's face the night
he told me about his father. I'd taken it for granted that
he'd never seen him again after the brutal incident of the
broken hip—that Mike, in his white hat, had stepped in
and banished the bad guy forever. Fade out, the end. But
life often made less sense than a movie. Who should've
known that better than I?

"What're you drinking, Liam?" Dev asked, leveling a
look at his father that made me understand that this scene
had been played out before, many times.

"Whiskey, what else?" Liam Hannagan lowered himself
slowly onto the opposite end of the sofa from me, without
removing his coat. "Emily, is it?" The smile was not without
charm. But I was in greater danger of succumbing to the
black plague than to any charm of this man's.

"Yes, Mr. Hannagan, it is," I said coldly.

Dev handed his father a whiskey without ice. I noticed
he hadn't made one for himself, nor had he offered one to
me.

"Will you not drink with me, Dev?" Liam Hannagan
asked as he raised his glass in a toast gesture.

"I won't, Liam." The exchange was part of the ritual.
Dev crossed to his Eames chair and sat, arms folded across
his chest. "How have you been?" he asked.

"Passable. Business isn't so bad. New crowd, you'd be
surprised. Yuppies looking for their roots. Gaelic lessons,
even, they're taking, if you believe it. Fathers are lawyers,
doctors, fancy stockbrokers—imitation Yanks." He
knocked back a chunk of his drink. "Wanted to forget they
were Irish at all," he said, turning to me. "But their kids
didn't forget. It was there waiting in the blood. Some joke
on those dads! So the kids come to The Troubles, throw
some darts, beg me to tell them about the days of the
Struggle, teach them the songs." The smile reappeared and
made its way around his face. "They all know I have a son
called after Dev," he said with pride. As I listened, I wanted
to deck him. And I wanted to cry.

"My father and his wife own a bar in Inwood," Dev said in the neutral tones of a narrator. "That's at the top of Manhattan. The bar is called The Troubles." His lips compressed, thin and white.

"We'd be honored to have you, Dev. Anytime, you know that. Ethne always asks for you. She thinks you walk on water. And you're a celebrity at The Troubles. The book, I keep it on a little shelf right above the bar, and I tell them all that my son—"

"Knock it off, Liam. I don't want to hear it." Dev didn't raise his voice, but it cut with the force of a backhanded slap.

"I'm sorry," his father said quietly, his shiny eyes brimming suddenly with tears. "I forget you don't like it." He turned to me and studied my face. "Have you any children, Emily?" he asked.

"No."

"You're missing a great joy—and a great sorrow. But you'll see that for yourself. And watch you don't wreck it. It's easy to do that, you know. So easy. I had a little boy. A fine little boy, and you know what I did?"

I wanted him to stop. I wanted to avert my eyes, to not see the pain in his. I wanted to scream at him that he didn't have the right to grieve. But I just sat there.

"I broke him. I tossed him and I broke him. Careless, I was. So careless. Oh, I could say it was the drink, that I didn't know and all, but it wouldn't be true. I just couldn't make the devils go away when they clawed inside me. And so I broke him." The tears overflowed now and he made no effort to stop them. They rolled down his reddened cheeks onto the stiff white collar of his shirt.

"That's enough now, Liam," Dev said in the calmed tone of someone fighting to stay in control.

"I'm sorry, Dev. I'm sorry." Liam Hannagan crossed himself, the movement as reflexive as a blink.

"I know you are," Dev said, his voice rough now, but not unkind. He stood up, walked over to the sofa and took his father's arm. "It's late. You ought to be getting home. Ethne'll be worried about you. You tell her I said hello." Gently, he pulled the man to his feet. "Take this twenty and get yourself into a cab."

Liam Hannagan put up his hands and drew away. "I'll not take money off you. Don't——"

"You will," Dev snapped, "and don't give me your bullshit. That's the last thing I need right now." Dev thrust the bill into his father's coat pocket.

Liam grabbed Dev's hand and squeezed it. Then he turned to me and delivered a parting smile. "He cares what happens to his old man," he said, shaking his head in wonder. "After all, he cares. Can you beat that?"

And he was gone.

As I listened to the footsteps descend, I was overcome by a feeling entirely new to me: an unimaginable wave of relief that my own father was dead. I kept my eyes fixed firmly on my lap. I thought that if I looked at Dev, I wouldn't be able to bear his pain.

"He does that . . . sometimes," Dev said.

Something I'd never heard in his voice, an uncertainty, made me look up. He was standing there—just standing, as though he were in a strange place and had no idea where to move. I stood and took a few steps toward him. "I am so sorry," I said.

"He started coming here thirteen years ago." The words did not flow easily. "I hadn't seen him—not since I was ten, but when the book was published, he tracked me down." His jaw worked as he scanned my face. "I know what you're thinking. Why do I let him? How can I stand it? Cordelia Otis's granddaughter judges again!" He made a mock flourish with his arm and smiled bitterly.

Was I asking those questions? Maybe, but they took a backseat to another one: Was that why Dev couldn't write anymore, because writing had brought back his father? Penny psychoanalysis, the kind I'd always scorned as some simpleminded party game, but . . .

He turned quickly and walked to his bed. As I watched his retreating back, I noticed the limp afresh and swallowed hard to keep from crying. He threw himself on the bed and turned to face the wall. Before I realized I was in motion, I found myself there, sitting beside him.

I didn't say anything, or touch him. I wanted urgently to have the right words—healing, magic—but no good ones presented themselves. And to touch him right then would have been, I knew, intrusive. So I just sat there and stared at the curve of his shoulders.

Fathers. Dev and I had certainly done a poor job of picking them. Why couldn't either of us manage to just write them off? It's a wise child who . . . I felt my head drop abruptly with the weariness of insistent sleep. As I jerked it up, I mumbled to myself, "I'll match my father against your father anytime."

I saw his back begin to shake, and I thought he was sobbing.

"God, I'm sorry," I began, "I—"

He flipped over to face me and pulled me down next to him. And I saw that he was laughing, really laughing. But his eyes were streaming tears.

CHAPTER
TWENTY-THREE

I woke with a shuddering start to the glare of sunlight, and knew instantly that Dev was gone. I was still lying on his bed, fully dressed, even to my sneakers. We'd fallen asleep like that—the philanderer's daughter and the abuser's son. Two damaged specimens clinging to each other in the dark.

My heart started to pound like a clock gone crazy. I wondered whether I'd missed my date with Irene, but somehow I felt pinned there, unable to move. For the first time since I'd heard the voice in the movie theater, I wanted to run away from all of it. Leave it alone. Let my parents be dead, their lunatic lives remain pieces of history, forgotten except for the unlucky few.

With conscious effort, I lifted my arm. I studied Mike's heavy watch on my wrist as though it were an object I'd never seen before. And I knew that I couldn't run away, not because of my parents but because of him.

Eight forty-five, but I should make Irene's in time if I hurried. I pulled myself up from the bed. My clothes felt molded to the skin, as though I'd been wearing them for months. I walked toward the bathroom, wondering where Dev was off to and whether he'd lit out early to avert any possibility of discussion about last night. My eye caught a sheet of paper lying on the phone table. I switched directions and went to it.

"Emily," the note read, "Gone fishing—in the Logan pond and others. See you later. *Ma semblable, ma soeur.* Thanks."

I felt an ache I couldn't assign to any specific part of my body. Though I knew I didn't have the luxury of much time, I detoured around to the bookshelves at the back of the room. It took me about ten minutes to find Dev's book, jammed against the wall behind the *Oxford English Dictionary*. The jacket was dark blue blending into dark green. The photo on the inside flyleaf showed a young Dev, relish for the world's possibilities clear in his eyes. As I looked at it, I could've strangled Liam Hannagan.

The review blurbs on the back hailed "a budding American Joyce—a new voice, keen in perception, pain, and humor."

It was the title, though, that hit at my gut and shook the foundations of my amateur shrink deductions. The book was called *The Troubles*. I stared at it for a moment. The blue and green cover seemed to roil around the white letters like a churning sea. Then, without knowing exactly why, I put it into my shoulder bag.

Within fifteen minutes, I was showered and dressed respectably in sweater, skirt, and pumps. I even found my coat, still in its plastic cleaner's wrap. As I hustled to the subway, the February air chilling my still-damp hair, I tried to pry my mind off Dev and onto my mother in preparation for my visit with Irene. But it didn't work. Each time I reached to grab a memory, it slipped away from me and he reappeared in its place—the changing purple of his eyes, the rolling limp of his gait, the ironic smile. It occurred to me that he was speaking truth when he told me he ought to have a warning stamped on his backside.

I was ten minutes late. And the old man who answered the door looked annoyed.

"I wondered if you'd changed your mind," he said, rubbing his hands together as though already washing them of me. He was a small man with wispy white hair and a white mustache, which had probably, in its day, bristled. His brown eyes, sharp and magnified behind thick, round horn rims, gave him the look of a skeptical owl. He moved agilely, but I figured he must be close to eighty.

"No. I'm sorry. The train got stuck for a while," I lied. I felt unprepared, caught off base and dubious about this meeting that yesterday had seemed crucially important. "I hope I didn't inconvenience Irene too much," I added, wondering where she might be, and why he was answering the door. "Are you Dr. Rosten?"

"Yes. Yes, I am. Look, Miss Otis—"

"Emily. You can call me Emily." All the closed reluctance I'd been pleasantly surprised not to hear from Irene was here in her husband's face.

"Emily, then. Before I take you into Irene, there's something you must know." I waited for him to continue. "She is not a well woman. Multiple sclerosis. Past two years it's begun to exacerbate again. Movement of any kind is extremely difficult for her, and she tires easily. Very easily."

"I'm sorry," I said, wanting to turn tail out the door and forget the whole thing.

"The resemblance is remarkable," he said, almost an accusation, the owl eyes like some medical instrument examining my face.

"That's right, you knew my mother too, didn't you?" I asked, uncomfortable under his scrutiny, but forcing myself to not turn away.

"Oh yes, I knew her." The words dripped with underlying meaning, making me feel suddenly far more vulnerable than I'd expected.

"Maybe I could see Irene now," I said. "I'll be careful not to tire her."

He nodded curtly and indicated with his hand that I should follow him down the hall. The apartment was vintage 1920s Park Avenue—rooms large, ceilings high, and, for those lucky enough to live on a high floor, as the Rostens were—good light, even when a more recent addition to the landscape waved itself in your view. All in all, it looked like the apartments of three quarters of the girls I'd gone to school with.

We walked past the entrance to a formal living room, which looked as though it hadn't been used in years. In fact, the whole apartment had an aura of preserved disuse—of objects kept carefully dusted and polished but otherwise never touched, of cushions fluffed up but seldom sat on.

Dr. Rosten stopped at a pair of closed French doors backed with sheer, stretched curtains. He opened one and preceded me into a room determined to be cheerful. It was painted a soft yellow, the sofa and two small easy chairs covered in a sunny, flowered chintz. A few polished wood tables of various sizes held plants and vases of cut flowers. Irene sat in a cane-backed wheelchair in the center of the room, an expectant half-smile on her mouth.

At first look, she was astonishingly little changed. The short blond hair was paler now—almost as creamy as her skin against the daffodil cardigan she wore. Clear blue eyes, small, heart-shaped face as classically chiseled as a cameo. As I looked more closely, I saw the years and the strain of being ill.

"Em-i-ly." She drew out the three syllables as though savoring a discovered treasure. She held out her hands. The small, withered fingers shook with the effort of the gesture.

"Irene, you promised you wouldn't." Herb Rosten was at his wife's side in a split second, taking her hands and replacing them in her lap.

"No!" Irene didn't shout, but the snap in her voice meant business. "I want you to leave us alone, Herb." He hesitated, the command in his face dissolving into confusion. "Go ahead, now. Make us some coffee. That's what we said, remember?" She soothed his feelings now, and the effects were instantly visible. "And bring us those nice little pastries—the ones from Dumas. You bought them, didn't you?"

"I did, love. Of course I did." He smiled at her, still apprehensive but mollified, and left us.

"Sit down, Emily." Irene's eyes crinkled as she looked at me. "There. That chair"—she indicated with her chin— "so I can look at you." I sat. "You *are* Celia."

"And you are Irene," I said with a smile that seemed to take over my whole body. "You look beautiful." All at once, my impression of a cameo crystallized into a specific memory. "When I was very little I thought my mother's cameo was a picture of you."

"Ah, you're sweet to say it, but I'm afraid this damned disease has claimed my looks—along with everything else." She smiled ruefully, as though about some faintly ridiculous minor inconvenience. "That cameo was your grandmother's," she said after a few seconds.

"I didn't know my grandmother ever gave my mother anything."

"Oh no. Not the Dragon, your *other* grandmother. Do you remember her at all?"

Did I? It struck me afresh, for the first time in years, how hermetically sealed my upbringing had been—how totally without the reinforcement of family photos, anecdotes, all the props of which memories are made. "Look, honey, there you are with Grammy. You are crying because you dropped your ice cream. Remember?" And you do, of course—or believe you do after you've looked at the picture a few times. *Grammy.* The name struck an almost inaudible chord.

"I'm not sure I do remember her," I said. "It was . . . a very long time ago."

"I know, dear. It was all Otis for you after . . . it happened. But you *do* have another heritage. Your grandmother Silver was an extraordinary woman." She paused. "Shall I tell you?" Her young girl's voice shaded the question in a way I couldn't define. I nodded, not trusting my throat to work. "The most important thing in her world was her beautiful daughter. Your mother was an only child, you know, just like you. And she had a difficult father too." Irene's delicate face clouded.

The door swung open. Herb carried in the coffee tray and deposited it on one of the tables. He then opened a mahogany cabinet and pulled out a flattish wooden tray with clip-on gadgets that let him attach it across the front of Irene's chair.

"Isn't this contraption foolish-looking, Emily," she said, making a face. "I'm like a child in its high chair." She gave her husband a smile that seemed to me calculated to make him feel good. "And Herb takes such wonderful care of me." Calculated or not, it worked. The glow in his owl eyes lasted the whole time he was serving up the coffee and miniature Danishes. He patted Irene's hair lightly and left.

"How do you mean, difficult, Irene? My grandfather." It had been clear that she'd have nothing good to say about my father. That was no surprise, but I didn't want to talk about him—not yet. Though no more than an hour ago I had longed to drop the whole thing, I found myself tingling with excitement, straining at the bit to learn about the Silver side of my family.

"He was a tyrant—more than a tyrant." And you, the thought penetrated my eagerness, are an actress, with an actress's gift for dramatizing a story. It takes one to know one. I'm going to have to swallow you with a couple of grains of salt.

"He was a haberdasher. A haberdasher in Cleveland. Very handsome. Eric was his name. You owe your looks to him, but not much else." Carefully, she brought the cup to her mouth and took a small sip of milky coffee. "Your grandmother, she was Esther. Estee, everybody called her, just like the cosmetics woman, except that your grandmother was no beauty, and she'd been raised in an orphanage, so she didn't even have a mother or father on hand to build her up a bit—tell her she had pretty eyes, nice ankles. So of course when this Adonis began to pay attention to her, you can understand that he simply swept her off her feet." The puzzlement must've shown on my face. She broke off her animated narrative. "What is it, Emily?"

"Nothing, really. Just that I'm a little surprised you know so many details. Are you from Cleveland too?"

"Good Lord, no. I'm from Boston. And thank you for not guessing. I spent years trying to erase 'Haavad Yaad' from my tongue. I know the details, my dear, because I loved your mother."

I had a flash premonition that she was going to confide a lesbian love affair, and I labored to suppress a sudden giggle. My parents had certainly been . . . different.

"Oh, I don't mean sexually. No, neither of us inclined that way." Irene leaned her head forward a bit, her neck popping tense cords with the effort. I could see she was pushing to underscore the words she was about to speak. "Celia and I were close—close as sisters. Closer perhaps, because we didn't have the rivalry that sisters always do. We talked about everything. Told each other everything. I believe I know almost as much about the Silvers as I do about my own family."

"Go on, Irene," I said. "Please go on."

"Estee worked at Douglas Martin. That's what the store was called. Family business. The Silvers were German Jewish immigrants, but they decided that a made-up WASP name for the store would play better in Cleveland than their own. Perhaps they were right. The store was quite successful. Very upscale. Estee sold neckties there, or some such. Everyone was surprised that young Eric took a fancy to her, a plain girl, no money, no family. But he did, and they married, and before very long it became crystal-clear what Eric was after. He wanted a slave, someone to wait on him hand and foot, cater to his every whim. Estee did that. Willingly. And counted herself lucky—a girl with no family, no money, no looks.

"Then your mother was born, and for a while everything seemed to improve. Eric was elated with his little daughter—beautiful in his own image. Celia was a good little girl, too, sparkling, talented, and Estee dressed her like a little princess, which delighted her daddy. And Celia was never allowed to stray for a moment from that path—from delighting her daddy. Because if she did, he would punish her. Wherever they happened to be, he would pull down her panties and spank her bare bottom. Estee hated it, but in the beginning she was afraid to say anything. Eric was lord of the manor. It was unthinkable for her to defy him. Besides, it wasn't as though he were *beating* the child. What could she really do? It was, after all, his child, too.

"But then things changed. Eric seemed to look for things to spank Celia for, to manufacture them. He started to take her up to her room and make a ceremony of lowering her panties. By the time she was eight, he began to do other things as well. Warned Celia never to say a word to her mother, and she didn't. She was terrified. Also, she was used to doing what Daddy said, no questions, no protests. But Estee began to sense something. She noticed changes in Celia's behavior—a new quietness, a listlessness, a drop in her schoolwork. And she dug, Estee did, until Celia told her."

I shut my eyes for a moment, overcome with pity—and more. My mother had been only a couple of years older than I was now when her life ended. There had been precious little in it to make her happy. And I'd failed her too. I was, as she'd known, my father's. I wondered if I'd taken her name in expiation for that sin. The joke was that even the name was wrong. Eric's name. Eric Silver, the child molester. My grandfather.

"What did Estee do when she found out?"

"Left. Took Celia and left."

"And Eric didn't put up a fight? He had the money, the influence."

Irene's mouth tilted in a faint smile. "I imagine he would have, if he'd lived."

"What happened?" I asked, my nails digging into my palm in apprehension.

"There was a fire in the house," she said, eyebrows raising, it seemed to me, in actor's emphasis of an unspoken point. "It started late one night a few days after Estee and Celia left."

"Irene, please don't play with me. Are you saying my grandmother murdered him?"

"No, Emily. I'm simply saying that Estee had the courage to rescue her daughter from an evil man, and fortunately, that man died, so that he couldn't torture either of them anymore. He deserved to die. Perhaps God agreed. It also didn't hurt that Eric was a heavy smoker, as well as a hoarder of newspapers and magazines beside his bed—used to scream abuse at Estee if she tried to clear out the huge pile, or if she objected to his bedtime cigarette. A poetic justice there, don't you think?"

I didn't answer. No answer was really called for.

"The Silver family dropped Estee and Celia cold, and Eric carried no insurance to speak of, so there wasn't much money. But Estee moved to New York—got a job sewing in the garment industry, and managed for the two of them. So you see, that part of the story at least had a happy ending."

"Right," I said curtly, my face stiff, stomach sick. Irene, with her cameo face and bell voice, had just let me know that in my family, death by violence was no mere aberration, but a tradition.

My grandmother zoomed into my head quite clearly now—short and square, lively eyes, quick laugh. I had a flash of her holding my hand near the seal pool at the Central Park Zoo, then swooping me up over her head so I could see the sleek dives and underwater glides. Was I three? Four? It seemed to me not much later that she died. I remembered my mother's face twisted with what had seemed a frightening fury, but must have been fierce, terrible grief. "Mama's gone," I'd heard her moan. "Take me, Mama. Take me."

She'd dug her long fingers painfully into my upper arm as she pulled me over to the coffin, whispering urgently in my ear, "It's closed. You mustn't be afraid." I *had* been afraid though—less of the ominous box than of the overwhelming power of my mother's emotion. I must have been older than four, I realized, because I stayed home from school to go to the funeral. Where had my father been? I was fairly sure he wasn't there, and I wondered why not. Other questions bubbled at my lips too, but I couldn't bring myself to ask them, somehow.

"I'm sorry," Irene said softly, as she laboriously raised one of the small pastries on her tray to her mouth, "I didn't mean to upset you with the ugly part." She polished it off in two dainty bites, and licked her lips like a fastidious cat. "It's just that I have such admiration for Estee, for the way she overcame her own fears for Celia. It was always that way, as long as she lived—anything for her daughter. She sent Celia to the American Theatre Wing to study acting. It was the best school there was then," Irene said proudly. "I went there too, you know. That's where Celia and I met. Only my parents didn't help me—not one bit. They almost disowned me when I said I wanted to come to New York and study acting rather than try for Smith. Estee and Celia took me in."

"You lived with them?"

"Oh yes. For three years, until a great aunt died and left me a small inheritance that my parents could do nothing to interfere with. But let's get off me. I want to know about you—about your career, your life. Have you considered moving back to New York, making the stage your main career rather than films or television? Or perhaps you're married to someone out there. Are you?" Her questions flowed with the unself-conscious ease of genuine interest. I found myself warming to her again.

I told her about how I'd happened to go to California and about Mike—the abridged version: how I'd jumped into his scenery truck after dropkicking my nascent screen career into oblivion; how happy I'd been living with him; that he'd recently died. "So maybe now I *will* move to New York. Mike left me enough money so that I could give it a try, see if Broadway's waiting for Emily Silver."

"Emily Silver." Irene nodded appreciatively as she popped another pastry. "I love that you took Celia's name. But I'll bet that the Dragon had a fit! I imagine she'll be leaving you money as well, won't she? That is, if she's still alive. Is she?"

"She is, and I don't know the terms of her will." I felt a flash of stiff-necked reluctance to discuss Gem with Irene. I also recognized it as absurdly inconsistent. So Irene didn't like her, called her "the Dragon." So what? I didn't like her either. And I'd called her worse. "Did you ever actually meet my grandmother? My grandmother Otis, that is," I asked, more to mitigate my snappish tone of a second ago than because I wanted to know.

"No." Irene looked up from her coffee, her blue eyes suddenly chilly. "You must understand, Emily, I had very little use for your father or anything connected with him. I . . . I suppose, because you look so astonishingly like Celia, because you chose to take her name, I assumed that you were on her side. But that woman did bring you up, of course. No matter what quarrels you may have had with her, that's probably where your loyalties lie."

I felt the blood rise in my face. I'd have given her an honest response, but I didn't have one handy. My loyalties were not easy to sort out these days. Instead I asked a question that had been playing around the edges of my mind since I'd first spoken to her on the phone yesterday. "You knew me very well when I was little, Irene. You were at our place all the time. I remember that. How come . . ." My voice shook and I had to start again. "How come you never kept in touch with me? Never even called?"

Her face softened. "Oh dear. You couldn't know. Of course you couldn't know. I *did* try, Emily. I did. Your grandmother blocked me. 'It would be better cut off

cleanly,' she said." Her imitation of Gem wasn't bad—not
as good as mine, but not bad. "Can you imagine? 'Cut off
cleanly.' As though she were amputating an infected foot!
I'd have persisted—found out where you went to school
and waited to meet you. But I got sick, you see. Just a week
after Celia died, this *thing* started and I landed in the hospital. After that, I wasn't my own person in the same way
for a long time—a very long time."

"I'm sorry, Irene. I tried to call you too, but I never got
any answer, and then, a while later, when I called again,
your phone had been disconnected."

"Yes. After I got out of the hospital, I married Herb.
Finally." She smiled a bit sadly. "He's had to put up with
a great deal."

"He doesn't seem to see it that way. It looks to me as
though he's entirely in love with you. Sick or well, that's
not so bad after twenty years. Better than my mother or
grandmother had. Both grandmothers, come to think of it.
Herb knew my mother too, I gather. I also gather he didn't
much like her."

The tinkling laugh. "Didn't much like her? Herb was in
love with Celia. She knew him before I did, but she wouldn't
look at him, of course. We used to joke about old Herb.
We were very mean."

I downed a gulp of cold coffee to fortify myself for what
I was going to ask. "Irene, you've made it clear that you
hated my father, and I understand why—so we don't have
to go into it. But my mother confided in you, about everything. You said that." She nodded. I ran my tongue around
dry lips. "Do you know who my father was involved with
at the time my parents died?"

"Alphabetically?" she asked bitterly, her eyes holding
mine. "I don't think you quite understand, Emily. It was
never simply one person at a time. Your father, despite all
his high-flown talk about spiritual communion and all that
rot, had the morals of an alley cat. At that time, let's
see, there was an actress who was just about to go off to

Hollywood, a chubby little convent girl of some kind, poor Nick Kennoyer of course. Shall I go on?"

At that moment the door opened and Herb Rosten strode in looking purposeful. "This is it, Emily," he said curtly. "Irene takes her nap now."

"But Herb," Irene wheedled. "Just another fifteen minutes. Emily and I—"

"Nope." He wasn't having any this time. The doctor was in. "You know how bad it is when you get overtired."

"He's right, Irene," I said with no more than a second's hesitation, maybe more relieved than I wanted to admit to escape hearing more about my father and his appalling ways. I walked to her chair, leaned over and kissed her forehead. It was papery and cool on my lips. "I'll come and see you again, if that's okay."

She gave me one of her embracing smiles. "I hope so," she said, but her tone seemed to doubt it, and I watched a shadow of regret cross her face. Just as I reached the door, she called my name sharply and I turned back. "Emily," she repeated, "I think I've said too much. The excitement of seeing you—I . . ." Her face twitched with sudden spasm. "Leave it behind you," she almost whispered. At that point Herb took my arm and virtually pulled me out the door.

CHAPTER
TWENTY-FOUR

WHEN I emerged from the tasteful darkness of the lobby into the clear sunlight, I welcomed the fresh, cold air on my face, breathed it deeply into my lungs.

"Cab, miss?" the doorman offered. I shook my head and almost ran down Park Avenue. Memories, like newly wild dogs throwing off years of domesticity, were slipping their restraining leashes and claiming the run of my whole being, bounding from head to gut and back again.

My father's phone calls, hushed and intimate, ending abruptly with my peremptory call of "Daddy! Stop talking and come play." And I'd hear him chuckle into the phone, "My Wild Princess calls," right before the welcome click that meant he was mine again. The exquisite little pastries from Dumas churned in my stomach. Who had he been talking to all those times? Nick and the actress and the convent girl and God knew who else.

My mother and Irene and I—the girls, Irene used to call us—sitting in our living room munching Oreos and Mallomars. Laughing, laughing, until I'd say something that struck my mother wrong and her laughing would cut off. "Stop it," she'd snap. "Don't ape him." That burning look, the one that made me scared she'd lock me up, would take over her eyes and they would glitter with the angry tears that told me I'd betrayed her.

The fights, hissed and vicious. The ones I buried my head under the pillow not to hear, but heard anyway.

My mother: "Disgusting pervert! This is the *worst,* even for you. You're crazy, you know. You'll kill us both."

My father: "I suppose so. With regrets, my love. You're like some strangling weed. I wish I could just root you out and go on breathing free. But we both know how unlikely that is, don't we?" My father's rippling laugh, turned inside out and ugly.

I stopped in my tracks, as abruptly as a cartoon character skidding to a halt at the edge of a cliff, and stood there panting, my open mouth taking in gulps of chilly air. That particular snatch of dialogue had lodged in my brain, sleeping there all these years. I thought—was almost sure—that I'd heard it the very night they'd been killed.

He'd threatened her. Lightning struck behind my eyes. Could it be that I'd been wrong? That he had killed her? I shook my head to try and clear it. No. The voice I'd heard that night was real. And Mike was dead because of it.

I replayed my parents' furious exchange in my head. A threat? Not necessarily. Couples say things like that to each other in the heat of anger. Maybe not in such florid terms, but she was an actress, after all, and he a playwright. I'd flung some pretty dire language at Mike from time to time in battle—hollered how I wished he'd drop dead and get off my back about whatever. Mike would just laugh and tell me to knock off the tantrum stuff, before he put me over his knee. But then, Mike had had little taste for high drama.

I forced my breathing slower and looked up at the street sign. Seventy-ninth already. I was halfway to Gem's house. I started south again, teeth clenched in resolution now. I'd show up and make her talk to me. I wouldn't pussyfoot this time. Even though she was ill, I wouldn't. She'd have to tell me what she knew. If she knew. It struck me that maybe she didn't. Maybe Mac and Mackey were somehow involved in it on their own. But in *what?*

* * *

I rang the bell and waited for Mackey's predictable heavy steps to respond, but they didn't. I rang again. And again. I checked my wrist. Almost one. My nails dug at my palm in frustration. Gem was out at one of her luncheons, of course, and the MacNiffs were shopping or running some errand—or, for all I knew, up to something a lot darker than that. As I turned away from the door in defeat, I found myself looking down at Mackey, who was standing on the sidewalk at the foot of the steps, the collar of her stiff navy-blue coat turned up against the cold.

I had the idea that she'd arrived right behind me, had been there the whole time, watching my fruitless ringing. And the idea got my blood up. "Mackey, where's my grand-mother?" I asked less than politely.

"Not home, looks like," she almost muttered.

So, no gloves. "I asked you a question. Now answer it."

I could see her hesitate, her broad brow furrowing as she considered her options. "Mrs. Otis is in the hospital," she said, her voice devoid of any expression but the faint ring of challenge.

"The *hospital?*" I was down the steps and at her side in an instant, everything scrubbed from my mind but sudden, urgent fear for my grandmother's life. "What . . . What happened?"

"Why?" she fired at me, taunting. "Don't try to tell me you care."

"Answer me."

"You run away, you break her heart twenty times over, and now all of a sudden you're so concerned? You were always a bad girl, a pagan, evil girl. The money, that's what concerns you."

It wasn't her hatred that got me, it was her satisfaction at having the upper hand, at making me suffer for the information. I grabbed both her arms and shook her body as though it were a stumpy apple tree. "Tell me. Now!"

"A stroke. Mrs. Otis had a stroke," she said defiantly, as though the words had been, "There, take that."

I dropped her arms and stepped back, my face breaking out in a cold sweat despite the temperature. I'd been party to more than a few disasters, and each one had taken me by utter surprise; not because I was an optimist—I was far from that—but because the disaster that happened was never the one I was prepared to face.

"Better get to the hospital fast," she taunted. "Maybe you can make sure you're still in the will."

I didn't reply. I didn't think. It was as instinctive as that day on the set with Bruce DeRenkin. My arm drew back under its own steam and slapped her across the face. Hard. The bitter satisfaction that blazed out at me from her eyes had all the impact of the slap returned.

I covered the eight blocks in record time, and arrived hot-faced with running. I knew where to go without having to ask. Gem had been an active board member at New York Hospital as long as I could remember, and as far as she was concerned, there *was* no other hospital.

They told me that she was in the neuro special intensive care unit, and that immediate family was admitted for a few minutes every half hour. I took the elevator up to the sixth floor and checked in with the nurse in charge. She told me that my grandmother was critical but stable, and still unconscious. Then I joined the small group of other patients' waiting relatives, some pacing, others just sitting, all sharing the same dazed yet intense expression. A pair of middle-aged women, expensively dressed and obviously sisters, were engaged in a whispered debate about arrangements for "him." The others were silent. I joined the pacers, under some illusion that it moved the clock along faster, or maybe, it occurred to me, I was simply—like my mother—constitutionally unable to keep still under stress. Finally, it was two o'clock and the keeper of the door opened it to let us file in.

Gem was the waxy yellow white of an embalmed corpse, an electronic army taped to her arms and chest—grotesque parasites feeding off the motionless, wasted body that propelled their ominously beeping indicators. She looked every bit as dead as Mike.

"Gem," I said softly. "Gem, it's Emily. I'm here." I put my hand on her cool forehead. She lay entirely still, except for the small, regular movements of her shallow breathing. I sat on the straight white chair at her bedside, close to hypnotized by the sounds and motions of the machines that told me she was still alive.

If she dies now, we'll never have our chance. When I'd seen her, there'd been something different between us. I wasn't just imagining that. I told myself I wasn't—that it was real. She would've talked to me, told me . . . *If she dies now, I will never know what she knew.*

I spent the remainder of the afternoon moving with the metronome rhythm of the intensive care unit—in for ten minutes, out for twenty, in for ten, out for twenty, all track of real time lost. Down to the cafeteria for a cottony tuna sandwich and weak coffee. Back and forth to the phone— maybe Dev had gotten home. But he hadn't, and I didn't want to talk to the machine. Since I was standing there with time to kill and a handful of change, I checked my messages at the Ramada. Sergeant Stivic had called two days ago, also Mike's Aunt Clara, yesterday. I rang Stivic, half hoping he'd be out. He wasn't.

"Eh, Ms. Silver. I was giving up hope on you." He sounded in a jaunty mood. A ripple of distaste ran through me.

"I'm sorry I didn't get back to you sooner. My grand-mother's been very ill," I said formally. "What can I do for you?"

"Ah, well at this point, probably not much, but I think I'm going to be able to do something for *you* pretty soon." His tone invited me to join the game.

"And what's that?" I made no effort to mask my skepticism.

"How well do you know these partners of your . . . of Florio's?"

"Not partners."

"Huh?"

"I said, they were not his partners. Mike didn't have partners. He simply left Hank and Jerry the right to buy the business at terms he considered fair." I could hear Gem's icy precision in my tone, and wondered why I was bothering to summon it up for Stivic.

"Whatever. You know these guys well?"

I pictured the two of them—a couple odd enough for a sitcom. Jerry, with a ready laugh and a joke for every occasion, the man of many words. More of a boy really, despite being almost Mike's age. Short, slim, his hair still in its sixties Beatles cut. Hank, the man of not too many words, his size and the hard times etched in his dark face adding weight to every one of them.

"Not really," I answered. So he was sniffing along that path now. I looked at my wrist. Almost time for the next ten-minute vigil at Gem's bedside.

"Any idea where they might be?" he asked with a casualness that a child could've spotted as heavily sly.

"Do you want to tell me where you're going with all this?" I snapped.

"Pardon *me*." He should have left sarcasm alone. He didn't have the touch. "I had the idea you might want to help us get to the end of this thing." Pause. I didn't speak. "Both these jokers have disappeared, Ms. Silver"—insolent accent on the "Ms." "Now, what do you make of that?"

I remained quiet, but this time because he'd astonished me. Hank and Jerry disappeared. It was Hank who'd first told me about Stivic's suspicions. "Not ridiculous," he'd said when I'd scorned the very idea. "Not true, but not ridiculous." Was it possible Stivic really had something?

No, Emily, it is *not* possible. "I don't know what to make of it, Sergeant," I said, chewing on my lip. "What do *you* make of it?"

"Let's cut the crap, okay?" The game had palled for him. It wasn't going the way he wanted. "You have any idea where either of these guys are?"

"No," I said. "Do you have anything else to tell me?"

"No," he said. And hung up.

I put in my ten minutes, my eyes trained on Gem, but my mind three thousand miles west. At the next interval, I rushed back to the phone and called Mike's office. "Florio Trucking," the voice answered, but it was an unfamiliar one. When I asked for Lucy, the temp told me she was on vacation. I slammed the phone back in its cradle with a force that threatened its purchase on the wall and earned me several dirty looks. I went through the charade of tracking down her home number through Information, and was answered by the predictable machine. I tried Dev again. Machine again.

I trudged into my next audience with Gem, not so much at a loss for answers but bereft even of questions that made any sense.

On the next break, I dialed San Francisco. Clara Santangelo's voice, blaring at me live, not on tape, gave me an instant shot of well-being.

"Clara!" It came out with the unspoken "Thank God" plain. I wasted no time on preliminaries. "Look, do you know about this thing the police think they're onto about Hank and Jerry?"

"Yeah." Cautious, alert. "You talked to Stivic, huh? I wish you called me first. What did you tell him?" Her tone grew sharp and tense.

"Nothing. What *could* I tell him?" Frustration heated my voice. "Would you tell me what the hell is going on here? You apparently know something I don't." It occurred to me that our positions were the exact reverse of what they'd been at Mike's funeral, and I recalled how unwilling I'd been then to lay any of it on her.

"You listen to me, Emily." Clara spoke slowly and with all the authority of a woman who'd taken it on herself to divorce a Mafia don. "Everything's taken care of. You got no cause to worry—and nothin' to do. Right? You just go on seein' to what you're seein' to there in New York, and no problems. All I wanted to tell you was, keep your distance from Stivic and don't try and get in touch with Jerry or Hank. Capish?"

"Oh, I capish, Clara, but you can't just leave me out. "It—it's not fair!"

"We're not talkin' fair, we're talkin' efficient. You got somethin' up your sleeve, and don't try and deny it. So I got somethin' up mine. I'll get the eye for the eye, maybe you can get the tooth for the tooth."

"Are you sure, Clara?" I asked slowly, my nails almost piercing my palm.

"I don't do anything, I'm not sure," she answered just as slowly.

Gem's condition did not change. Critical but stable. But something *did* change. As the cycle repeated itself again and again, I felt, unlikely as it was, a resolute calm begin to grow inside me—not the paralyzed freeze of grief that had followed Mike's murder but the still strength of indomitable will: Gem's kind of strength, her kind of will.

Perhaps that was why the plan came to me. When her doctor arrived, he told me that the stroke had happened last night, that her vital signs were surprisingly good but that essentially it was even money whether or not she'd pull out of this, and in what condition—and that we should know something more definitive by tomorrow morning.

"I'll be staying at my grandmother's home, Doctor," I said. "Please contact me there if anything should change overnight."

CHAPTER
TWENTY-FIVE

I rang my grandmother's door-bell for the second time that day. It was past seven and pitch-dark out now, but I saw a light in the downstairs window—the servants' quarters. I only hoped they'd open the door before figuring out who it was. I huddled in the shadow, trying to obscure myself. Waiting.

Finally, I heard a step. I bit my lip and raised my chin in preparation. The door opened a crack.

"Yes?" Mac's reticent voice. Him, not her—that was a break.

Quickly, I stepped forward. "Mac, it's me. Emily."

He started, pulled back, but he couldn't shut the door, even if he'd dared to try, because I'd placed my foot in the small opening. "Oh, miss." His soft burr had the edge of alarm. "I'm afraid . . . that is to say, what can I do for you, please?"

"I've decided to stay here tonight," I said calmly, keeping my eyes leveled at him, even though he chose to avert his.

"Oh no. I . . . That's not possible."

"Oh yes it is. I told Dr. Fleischmann to reach me here if there was any change in my grandmother's condition over-night. He expects her to regain consciousness by morning," I added, slipping my shoulder into the doorway while he absorbed the implications, and hoping that he'd be too frightened of Gem's reaction to risk shoving me out and slamming the door. It worked.

"Just a moment," he mumbled as we stood face-to-face in the vestibule. "I'll let Mackey know you're here."

"That's all right," I said, sailing past him. "I'll just go upstairs to my room. I know the way. I did used to live here."

Oh yes, I did used to live here. I felt, rather than imagined, my nine-year-old self running up those stairs. And I realized that, in some way, I'd always been nine years old in this house—a gangling, awkward kid, raw anger just under the skin, ready to boil over. Living with Gem's cold discipline had given me no joy, but I'd given her no joy either.

My room, fourth floor back, was unchanged—a big, moss-green box, a color I'd never liked, yet I'd parried each of Gem's offers to change it. The twin beds were still covered with violet-printed spreads that matched the tied-back curtains. I sat on the bed that had been mine and let my heart slow down. Would he send Mackey up here? Somehow I thought not, but I found my ears straining tensely, dreading the prospect of her heavy tread.

I concentrated on Gem's spirit, drawing it in, turning my body over to it—doing exactly what Nadia Gregoriu had taught me to do to prepare for a part. I beat back the tension, trying to recapture the calm I'd felt in the hospital. I was going to need every resource I could summon to deal with Mackey. It was one thing to haul off and strike her in a moment of provoked fury. I didn't even feel bad about that, never mind that she was seventy. But it was quite another to confront her, overcome her will to the point where she would give up her secret about Andy Logan in time for me to shout to Clara and Stivic, "Stop, you're wrong. That's not the way it happened." And to do it while Hank and Jerry were still alive.

The house was utterly quiet. As I lay there facedown on the bed, my eyes shut, I felt weightless, suspended in time and place. I imagined a hand stroking my hair, then reaching under the heavy mass to massage my neck. A delicious thrill ran down my back as the magic touch descended along my spine and played teasingly at my waist. Then the fingers reached lightly under the band of my jeans and inside my underpants, to caress the curve of my buttocks. I heard myself groan softly with pleasure as the hand slipped between my legs.

"What the fuck are you doing!" The door burst open and she stood there silhouetted in the entryway, elongated and powerful—a terrifying avenging angel. He and I sprang up from the sofa and faced her like a pair of guilty children waiting for punishment. "Emily, go downstairs to your room." Her smoky voice was distorted with fury. I abandoned him and ran for my life.

Now I sat bolt upright, eyes wide, jaw slack, stunned by the long-buried memory. I'd been terrified that day—but of the wrong person. My mother had been my protector, my father my violator. Nick Kennoyer had been mistaken—Tuck hadn't stopped short of his daughter in his crazy quest for "communion."

My heart ached for my mother for the second time that day. Poor Celia, she'd had no luck with father or husband. Or daughter. I'd pulled away from her always, bending to him as though I were some heliotropic plant.

When had that particular incident happened? Was it an isolated one? Had it ever gone farther? I forced my eyes shut and tried to storm the locked vaults in my head. The best I could come up with was an impression that I'd been in the third grade at the time my mother'd walked in on us, and a sense memory that Daddy stroking me all over was something I'd enjoyed not just once. Had he done more than stroke? I didn't think so, but I was far from sure.

I lay back down on the bed, my head throbbing with a dull ache that it seemed to me had been present for hours but had had to wait its turn for my attention. I tried to get back to concentrating on Gem, but it didn't even begin to work.

I reached for the phone on the nightstand beside me and

held the receiver to my ear listening to the buzz for a full
ten seconds before I remembered why I'd lifted it. I dialed
Dev's number. He was probably wondering where the hell
I was. After four rings the machine clicked on. Eight
o'clock. Why wasn't he home? "Fishing in the Logan pond
and others," his note had said. What if . . . "Where are
you?" I asked the machine. "I'll call again later."

I stood up and tried to swallow a sudden rush of panic,
to scrub my mind clean of the bloody pictures that had
begun to form there. I caught myself formulating bargains
with God. If you'll let him live, I'll . . . what? Drop all
this? Ask no more questions? I could hear Dev: "Declaring
yourself again. Making deals. With whom?" He was right.
Except as a sweep of omnipotent, punishing power, I didn't
even believe in God. Come on, Emily. You came here to
do something. Now do it!

I kicked off my shoes and walked out into the hallway,
closing the bedroom door quietly behind me. Then I made
my way down to the third floor, my grandmother's private
domain. I opened the door of her study—the room where
I'd sat with her the other day—clicked on a brass lamp on
the polished walnut writing desk, and quickly shut the door.
I felt myself hesitate for a moment before proceeding. This
was the room of discipline, of lectures, even its correct
English furniture straight-backed and disapproving. I took
a deep breath and pulled open the top drawer of the desk.

Fifteen minutes later, I knew a great deal about my grandmother's social and charitable commitments, also her medical and hairdressing appointments. But I had no trace of
an answer to any of the questions I'd come here about. No
records of private detectives, no mementos of my father's
life or death, and no mention of Frank Strohmeyer or Andy
Logan. I did notice that one of her check stubs, neatly
marked "charitable contribution," was designated simply
with the initial "T," but that alone told me nothing.

My heart skidded just slightly in its cavity as I prepared
to give up on the study and broach Gem's bedroom. If

there was anything to find, I knew instinctively that was where it would be. I just hadn't been up to starting there. Incredibly, I'd been inside Cordelia Tucker Otis's private chamber only twice in my life: the first day of my life here, and the last.

That first morning after she'd claimed me at the hospital and told me I was to live with her now, I awoke early, face numb from having fallen asleep crying, hunger pangs raking my stomach, and crept downstairs like a foraging cat. I found the kitchen empty and spied a loaf of fragrant, un-sliced bread. My hunger turned suddenly savage, ungov-ernable. I tore at the bread, stuffed chunks into my mouth and followed them with others before I'd completed chew-ing and swallowing the first. Then, all at once, my eyes, scanning with the wary instinct of an animal protecting its prey, settled on a newspaper lying almost out of sight on the counter across the room. "SOCIETY DOUBLE DEATH." I ran to the paper, grabbed it. Photos of my parents. I read the words. ". . . shot his wife, Celia, and then turned the gun on himself." I felt the bread expand like a poisonous sponge in my gut. I doubled over with stabbing pain. After a paralyzed minute, I managed to hobble to the sink, where I threw up in spasmodic bursts that left me gasping.

Then I ran up the stairs to find my grandmother. Ur-gently, I flung open every closed door I came upon, until I found her room. She was in her bed, her head turning drowsily on the lace-trimmed ivory pillowcase at the sound of my invasion. The tousled red-gold curls, delicately square shoulders covered demurely by fine batiste, gray eyes, na-kedly blind without their glasses—all of these made her seem to me vulnerable, approachable.

"There's a mistake," I shouted. "The paper told a lie. They said Daddy killed—"

"Hush!" In less than an instant she was out of bed, ma-roon wool bathrobe pulled tight around her, silver-rimmed glasses arming the gray eyes to take their rightful command.

"But they're wrong! I told the policeman. I heard the voice. It was the *voice* that killed them."

Her face went white. "I am sorry that the newspaper upset you," she said stiffly. "It should not have been left there. I shall speak to Mackey about her carelessness." Our eyes locked in combat. The first skirmish. "There was no voice," she said tonelessly, one word at a time.

"There was. I heard it." Anger scalded away my fear of her, for the moment. "I'm not crazy, you mean old lady. Don't you *care* that somebody killed your son?"

I thought she'd go for me then, slap me, kill me maybe. But I didn't care. She didn't move, just stood there, chin high, hands resolutely at her sides. "My son killed himself and your mother. That is all there is to it. Understand, Emily, that we shall never speak of this again," she added, the magnified gray eyes drilling into mine. "Now go and have a bath before breakfast."

Now my hand turned the egg-shaped brass knob, half expecting the door to be locked. The door swung open into the mauve and ivory room. It was just as I remembered, yet, in another way, not at all as I remembered. Fragile colors; gleaming fruitwoods; except for a silver-framed photo of her parents—the great Samuel Tucker and his delicately pretty wife, Gwyneth—no trace of any family at all. I'd seen this room as the chamber of the Ice Queen. Now I saw the sanctuary of a sheltered, virginal girl.

I lifted my chin, Gem-like, and set to work. Drawer after drawer of precisely folded underclothes, handkerchiefs, scarves, gloves—all with the faint astringent smell of lemoned lavender, which I thought of as uniquely hers. No secret box. I disarranged French watercolor landscapes. No hidden safe. I opened the door of the huge walk-in closet, and entered a mini-world of garments, shoes, purses, meticulously arranged by season and cross-referenced as to color. I paced back and forth, opening purses, hatboxes,

Lucite-fronted drawers, knowing all the while that they wouldn't hold what I was looking for. I paced some more. There had to be something. *Something.*

And there was.

As I patrolled the closet yet again, my stockinged feet noticed an unevenness in the carpet—a hillock maybe a foot or so long and a little less wide. I squatted down and felt around the outline with my hand. At one end, almost imperceptible among the thick, velvety mauve fibers, was a seam, a carpet-layer's expert piecing. I worked my fingers under it and jerked it up. My head gave a throb, hard as a punch, releasing a torrent of hot blood into my cheeks as I stared down at the smooth, dark leather portfolio fitted neatly into a depression specially carved out for it.

Right there on the closet floor, I opened it and examined in the dimmish overhead light what it held. Last Will and Testament. I laid that to one side. Photos, some fuzzy with age: My father—couldn't have been more than seventeen, but the charm of his smile identical to what I remembered. Me up at Orchards sitting on the horse she'd given me for my tenth birthday, me playing Romeo at Fletcher. Me again but, I realized with a start, *recent,* striding down Hollywood Boulevard, Mike's arm around my shoulder. Another of me, caught this time in animated conversation with Trip, coffee cups in the foreground. More photos of me, going back to when I'd first arrived in California. Tears stung my eyes. She'd commissioned snapshots. She'd wanted me and had had to settle for a private detective's reports and snapshots. "Don't die," I said aloud.

The file of investigative reports on me, grouped together with a thick rubber band. I resisted a fleeting temptation to read them—waste of time. They'd tell me nothing. I already knew what I'd been doing for the past eleven years.

Another photo—this one sepia with age—of a short, stocky man I didn't recognize. Bushy brows, fierce smile as he faced the camera in what looked like tennis whites. Something about him reminded me of Dev, though he didn't look at all like him. No, if anything, this man was Semitic-looking.

Letters. My fingers trembled as I unfolded one in handwriting it took me a moment to identify as my father's. It was dated August 3, but no year.

Dear Red Queen:

I needed to let you know this, but it seems I don't have the guts to do it in person. *Mea culpa*, but then it always has been. My punishment is to know always what a disappointment I am to you.

I've just gotten married. Her name is Celia Silver— well, Celia Otis now, officially, but since she's an actress, I expect the Silver will continue to shine. The truth is, I've married her because she is pregnant, and suddenly, presiding over the development of a primitive, squalling mite into a triumphant, perhaps magical creature, seems the most exciting game in town.

I can see you shaking your head, that furrow deepening in your distinguished brow, thinking that this is just another of "that profligate boy's follies." But no, my liege, this is real! And Celia, though at times alarmingly intense, is astonishingly beautiful and—I mean this—a very talented actress.

My new play is in fact going to be performed at a very good small theater on Bleecker Street. No money, of course, but potentially, this could be the important step. Speaking of money though, I'm seriously short—yes, again—and I throw myself on your tender mercies one more time.

Your blessing, please.

It was signed, "Your loving pawn, Tuck."

Oh Jesus! If any scales remained before my eyes, they dropped. I knew manipulative when it hit me in the face. Certainly, Gem did too. But she'd kept coming across for him anyway. For the first time in my life, I felt myself standing shoulder to shoulder with her, my idolized father on the opposite shore of a fast-widening gulf.

I noticed the brief letter I'd left on her bed the second time in my life I'd entered this room.

> Gem:
> I'm sure this will be as big a relief to you as it is to me. I'm leaving. Vassar can probably manage without me as well as you can. Acting is what I want. It is my heritage, after all.
> Don't try and bring me back. I'm over eighteen now, and you can't anyway. All you can do is disinherit me. Be my guest!

I winced at the snotty cruelty. *Don't die. Let me at least tell you I'm sorry for that.*

Then I spotted another letter, one that pushed everything else to the sidelines. It was neatly typed on cheap, plain paper.

> Dear Mrs. Otis:
> I didn't want to bother you on the phone or come to the house, as we agreed I wouldn't. But I wanted you to know that the matter is taken care of. He won't be making any more waves, and nobody hurt, like I promised.
> You are a wonderful lady. The best.

The date was April 22, 1972. The signature was "Andrew Logan."

I stared at it, almost not breathing, as though by concentration I could make the words bend to my will and disappear. But the words were indelible, and so was what they meant: that my grandmother had been involved in my parents' death.

"What do you think you're doing!" The voice hit my ears with a faint echo, from the end of a long tunnel. I looked up, dazed, to see Mackey standing at the closet door. In her hand was a serious-looking carving knife.

CHAPTER
TWENTY-SIX

For just an instant I was a child again, caught intruding where I didn't belong, and as terrified as I'd been all those years ago that the penalty would be death.

The silver crucifix on Mackey's chest heaved slightly with her labored breathing. The silvery blade of the knife in her hand hung down at her side, perfectly still. Cross and sword—the righteous avenger. Laughable, pathetic, frightening. All of those. And yet, after the fleeting panic, I felt none of the appropriate emotions. I felt nothing at all aside from a faintly prickling numbness.

"You got no right to be here," she said, her mouth hardly moving. "No right at all."

"That is a matter of opinion. I say I do."

"Digging for the will, are you? And Mrs. Otis fighting for her life. You ought to be ashamed. You have no shame though, have you? Just like—" She broke off, her raisin eyes bright with hatred. I thought I saw something else as well: a flicker of fear.

I rose slowly, never taking my eyes off her. "My father?" I watched her jaws clamp shut. "Is that it? Is that why you hated me so much—because I was his daughter? For Christ's sake, I was a *kid*. I was nine years old!" She flinched. "That's right, for *Christ's* sake, you religious hypocrite."

214 · *Carol Brennan*

"Blasphemer! Blood will tell," she said, her tone dark with meaning.

"Yeah, well, I've got my grandmother's blood in my veins too. And you'd better not forget it." She started to say something, respond to the challenge, and, with visible effort, stopped herself. "I wasn't looking for the will, Mackey," I said coolly. "But then you know that. And you know what I *was* looking for, don't you? *Don't you?*"

Her eyes broke contact and fixed on the floor.

"I found it," I said. She looked up quickly, urgently, to search my face, the fear in her eyes intensifying. "I know about Andy Logan."

Without warning, she lunged at me, the knife blade flashing as it caught the overhead light. *"Devil!"*

I moved without knowing it, felt a sting on my left arm, grabbed for her wrist and missed. I grabbed again and caught the forearm of her knife hand, but not before it had delivered another sting, deeper on my right. All the while, screams—hers, mine, no telling them apart now—blended in a bloodcurdling duet.

"Stop!" A new voice. Male. Large hands forcing us apart. My eyes blinked shut, blurring, burning with the salt of sweat and tears. When I opened them, I found myself looking into the face of Andy Logan.

Dark, spiraling circles forced themselves in front of me, threatened to make him disappear. I kept my stare fixed on him, unable to speak, thinking only, Keep him. Don't let him go.

I sat down hard on the carpet, still looking at his face—concentrating on not letting my eyes close. I reached my hand up to rub them, and a warm stickiness covered the side of my face.

"For God's sake, go get some towels, bandages." His voice was raw, urgent, not as I remembered it, but somehow I had a sudden shadow memory of having heard this voice recently. I saw him move toward Mackey, take hold of her shoulders. I tried to turn my head to get a better look, but

I couldn't seem to manage it. "Don't you see how she's bleeding? Now *go!*"

The circles overcame me then, despite my hardest fighting. As they reached out to swallow me up, I remember seeing Dev's face, right in the center, looking out quizzically at me. "I blew it," I thought. Or maybe I said it.

My mouth burned, and my throat. I lurched forward, gasping for air.

"Okay. You're okay now. Just another sip." This was the voice I'd heard when I'd woken up at St. Vincent's twenty years ago.

Suddenly, I remembered and was suffused with panic. Andy Logan had me. He was going to kill me. My eyes flew open. I was lying on my grandmother's mauve silk bedspread. Andy Logan's gaunt face wasn't more than eight inches away. I realized that one of his hands cupped the back of my head while the other held a glass in front of my face. I tried to raise my arms to ward him off, but they felt heavy, bound up.

"Easy, Emily. You're going to hurt yourself. Come on, just one more sip." He brought the glass to my mouth, and I identified the smell of brandy. Poisoned? As the mist in my head began to clear, I realized that if he'd wanted to kill me, I'd be dead now. My eyes, still bleary, scanned the room. Mackey seemed to be gone.

I cooperated in a small sip of the brandy. Then I looked down at my arms. Each was wrapped in a white turkish hand towel fastened with two large safety pins. "I'm no doctor," he said, "but I've patched up knife wounds before. The towels'll help keep the bandages in place. I've seen worse. You were lucky."

"That's me," I said grimly, "lucky." He smiled just as grimly, but didn't say anything. "What are you doing here?" I asked. Silence. His smile disappeared, replaced with a look of bleak, indelible sadness. "I think I have a right to know," I said, "don't you?"

He nodded wearily. "I suppose so. Right. Wrong. I used to be more of an authority about that stuff."

Some authority! "What's your hookup with Mackey?" I asked.

He hesitated a beat, as though checking out whether there was a last exit before the bridge. "She's my mother," he said, his voice devoid of any expression at all.

I kept staring at his face, searching it maybe for some sign, some clue that would begin to make me understand. Gem, Mackey, the voice, my parents. I had the odd feeling it was all laid out there for me to see—except I didn't. I didn't see at all.

"You didn't kill my parents."

"No. I didn't kill your parents." Still flat: name, rank, and serial number. But his eyes, raisin eyes like Mackey's—I saw that now—seemed to be trying to tell me something.

"Mike?" My heart began to thud hard. "Dev?"

His brow creased in what looked like honest puzzlement. "Who's Dev?"

"Paul, I mean. Paul Hannagan." It was hard to breathe.

"Is Hannagan dead?" Either he was utterly surprised or he was an actor fully worthy of Nadia Gregoriu's master class.

I gulped a relieved lungful of air. "Not that I know of. But you did break into his apartment. That was you, wasn't it? You duped my tape and played it back on the phone. What did you think, that I'd swoon with terror and run? You're good at terror, aren't you?"

"I was. Just once in my life, I was. I terrorized a man and he broke apart. It was necessary. I had to do it, but it broke me, too. For years I'd wake up with the cold sweats. I'd see him there shaking, front of his pants soaked, begging for his life. And I'd feel like some Nazi. Yeah, that was me at Hannagan's place. And yeah, I tried to spook you with the tape. Only for your own good. It would have been better if it worked."

"For whom? Did you try to kill me in the subway for my

own good too?" Nothing but his resigned stare wanting me somehow to see things his way; knowing I wouldn't. "Mike," I said. "Mike Florio." *Did you kill him?* The direct question lodged in my throat like a bone, choking me. Suppose he said yes? What could I do, arms swathed in towels and no weapon?

"Emily." He sat down at the foot of the bed. I thought I could see him weighing options—not liking the play-out of any of them. "Emily," he began again, reluctant decision evidently made. "I didn't kill Mike Florio. I killed two people in my life—a pimp named Ignacio Sánchez and a crack dealer named Luther Bubbles. One came at me with a machete, the other one with a gun."

"But you know who did, don't you? You know who killed Mike. You were part of it, right? Maybe you set it up."

"No, I didn't set it up. I almost wish I could say I did, hand you that knife of my mother's—let you finish me off and be done with it. I'd've taken care of it myself, but I'm stuck with being a Catholic."

"Didn't stop your buddy Strohmeyer," I said nastily.

The look that crossed his face gave me a glimpse of the man who'd terrorized Nick Kennoyer—held that cigarette and ground it into Nick's cheek while he talked of finger breaking and castration. The picture torched my fury.

"And it didn't stop your pious mother from going at me with a knife, or you trying to kill me under a subway train."

"You don't understand a damned thing," he snapped. The ragged edge of his voice again nudged my memory—but not far enough.

"On that we agree," I fired back. "So *tell* me." The hesitation again. "I am going to find out, Logan. Unless you finish me off, I'm going to find out. So you might as well tell me."

His tongue flicked around his reddish lips. Then he began to talk, the words coming out as though on a Teletype, his eyes on me the whole time, but whatever lay behind them blocked—or dead.

"I have a sister. Well, half sister, I guess. I was the child of my mother's first marriage. Jim Logan—I never knew him. He died shortly after I was born. He was a cop too. Kicked in the wrong tenement door without having his gun in position. I was seven by the time she married Gordon MacNiff. He's a good man, was a good dad to me. Doesn't talk much—never did, and hardly at all now, but not an ounce of meanness in him.

"The two of them never thought they'd be blessed with a child. It didn't seem to happen. Wasn't God's will, at least that's the way they looked at it. But then, five years later, He smiled at them. That's what my mother said when she told me she was pregnant. 'God's smiled on us, Andrew.' You wouldn't have recognized my mother then. Before it all happened. She was different. Very different."

"That shrine in your parents' room. All those photos. Did your sister die?"

I could see that I'd surprised him. "Who showed you those pictures?"

"No one. I sneaked into their room once when I was a kid." Something in his face made me ashamed to admit it, even after all this time. "Your mother caught me—and my grandmother. She smacked my face. What *is* it? What's the mystery about your sister? Is she dead? Did somebody kill her, too?"

His eyes shut again, as though flinching from the beam of a strong light. "My sister was like no other child I ever knew. From the moment she was born, she was only good. Pure good. I can see what you're thinking—that it was some kind of family myth, or something. The parents idealizing the prayed-for child, the doting big brother too old to get into being jealous." I itched for him to go faster, get to the point, but I welded my teeth together and stayed silent. "But it wasn't that. It wasn't in our minds. It was *her*. Everybody who ever met her saw it. When she was eight, I joined the force. Still lived at home though. Those days, people did if they weren't married. We had an apartment up in Washington Heights. Not fancy, but homey. Nice. Dad was a longshoreman, Mom did some housecleaning." Mac and Mackey: Mom and Dad. Maybe I was closer to the spoiled miss than I knew. I'd never thought of them as having any life other than the one I saw.

"Of course, my pay helped out too. We managed—better than managed—until Dad had his heart attack and couldn't handle that kind of work anymore. That's when Mrs. Otis came into it, God love her. She hired them to come and live here—do for her."

"And what about your sister?" Another child, another girl in this house. Why had I never seen her?

"She was thirteen by then. Mrs. Otis saw to it that she got into Sacred Heart Convent up in Westchester, paid her tuition, too. My parents were high as a kite about it. What a chance for a working-class kid! The only ones who felt bad about it were Frank and me."

"Frank? Frank Strohmeyer?" Okay, here it came.

"Right. Frank and I were rookies together at the Academy, and then we were both assigned to the one-oh in Chelsea. You called him my buddy. That was right, ever since I was twenty and he was even younger—eighteen. Frank was religious, like we were. Cops can get pretty raunchy, not just the language but their whole lives. The two of us had the church in common, and it made us pretty close. There was a difference though. Sure, I was born into it, knew it was God's true faith, and had to be obeyed, letter of the law. But Frank really believed. I mean *really,* like my mother and . . . my sister. Only my sister was different. Not just different, better. Frank spotted it early, and he fell in love with her."

"In love! With a little girl?" I didn't mean to make it derisive, insinuating, but it came out that way.

"Wash your dirty mind out, will you." The flash of anger flushed his face. "I've been a vice cop for twenty-two years, lady, and I've seen perverts would make you heave your guts up. So I know it when I see it. Frank's love was pure, get it? He was waiting for her to grow up. You want to dig up filthy stuff, you better stay closer to home."

"If you think you're going to shock me with bulletins about my father's disgusting habits, you're a little late." His jab at that still-open wound didn't shock me—but it hurt. No way was I going to show him that, though. "So Frank Strohmeyer was the purest of the pure and your sister was Mother Teresa."

"How—?" He cut himself off. His face paled suddenly. I had the feeling that my response had thrown him off balance. Then he chuckled. "Very good," he said, enjoying his private joke. "Very good."

"Look," I cut in, impatient. "You, Strohmeyer, your sister? What do all of you have to do with my parents?"

His face sobered and he looked at me; the emotion plain in his dark eyes was pity. "Think about it," he said quietly.

I did as he said. I thought about it. And with a wave of sickening anger, I knew. What was it Irene had said when she was ticking off my father's conquests? A convent girl.

"My father," I said softly, finding it hard to meet his eyes, but doing it anyway, "and your sister."

He nodded, but not, I thought, at me. He was back somewhere behind his expressionless eyes, what he saw there whipping him into agony. "Animal," he muttered through almost motionless lips, "pervert." His voice broke. "Fucking faggot!" he screamed, and seemed to wake himself out of a trance.

"Tell me, Andy!"

"He'd see her here sometimes when he'd come to pry some money out of Mrs. Otis. And he started in on her— filled her head full of mystical bullshit to get her into bed. Told her that it had God's blessing. What could that pig know about God? I pity you being spawned by that filth. He got her pregnant, of course. Can you imagine her terror? I think about it still, and I sweat and I weep.

"I was the one she finally told. I went there with her that

night to face him with it, tell his wife, too. It was right she should know what she was married to."

Oh, she knew, I screamed silently. You think she didn't know? "Your sister. She's the one with that strange voice."

"Yes. Nodes on her vocal cords. She was born with them. Mrs. Otis took her around to all these surgeons, but they wouldn't touch her. Too much risk of—you know—losing her voice altogether."

"Where did she get the gun?"

"She?" Alarm tensed his body like a small electric shock. "Oh no," he said, quickly recovering his balance, "it wasn't her. My sister? Is that what you thought? That she could *kill?*" His forehead broke out in a sudden sweat, his eyes wild. "No, *he* did it. He grabbed my gun and did it."

"*Your* gun. So you're telling me that my father used your gun to kill my mother and himself, and Strohmeyer covered it up. How convenient, your good buddy being in a position to do that for you. Otherwise, it might have been difficult to get anyone to believe your version, don't you think?" If my sarcasm nettled him, he gave no sign of it.

"He didn't do it for me. Do you think any of this was for *me?* It was for *her.* No way we were going to have her pushed into that sewer—picture all over the papers, like she was a—"

"*My mother's* picture was all over the papers," I said through clenched teeth. "After your sister shot her."

"No!"

"Yes! I must have thrown all of you a curve, hearing that voice of hers. She called out to me, trying to find me. What were you going to do with my body? Let them think my father decided to kill me, too?"

"You were never in any danger. Sure she wanted to find you. But not to *hurt* you. You were her first thought when it happened. She was frantic. 'Oh Jesus, the kid!' I can still hear her praying out loud, begging for His help. She wanted to make sure you'd be okay, not left there in a house with two bodies. *Don't you understand?*" he yelled.

Suddenly, something clicked into place in my memory. *"Roll, Emily. Now!"* It was that same ragged yell. "You hollered at me to roll, didn't you? You pushed me off the platform, then you changed your mind. Why?"

Again, I watched him calculate—what to say, what to omit? "I didn't push you."

"Right. I tripped. Big coincidence."

"Frank did." On his face was the self-loathing of someone forced to betray his best friend. *Just as Nick had been.*

My mind flashed back to that afternoon on the subway platform—the crowd waiting impatiently for the train; Andy Logan, alarmed as he sees me spot him. He turns to the side, looks down. *To talk to someone shorter.* Hadn't Dev said Strohmeyer was a powerful fireplug of a man? I imagined him barreling through, around behind and . . .

I had a sudden glimmering. "Strohmeyer killed Mike, didn't he?"

Andy didn't speak. It didn't matter. The torment on his face gave me my answer. And the first thing I felt was cheated—cheated out of my revenge. Frank Strohmeyer had beaten me to the punch, died in an instant with a gun in his mouth. But Mike hadn't died instantly. No, that had been slow.

"It was a mistake. Florio was never supposed to die— just be scared enough to back off."

"A *mistake?*" I lunged at him then, bandaged arms or not. I butted with my head, sank teeth into his thick wrist, managed to raise one hand high enough to tear his cheek with my nails. My attack took no more than seconds, and he made no sound of pain or protest. Then I felt my shoulders forced gently but firmly back onto the pillows and held there until I stopped struggling and my dry, panting gasps subsided gradually into exhausted but regular breathing.

His hands continued to restrain me. I stared at his white shirt cuff, spotted with dark red droplets of blood from the tooth wounds I'd inflicted on his wrist.

"You have to understand. All these years, it . . . It was never okay, but we all thought it was finished. At least she was safe. And then, all of a sudden, here's Florio nosing around, asking questions." He spoke quietly, reasonably, turning my mind agonizingly back. If I hadn't been in that movie theater; if she hadn't. *If I hadn't told Mike.*

"Of course, we knew about you and him. Mrs. Otis kept tabs—I helped her with that. So we knew that it was you raking it up. Frank went . . . berserk. Made a call to some guy he knew who was connected out there. If he'd only gone there and handled it himself, it wouldn't've come to . . . I promise you he never meant the man to die, but I agree that doesn't matter. The blame was his—and mine, too. The weight of it finished him off."

"Finished him off too easily," I said.

His short burst of laughter was almost indistinguishable from a sob. "Easily? No, not easily. Frank is burning in hell now, and he burned in hell before he died. You're not a Catholic, and even most Catholics don't live it the way he did. Frank Strohmeyer loved God. The thing was, he loved my sister more. And that led him to mortal sin."

I listened to him, amazed at the unself-conscious literalness, at how real it all was for him—not some cloistered friar in brown robes, but a New York vice cop. Burning in hell? I glimpsed for just a split second what it must be like for the true believer—giving up control, depending on God. But in the clutch, they hadn't. They'd welshed on their beliefs and seized control themselves. Strohmeyer and Mackey and Andy Logan. And it had destroyed them all. But what about the mysterious sister? The still point in everybody's lunatic gyrations—including my own.

She'd killed my parents. I didn't for a second believe what he'd said about my father doing it. A sheltered, devout girl, seduced, pregnant. Ashamed, scared, angry—I could even sympathize with her. But the fact was, she'd done it.

"Your sister seems to be the only one who's walked away free—just wafted off into the sunset and left the rest of you to clean up, right?"

I looked at the claw marks I'd made on his face and at

224 · *Carol Brennan*

the look of grim satisfaction—the face of a patriot giving his life for his country. And I realized with a sudden, sinking feeling that despite all Andy Logan had revealed, he'd succeeded in what had always been his goal: protecting his saintly sister.

"Will you tell me her name, at least?" I asked carefully.

He smiled sadly. And then, before I had a chance to know what was happening, he flipped the bedspread up around me, covering my head, and twisted it tight. I wasn't trapped for long, even with my lumbered arms. But it was long enough to give him a good head start down the stairs.

Before I even reached the top of the parlor-floor stairs, I heard the sharp slam of the front door that told me he was gone.

CHAPTER
TWENTY-SEVEN

SLOWLY, I walked the stairs back up to my top-floor green bedroom. I'd seen all I needed to in my grandmother's secret file. She knew. She'd known it all along. Approved it. Helped. The way I looked at it, she wasn't blameless in Mike's murder either. Oh, she'd never have sanctioned such a thing, but without her complicity, the truth would've surfaced twenty years ago— there'd have been nothing for Mike to go digging for. And without her goddamned private detective, they wouldn't have traced Mike to me. So, responsible she was.

"People are responsible for what they do, Emily." I heard her in my head, pictured her—erect, stern, righteous. But, I realized with a hard stab of pain in the center of my chest, the picture lied. I shut my door and turned the old, skinny key in the lock—not that I thought for a moment it could really keep anyone out, certainly not anyone determined, but at least I'd have the jump of a warning.

I dialed Dev one more time. Past two in the morning now and he still didn't answer. I waited for the beep and began, "I . . ." I never got past the one word. Something held me back from spewing out all that had happened, what I'd learned, where I was. It wasn't the stuff of a phone message. And I tried to tamp down a growing fear that he might never hear it anyway.

I lay on the bed, suddenly in the throes of a deep chill.

I felt my body beginning to shake. "Stop it!" I said aloud through chattering teeth. "Stop it, stop it, stop it."

"Once there was a girl named Emily." A voice in my head played back to me the words I used to quiet myself with. "And when she grew up . . ." Oh yeah, when she grew up . . .

As the shaking gradually subsided, I fell into an almost sleep—my eyes barely shut, blanking out everything. Then a thought pierced through that made me sit up, instantly wide awake, to reach again for the phone. I had to get to Clara, tell her about Andy Logan, Frank Strohmeyer—how wrong she was. Otherwise, Jerry and Hank would be killed—two more casualties. Mistakes. Eighteen rings sounded in my ear before I hung up. I got Hank's number from information. He wasn't home either. Jerry's number was, "at the customer's request," unlisted.

Just as I banged the receiver back in its cradle, the phone rang.

"Yes?"

"Miss Otis? Dr. Fleischmann. I didn't think you'd mind my not waiting until morning. I have good news for you. Your grandmother has regained consciousness."

The doctor's words seemed like an answer to a withdrawn prayer. Good news? I wasn't at all sure. "How is she?" I asked cautiously.

"Some motor loss, the right side—arm, leg, slight droop to the mouth and eye. I'm optimistic about physical therapy. Your grandmother's a very determined woman. The key thing is, her brain seems to be as sharp as ever—and as you know, that's pretty sharp. Also her determination." He laughed. "The first thing out of her mouth was to demand a private room. The second was to ask for you."

"When can I see her?"

"Soon as you can get here. I'll leave word at the front desk to let you up."

I hung up, acutely aware of the breathing sounds that had been background to our conversation. Mackey on an extension, I figured. Two-fifty, Mike's watch said. I splashed water on my face and ran a comb through my hair. Then I looked down at my towel-covered arms, the edges of my sweater sleeves above them ragged where Andy Logan had cut them off in the course of his first aid. My black skirt too was, I saw, stiff in many spots with dried blood. Whatever I felt about her, I couldn't let Gem see me like this. I'd just keep my coat on.

As I descended flight by flight, I noticed afresh the marble steps, their rich burgundy runner held in place by polished old brass, and I realized in a way entirely new to me that this had been my home. Much as I'd battled it, hated it, tried to make it not be so, this house, not my parents' Chelsea duplex, was where I was from.

When I reached the foyer, I surprised myself by walking, instead of out the door, down one more flight to the MacNiffs' quarters.

The door stood open and I entered. A dim-bulbed table lamp provided the only light in the small sitting room. My impression was that the room was empty. It took me a moment to register Mackey, sitting hunched in a bulky plaid armchair. She saw me too, but remained completely still, her round flat face as openly distressed as a lost child's.

"I'm leaving now to go to the hospital, Mackey."

"Yes." She nodded, and continued bobbing just the slightest bit, like one of those Chinese dolls. "I tried to kill you," she said after a moment, her tone matter-of-fact, bland.

"I know." Why had I come down here? Not for information, certainly. This was the last place in the world I'd get that. But, for some reason I didn't begin to understand, I needed to see Mackey, as though to confirm something. "But you *didn't* kill me. No matter what, you didn't."

"Devil!" Her face contorted. She rose from the chair and raised her outstretched arm in my direction. "You. You tempted me to murder."

The bedroom door swung open and Mac stood there, fully dressed in his usual white shirt and black pants but looking even more haggard than earlier, when I'd forced my way into the house. He walked slowly to his wife and put an arm around her shoulder. "There, Cathy, don't do this. You'll make yourself ill, you will." Her sturdy, rigid body collapsed against him, the power of its fury suddenly deserting it.

Mac's eyes shifted to me. "I think you must go, Emily," he said, patting his wife's arm all the while. The note of strength in his voice was nothing I remembered. "It's not your fault, I know that. But you see, you, us—nothing good was ever possible. You are your father's daughter. And we could never forget, or forgive."

It clicked into place then, what I'd come down for: to hear him say just that. "I'm sorry," I said. "I'm sorry for all of us."

Gem's private-duty nurse was waiting for me as I got off the elevator, a tall Jamaican who carried herself like a queen. I looked her over and figured the two of them would get along fine. "Mrs. Otis has been waitin' for you." The soothing ripple of her accent was a strong professional advantage. "But it's important that she gets her rest. She may want to hold you longer than is good. You know, she really ought to still be up in special care, but she said no—she wanted a private room and she wanted to see her granddaughter. And she wouldn't hear of waiting. Mrs. Otis is very determined."

Lady, you don't know the half of it! "I understand, Ms. . . .?"

"Carruthers."

"Ms. Carruthers. Maybe you should just come in when you think it's been long enough, and I'll go." She nodded and led me down the long hall, the squeak of her white rubber-soled shoes the only sound breaking the hospital-at-night hush.

The nurse opened the door, motioned me to enter by myself, and shut it quietly behind me. The bed had been adjusted to an almost sitting position. Gem, sustained by an IV drip bottle and monitored by several machines, was small and motionless, like an antique ivory doll, her skull wrapped in a white scarf. The one familiar touch was her silver-rimmed glasses. Evidently she'd bullied someone into letting her wear them. I could just hear her: "Young woman, or doctor, or whoever, I will not lie here blind as well as helpless. Please locate my glasses and bring them to me at once."

I walked closer to the bed and saw that the eyes behind the glasses were closed. I've thought many times since of that particular moment—what was really on my mind, in my heart. And each time I reconsider it, as through a prism, something different turns up. I was appalled, almost awed by her fragility. At the same time, I couldn't truly believe it. For me, my grandmother's commanding strength had always been a given—unquestioned, unquestionable. Might she not, at any second, leap from the bed and slap me for having trespassed in her bedroom?

I wanted to kill her for what she'd helped do to Mike. I wanted to shake her hard—force from her lips the truth of every lie she'd told under cover of moral superiority. I wanted to stroke her forehead, nurse her carefully. I wanted to apologize for every cruelly ungrateful act I'd ever subjected her to.

I hated her. I loved her.

"Hello, Gem," I said softly, bending in closer.

The eyes opened. Had the doctor mentioned the slight droop in the right lid, or was this some potentially dangerous new development? Suddenly I couldn't remember.

"It's all right," she said. Yes, yes, he *had* said the right side was slightly damaged. I could see it in the way her mouth moved. "Don't be frightened." The testy tinge of her voice sent a burst of relief through my chest. "Dr. Fleischmann believes I shall be able to correct this and speak properly again. Either that's the truth or he's jollying along an old woman."

"I don't think he'd dare jolly you along. Why is your head wrapped that way? It wasn't this afternoon."

She looked at me as though I were a bit dim. "I instructed my nurse to do that," she said briskly. "I can do nothing for the moment about my eye or mouth, but there is no point at all in being more unsightly than necessary."

"Right," I said. Some things never change.

"*Your* hair, Emily. You've cut it."

"Yes."

"Good. It's high time."

My hair. That mattered to her, even as she lay here. I thought of her collecting those photos of me, gathering information, mementos—saving even the bitter ones. My eyes burned with tears of confusion.

"Emily, take your coat off, and sit down." I pulled over a chair and sat near the foot of the bed where she wouldn't have to turn to see me. "It's warm in this room," she said. "Hospitals are always too warm. Take off your coat."

"I . . . I think I'll leave it on. I'm not warm. I guess I've gotten used to California weather."

She looked at me appraisingly, the magnified, droopy eye lending an eerie omniscience to her glance, as though it could penetrate the cloth through to my bandaged arms and bloodstained skirt.

"Emily, I was surprised to hear that you were staying at the house." The paralysis to the right side of her mouth slowed down her speech, seeming to add weight to every word. "Pleasantly surprised. When this thing happened, I experienced a sudden, blinding headache, and I knew something cataclysmic was about to happen to me. I . . ." She hesitated. "I am not accustomed to speaking to you this way. It does not come easily to me. I thought that now I should never have the chance . . . We should never have the chance to . . ." I could see her swallow hard. "Good Lord, I do think this has affected my brain, no matter what he says."

"Don't stop!" I cried out. "You see, when I heard about it, I thought exactly the same thing." Her eyes met mine in an intense, mutual yearning—like ill-matched lovers who think, for just a moment, that things might really work out. "So go on." I noticed my fingers, outstretched, tense, grabbing at the moment and I folded them and corralled them back into my lap. "Please."

"Things did not work out between us the way I had hoped," she said quietly. "I believe that in great measure I was at fault."

"I—"

"Do not interrupt, Emily." Her voice carried its usual snap of authority, despite her labored speech. "There," she said after a beat, with a small, rueful smile tilting the working half of her mouth, "you see what I mean. I expect I was rather stern, foreboding for you, after the . . . atmosphere you'd lived in . . . before."

"You mean the way it was with my *parents.*"

"That is correct. With your parents. You are quite right to object to the euphemism. Either one discusses something or not. Emily, if you hadn't come back to New York when you did, I would have contacted you—asked you to come." She saw my surprise. "Even apart from this"—only the smallest pause—"stroke, I do not have a great deal longer to live. A year more, six months—it doesn't seem to make a great deal of difference. And if I'm to be incapacitated, the shorter option is preferable to me. I shall be leaving you a considerable amount of money."

Disappointment closed in like a sudden storm. My temper caught me off guard and flashed. "Money? That's what's on your mind about the two of us—*money?*"

"You're too old to be that cavalier about money."

"And *you're* too old *not* to be cavalier about it. Besides, I don't want your money. I have all I need."

"I'm afraid you have no choice about the money, and I trust you to use it wisely."

"If you do, it'll be the first thing in memory you've ever trusted me about. Why didn't you trust me? Why couldn't you? They were my *parents*. Whatever they were, they were my parents. I had a right to know!"

"I'm sorry, Emily," she said, her eyes closing for just a second behind the glasses. "I am sorry about a great many things. If only . . . Words I loathe, 'if only.' They imply that facts can be altered."

"Gem," I said, the storm of anger dissipating as abruptly as it had gathered, "you talked about being stern and foreboding for me, after the way it was with my parents. Well, things were pretty terrible with my parents—not just between the two of them but for me. I knew it. I just pretended it wasn't that way—that everything in my life with them was rosy, and that you were the wicked witch who'd captured me and locked me in a tower. Look, I'm not saying you were a greeting card grandma, but I didn't give you much of a chance. I was no piece of cake."

"No. No, you were not. There was no rule you didn't feel called upon to break, no limit you didn't challenge. Rewards, punishments—I knew no other way. I remember feeling quite hopeful on your tenth birthday. I'd bought you the horse. Birthday, you named him. You were so excited you actually put your arms around me, kissed me. And then, when we were eating the cake, you cried. All you wanted really was your parents."

"And you told me about your husband, my grandfather, being an alcoholic and killing someone, just like my father. Why couldn't you just have . . . hugged me or something?"

"Why, indeed? Perhaps I was simply too old to raise a child. Not that I was a brilliant success at it when I was younger," she added.

"You sure you want to take the blame for the way my father turned out? It's a pretty heavy load."

She gave me a curious look. How much did I know? "Emily, you are certainly overwarm in that coat. Do take it off. At once." At once: always her final prompt to action—last chance to do whatever it was before penalties were imposed. Just then the door swung open and Nurse Carruthers stood there, silent and expectant.

This woman has just had a stroke for Christ's sake! Let it alone. Drop it right now. Kiss her on the forehead, tell her you'll see her later, and walk out that door. But if I did it—the prudent thing—I knew that the groping, fragile shoots of honesty we'd just put out, the trust neither of us had ever dared extend the other before, would be crushed forever. Dead.

I hoped I was doing what we both wanted, needed, but I was far from sure.

"I'm afraid we need a little more time, Ms. Carruthers," I said, the blood pounding hard in my ears. "My grandmother and I have a lot to discuss."

CHAPTER
TWENTY-EIGHT

CARRUTHERS took an unhurried reading of the various monitors, as well as Gem's temperature. The look on her face prevented even Gem from protesting. Then, with a scathing the-apple-doesn't-fall-far-from-the-tree glance at me, she turned and left.

Without a word, I stood up and removed my coat. Her gasp was faint, but I had no trouble hearing it. "Now listen to me, please. I'm okay. I'm fine. I did it this way not to be dramatic but to shortcut a lot of back-and-forth that would've upset you just as much."

"Andrew?" she whispered, the horror plain on her damaged face.

"Mackey," I said. "I was in your bedroom closet, going through papers. I don't think she intended to use the knife. She just went crazy. Andy ran in and took it away from her, patched me up."

"You know, then." Her eyes remained fixed on me—urgent gray lasers.

"I do, yes." I heard my voice, dry, emotionless. "And Andy filled in some blanks. Not that there were all that many. Would've been no point in holding back."

"I suppose not. So now you know about Teresa." *Teresa.* No wonder Andy Logan had been startled when I'd thrown Mother Teresa at him. "Very good," he'd said, and had a little laugh at his private joke. *Very good.* Suddenly something zoomed in clear.

"So she became a nun," I said. Of course she had. Everything in her life had programed her for it. Till my father had . . . "What noble task does she perform, nursing lepers?" I watched the sarcasm zing her, as I guess I meant it to.

"AIDS patients, actually." Zing, right back at me.

"Did she ever have the baby?" Incredible—the first time that question even entered my head. A half brother or sister somewhere. Instantly, the idea had a surreal excitement to it.

"I chose not to know that." The crash of disappointment surprised me with its intensity. "Emily, I understand that it is convenient to blame Teresa. Convenient for you. But she was a victim, the most sheltered of girls, seduced in the most appalling of ways—by someone she should have been able to trust. Teresa was simply a new challenge for him. I knew my son very well. That is all it was. She was the sort of girl one seldom meets. Pure, set apart. Everybody saw it. I met her when she was thirteen. Rather startling—the limpid innocence, that odd voice fault. I'd never seen a mother and child as intertwined as Teresa and Mackey. Far too much so. I thought that Teresa's going off to school would be useful for them both. And it was. The child was a great favorite with the nuns. The other girls there didn't taunt her about her voice, as they had in the local parochial school."

"The voice. You kept telling me I never heard it. I was a 'fanciful child.' It was all in my crazy head." In that instant I hated her with the searing-hot hatred of the deceived. "How could you do it, Gem? *Why?*"

I watched her swallow, unable for a moment to answer my cry of pain. "Because it was necessary," she said firmly. "Emily, people like you and me march through the world determined and largely unafraid, doing what we think is right, and damn the consequences. We have no need of God. The entire concept is irrelevant to our lives. We find it almost impossible to comprehend someone like Teresa, for whom the concept *is* her life." *People like you and me.*

"Is that what you thought was right? All that lying, covering up? That's what's poisoned it all these years for you and me—the lies!" My voice slipped my control—soared, trembled as I went on. "The truth is, no matter how naive she was, no matter what was done to her, she shot two people. Because of her Nick Kennoyer is a permanently terrified creature. *And Mike is dead!*" That last a shriek not even meant for her.

The door opened and Carruthers stared at me accusingly. "I think you must go now."

"My granddaughter and I are engaged, Nurse. Please leave us." Carruthers hesitated. "At once!" Not loud, but supremely commanding. The door closed and we were alone again.

"I wish it might have been me in Mr. Florio's place," Gem said, her voice shaking as she spoke in a way I'd never heard. "I had no idea about any danger to him until you told me he was dead. I will understand if you choose not to believe that."

"I believe it," I said. It came out a hoarse croak.

"I contacted Sergeant Strohmeyer and told him of my intention to speak with the Los Angeles police."

"And he killed himself."

"Yes. He was responsible for his own death, *as your father was*. On that point, I shall never waver. Your mother was an unfortunate young woman. I can't say I liked her, but I . . . have never blamed her."

"I should think not," I shot back, stung on my mother's behalf. "She was in the wrong place at the wrong time—not to mention the wrong marriage."

"Certainly that." I wanted her to say something more, but she didn't.

"My mother was talented, very talented. She worked damned hard, all the time. It wasn't only *your* money we lived on, you know. She always had a job. She never gave full time to her acting. She—"

"Emily." I had never heard my grandmother's voice compassionate. "Hush. You needn't."

We looked at each other for a while, maybe a long while, not speaking.

"You saved my pictures, even that rotten letter I wrote you when I left for California. You had your detective snap photos."

"Yes. I should have terminated his services when you became twenty-one. I knew that. I had no justification, really, for continuing once you'd become an adult. But I couldn't make myself do it, somehow."

"There was also a photo of a man. A very old photo. No one I recognized."

She smiled. I saw her debate with herself for a moment. "Jacob. Jacob Urman."

The name sounded slightly familiar, but I couldn't quite place it. "Do I know him?"

"No, you do not. But perhaps you've seen his name occasionally.He'd lived in Israel for a very long time. He died three years ago."

Of course! Israel's Gray Fox. He'd been one of the founders, almost prime minister a few times, the obit had said. Irgun fighter, one of the most daring. "Was he a friend of *yours?*" I asked, finding the disparity hard to believe.

"Yes, he was. A very dear friend."

Was I hearing what I thought, or spinning out romantic fantasies? "A lover?" The unthinkable question was propelled out of me by astonishment.

"Odious word, but yes."

"An *Israeli?*"

"You speak as though he were a Martian," she said tartly. "Jacob was an American, actually. From Connecticut. I knew him before I met your grandfather. He was a young lawyer in my father's firm then. We considered . . . But of course, it was impossible."

"What was? Marriage to a Jew?"

"That's right. It was then—for me. The times were very different. My father did not approve."

"Oh for God's sake! And you *obeyed?* The great Samuel Tucker stood on the mount and spoke, and you just col-

238 · *Carol Brennan*

lapsed? What happened to 'people like you and me,' who march through life doing what we think is right?"

"I developed the courage of my convictions later in life than you. Much later. Might I have done things differently, if I had them to do over? Is that what you're asking? It is a foolish question. It has no verifiable answer. One has one's regrets, but that is far from the same thing."

Her eyes shut, inadvertently this time, and her face looked suddenly wearier. I pressed my lips to her cool forehead. "I'm going to leave now, Gem. You need to sleep. I'm going to have to be out of town for a day or two. But I'll call to check on you. And I'll get back as soon as I can."

"I do trust you," she said softly, without opening her eyes. She spoke the words deliberately, one at a time. "Remember that."

CHAPTER
TWENTY-NINE

As I walked out of the hospital, the sky was showing bleak light—a pessimistic February morning. It was just after seven. I raised my stiff, bandaged arm, and almost immediately a cab swung into the semicircular drive. I gave him Dev's address and leaned back on the cracked red plastic.

Better late than never. Those words stood alongside "if only" among Gem's least favorite. She'd scorned them as the artificial optimism of the lazy or the foolish. "That will not do, Emily. Time is the absolute tyrant. To fail to understand that is to waste one's life." I could hear her voice echoing back over fifteen, twenty years—firm, certain in its conviction. All the while, doing just what she was warning against: killing the time with lies, just as I'd killed it with anger and spite.

Now the lies were over, and it was late for the two of us. Gem hadn't long to live. But gratitude swelled in my chest for what had just happened between us. "People like you and me march through life and do what we think is right. We have no need of God." *People like you and me.* I was sure now that that was true. Better late than never.

I rang Dev's bell, trying hard to think positively—to expect an answering buzz. I rang three times, as though the number 3 had the magic properties ascribed to it. Then I pulled out my key and let myself in.

My heart chilled as I opened the apartment door. The place looked exactly as I'd left it yesterday morning. I glanced around, still standing in the doorway, unable for a moment to cross the threshold. He had never come back at all. I made myself go in, shut the door behind me.

My last, deep-buried bone of hope vanished when I saw that the message machine registered two messages. I pushed play, just to make sure, and heard my own plaintive voice coming back at me: *"Where are you?"* "I . . ." I dug my nails into my palm hard. People like us don't fall apart, Gem. Right?

I punched in Aunt Clara's number. She answered on the first ring, fully alert, nervous. Unusual, given that it was four-thirty a.m. for her. I wasted no time on preliminaries. I told her that everything she and the police thought about Mike's death was wrong; that his death had been ordered from New York by a cop named Frank Strohmeyer, who'd since killed himself; that she must call a halt immediately to any revenge plans she had in the works, before innocent people were killed.

"Yeah, Emily. I get what you're saying." She sounded relieved. "Don't you worry, honey. No innocent people are gonna get killed. Not by me."

"What the hell are you saying, Clara? I just told you what the truth is. I'm not speculating. I *know*. It all has to do with me, with . . . Look, I can't go into it now on the phone, but how about"—my mind raced—"how about we make a deal. You stop anything you have in the works, and I'll come up to San Francisco in a day or two and explain the whole thing. And then you judge. Okay?"

"You come see me soon as you can, Emily." She hung up, leaving me with no idea at all whether she'd bought a thing I'd said. I dialed Hank's home number. No answer. My heart dipped sickeningly. Was it already too late? Had Clara gone ahead and . . . I shut my eyes for a minute while it coursed through me that if she had, there wasn't a damned thing I could do about it.

I had to find Teresa. It dawned on me suddenly with the inevitability of a simple truth that she was, of course, in L.A., and that Mike must have tracked her down. But how? How could he have done it—and so fast? He knew nothing at all about her, even that she *was* a her. Well, if he could, I could. A nun who worked with AIDS patients.

I called American Airlines and booked a seat on the 10:15 flight to L.A. from Kennedy. Then I rang Trip, hoping I'd catch him before he left for the Warner's lot. I woke Anthony, who got him out of the shower.

"Morning, E.S. Tell me you're coming home."

"I'm coming home."

"You're kidding."

"Trip, I need you to do something for me. I know you have to go to work, but get it done some way, okay? It's a major hit," I added. That was our code with each other, had been since shortly after we'd met, for "I need you now." We'd used it a lot in the bad times after I'd booted Bruce DeRenkin and couldn't get work, and in the worse times after Evan got sick. Now, I told him what I wanted him to do for me. Dead air for a long moment.

"What flight you on?"

"I'm leaving here at ten-fifteen, but don't even think of coming for me. You won't have time to get out to LAX after your shoot, and the traffic'll be zooey. I'll catch a cab and call you when I get home, and you can tell me—"

"Knock it off. I'll meet you at the gate." Click.

I stripped off my soiled clothes, gingerly unpinned the towels, and did as good a job as I could manage of washing myself without soaking the bandages on my arms. Then I changed into a long-sleeved white cotton shirt and black jeans out of the bag Dev had retrieved for me from the hotel. While I was doing these things, I forced myself onto automatic pilot, using every bit of actor's concentration I'd ever learned to keep my mind empty—off Dev and where he might be. And why, if he was alive and well, he hadn't left a message for me.

I zipped up the bag, put on my coat, and managed to get out the door. I was resolute. I had a plan. But I felt bleak as the weather and more than a little scared on every count I could think of. "I do trust you," Gem had murmured just before I left. But maybe I was not to be trusted, after all.

Mercifully, my flight left on time. An omen? I reminded myself with some irritation that I didn't believe in pagan religions any more than I did in Christian or Jewish ones. I fidgeted in my seat, unable to settle down or keep still. Celia junior in perpetual motion.

The stewardess came around with a cart of *USA Today*s. I took one and scanned the front page. The deficit was no smaller, unemployment was up, things in the Mideast were getting nowhere fast. It occurred to me that if Jacob Urman were still alive, he'd probably still be right there in the thick of slugging it out with the Arabs. Gem and Jacob Urman. I played with it in my head, trying to imagine scenes, invent dialogue for them—something that would make it seem real. Let's see, she'd've been in her early twenties, years younger than I. Even then, I could see her marching through life, doing what she thought was right.

"Jacob, this can never be. I will not defy my father." No, too stilted. She wasn't a dowager philanthropist then, she was a young girl in love, heartsick at having to give way to the tyranny of social rules—but doing it anyway. Had she wept? Had they held each other, lain together one last time? The embracing figures I'd constructed—the graceful, young Cordelia Tucker, the brilliant, feisty Jacob Urman—did a sudden dissolve into Dev's and mine, and I bit my lip hard to contain my own tears.

I flipped the newspaper open to another page, trying to find something neutral to fix my mind on. A news brief on page 4 caught my eye and almost ripped it from its socket.

SECOND TRUCKER KILLED

Jerome Staleigh, of Florio Trucking, was found dead last night in his truck on a deserted service road off Route 1, forty miles south of Los Angeles. Police say he had been executed mob style with a single bullet to the head. Less than two weeks earlier, Michael Florio, the company's owner, was beaten to death not far from the same spot. LAPD Sergeant Stanley Stivic refused further comment.

Jerry—lighthearted little Jerry with his dopey jokes. So Clara had gone ahead. When I'd reached her just hours ago, it had already been too late. No wonder she'd sounded so odd, so jumped up. *"Come see me, Emily."* Right, I thought bitterly.

But the story didn't mention Hank. Maybe he was safe. Maybe he'd gone into hiding. Maybe I could still get to him. I lolled my head against the seat back, hoping to stop its pounding. My face was glazed with a thin layer of sweat, chilling in the artificial dry cool of the cabin.

I reached my hand into my bag on the seat beside me to fish out a Kleenex, and felt the hard edges of a book. *The Troubles,* Dev's shining start as a writer. I'd forgotten having taken it with me. I realized with a pang that it had been only yesterday morning before I ran out to make my meeting with Irene. The world had changed enough for me since then that it could've been weeks, months, since I'd searched for this book on Dev's shelves, eager in the moment, despite everything else going on, to read it, to know about him.

I opened it now. The cover moved stiffly, the way it does when it hasn't seen much action. I turned to the dedication page. "For Michael Vincent Florio *Sunt lacrimae rerum.*" *Lacrimae:* tears. That was as far as my prep school Latin took me. The first story was called "Heroes." It began, "My father looked to his hero as a sailor does to the North Star. But his attention wandered and he drifted seriously off course."

244 · Carol Brennan

I spent the next four hours in thrall, absorbed utterly in following a child on his way to becoming a man: damaged, bitter, frightened—but also fierce, funny, and joyous. Alternately, I forgot it was Dev I was reading about, and remembered it so acutely that my throat clogged with tears of loss.

I felt the bump of wheels on tarmac just as I was beginning the last story. "Free," it was called. Reluctantly, I shut the book, put it in my bag, and gathered my stuff. I knew in one of those sudden, unwelcome surges of against-the-grain truth that I had little heart left for what I'd come out here to do. But how could I turn back, leave Mike's death— Dev's too, maybe—with no meaning at all? Accidents.

I stood up, took a long stretch, which shot twin stabs of pain through my sore arms, and walked off the plane.

Trip was holding slightly reluctant court with a trio of admirers at the gate. I hung back out of sight for a second or two while he signed autographs and gave Charlie Gracious Star handshakes. Then I turned myself loose and ran into his arms.

"His girlfriend," I heard one whisper knowledgeably to another. "Been together a long time. I forget her name though."

"Her name's not Teresa, it's Sister Magdalene," Trip said as soon as we were belted into his sleek little Jag. He lobbed it over at me casually, underplaying the accomplishment.

It knocked me off my pins. I'd figured when I asked my "major hit" favor of him, Trip might have a good shot at tracking down a weird-voiced nun who nursed AIDS patients, but I never thought he'd be able to do it this fast.

"You are the best! How the hell did you manage it?"

"Wasn't too hard." Pride found its way around the edges of his offhand tone. "Gay Men's Health Crisis got back to me in less than an hour. She works at St. Anthony's." We exchanged a glance of painful recollection at his mention of the hospital where Evan had died. "The word is, she's terrific."

I didn't say anything. Sister Magdalene: the repentant fallen woman redeemed by Christ. Just the kind of dramatic symbolism a troubled teenager would've been drawn to.

"What's with the hair?" Trip asked, his eyes changing expression. Hardening?

"I'll tell you sometime. Like it?"

"I don't know," he said. "Can't tell till I see the rest of you looking better. Skinny. Spook circles under the eyes. Pimple coming out on your chin. Bruised neck. You look like shit, actually. If you turned up on a lot like that, your director would cut your heart out."

I laughed nervously, caught off base by the resentment I heard growing with each word. "Don't try to spare my feelings," I joked, feeling anything but jokey. "Tell me what you really think." I leaned over and kissed his smooth, tan cheek. "It feels so good—" I'd been going to say "to see you," but I never got that far. He drew back and looked at me as though for the first time.

"There's a lot about you I don't know, isn't there?"

I hesitated a beat, knowing I wasn't going to like what was coming. "Yes."

"Important things."

"Yes."

"So whatever we have with each other isn't what I thought. Right?" His voice was tight with hurt turned angry.

"Not right. What I have with you is the most important relationship I've ever had with anybody—besides Mike. And my grandmother," I added, surprising myself as much as Trip.

"Your *grandmother?* I thought she was your big, bad bogeylady."

"I thought so too."

"Look, E.S., I feel like a jerk, okay? A jackass. I run around like a little doggie doing your mysterious errands— no explanation offered—and wait there wagging my tail for a pat on the head."

"Goddamn it, if that's the way you feel, why didn't you just—"

"Because you were my best friend." Were? An ice cube of fear began to freeze in my gut. "And because you said it was a major hit. And because Walter Grody of Cedar Rapids doesn't learn too fast. But finally even *he* said, 'That's friendship?' Bull*shit!* Hey, I trusted you with my whole story, embarrassments, warts and all—even the time I shit my pants in first grade, the time I got caught weenie wagging with that camp counselor. And you held out on me."

"No! No, it wasn't like that. I—"

"Yeah, it was," he said quietly.

I let them sink in, his words and the look on his face. "Yeah, it was," I said slowly, reluctantly. An unwelcome truth, but undeniable all the same. "You were part of my new start out here. I thought I could leave all my garbage tied up neatly back in New York and lose it. I lied to you, Walter Grody—by omission, but it was still a lie." Like the lies that had hung so long between Gem and me. For reasons, always reasons. "My reasons aren't good enough, Trip. If it's any comfort, I only told Mike about it all because we were sleeping together, so he heard my screaming nightmares."

"Some guy from Mike's company was killed yesterday. Was that part of your garbage? Your story?" His voice was calm, but his hands gripped the steering wheel hard enough to make the knuckles gleam white through the tanned skin.

"In a way," I said, the words painful. "Look, before I go back to New York I'll tell you all of it, Trip. I *need* to tell you—not just for you, for *me.* Can you trust me a day or two more without asking why?" I forced myself not to add that it was a major hit. I sensed that invoking the pressure of our old code again now would compound the damage I'd already done. I was asking him to trust me. I'd have to trust *him.*

It took a long minute before he said, "Okay," his eyes straight forward as he started the car. "Where to?" he asked, still not looking at me. "You hungry?"

"Yes, but there's something I have to do first. Could you take me to East L.A.?"

"Why the hell do you want to go there?" His head swiveled toward me in surprise.

"It's important." I caught myself ready to throw out an evasion. If I meant it about leveling with Trip, I might as well start now. "Hank lives there. He's the other guy that worked with Mike. I think he's in danger, if he's not already dead. I have to try and warn him. We'll need to pull up someplace and look at a phone book. I don't know the address."

Neither of us spoke during the forty-minute drive. My mind was not on Hank or on Teresa Magdalene but on my only close friendship, and whether it would join the growing list of casualties. What was on Trip's mind, I couldn't say.

Finally, after a few wrong turns and two stops for directions, he rounded the corner of Alameda Street and pulled up in front of a gray frame house with a slightly sagging, friendly front porch. Somewhere in the back of the house, lights were on.

"I have to go in alone, Trip." His beach-boy-blue eyes were frigid. "I'm sorry—I do. Not because I don't trust you, but because Hank barely knows you." Slight thaw. "If you're really pissed at waiting for me, I'll understand if you just leave."

He threw me an exasperated eye roll. "Give me a break, huh?" He reached across me and opened my door.

The first ring of the rusty-sounding bell produced nothing. The second time, I held my finger firmly down and was rewarded by the sight of lights flipped on and Hank's huge shadow through the parlor window.

As the door swung open our eyes met—his astonished, mine relieved. "Hey, Emily," he managed to get out.

"Hey, Hank. I thought you might be dead."

His teeth closed, biting the insides of his lips back as he took a moment to think. "You better come in."

I followed him through the vestibule into a comfortable,

248 · *Carol Brennan*

man-type living room—furniture giant-sized in worn
leather and tweed. He motioned me toward the sofa. He
sat himself in a tobacco-colored leather chair and waited
for me to begin.

"Hank, you have to disappear. You're in as much danger
as Jerry. I . . . I thought I could stop it. I tried, but it didn't
work. They're going to kill you, too." As my words tumbled
out, I was conscious of his face changing—but not in the
way I expected. Not alarmed, not one bit. He looked concerned—sorry for me.

"Cops think Jerry and me did Mike. What makes you so
sure we didn't?"

"Because . . . because I know why Mike was killed. And
it had nothing to do with the trucking business." I didn't
surprise him there either.

"Sometimes different folks want the same thing for different reasons," he said quietly, a huge hand rubbing his
chin as he spoke.

My heart took a sickening dive. "What are you saying to
me, Hank?"

He shook his head slowly. "I'm not gonna play games
with you, Emily. I didn't have anything to do with Mike
getting killed. Hell, I'd sooner've died myself." I let out a
deep, tense breath. Prematurely. "But it wasn't that way
with Jerry. Little dancing poodle, he got tempted, impatient." He stopped and bit the insides of his lips again. I
got the idea he was having reservations about saying more.

"Tell me, Hank. I need to know."

"I guess you do. I never had a lotta use for Jerry. Seemed
to me a lightweight, jollying everybody along the way he
did. But he made us laugh, Mike and me, and he was a
damned good driver—gotta say that. Also sold accounts,
made them laugh, too, I guess. I didn't have a good feeling
when Mike left those rights to buy the business to the both
of us that way. No special reason I could put my finger on,
I just didn't like it. I tried to tell Mike, don't do it that way.
But you know how Mike was when he got that Guinea head
set on something."

Oh yeah, I did. All at once I saw Mike, crystal-clear. But a second later, he blurred behind my eyes—as though he were someone I remembered dimly from years ago.

"You shook Jerry up pretty good with that call from New York about the message slips. He started acting funny, pestering Lucy to let him go through Mike's stuff. It was old Aunt Clara who really got him nailed. She's some piece of work, and her connections didn't hurt any. Once I told her the way Jerry was behaving himself, she knew just where to go for the answers. Sure enough, old Jerry was swimming around in some pretty polluted water. That lamebrain Stivic still hasn't got it straight—course now it couldn't matter if he ever figures it or not."

"What do you mean?" But I already had a pretty good idea of what he meant.

"Spelled out: if he fingered Mike, he'd get to be an instant entrepreneur—even have the buyout all bankrolled for him. So Jerry set Mike up, fixed it so the goon squad could get him in the right place at the right time. Now Jerry's over. Clara and me, we feel good about that. Hope you do too."

I sat there and sweated. I felt too many things.

"I sent Lucy off on vacation, so she wouldn't be around for it," he said. "She's a kinda delicate flower, Lucy. She was in tough shape—almost killed her what happened to Mike." He leaned forward in his chair slightly, and his tone sharpened now. "Clara says you know the guy in New York took out the contract, Emily. She says, all of a sudden he up and killed himself." He paused, eyebrows raised, waiting for me to confirm it.

"Yes." My voice cracked on the word.

He looked at me silently. "I'm not gonna ask you for the story—don't much care about it, long as the guy's dead. I figure that's what you went to New York for. You took care of it there. I helped Clara take care of it here. Mike can rest easy now. That's all that matters."

Was it? I'd thought so—been consumed with it. But now it seemed strange to be so sure. I wondered if I wanted to know whether Hank had killed Jerry with his own hands.

I also wondered if I owed it to him to tell him that I hadn't "taken care of it" in New York. I decided no on both counts.

I stood up. "Goodbye Hank," I said—stiff, formal to my own ears.

He stood too, and put a log-wide arm around my shoulders. "It's finished, Emily. Whyn't you go take yourself a vacation—get your strength back, so you can make some more of those movies?"

"Right," I murmured, not wanting to look at him.

I slid into the seat beside Trip. He started the engine. "What happened in there?"

I stalled only half a beat. Truth. Maybe it could get to be a habit. "He didn't need my warning. Jerry, the man who was killed, helped the guys who killed Mike. Hank found out about it and helped kill Jerry."

"Interesting bunch of people you know." Deadpan—the same way I'd said my piece of truth to him.

"You don't know the half of it. But you will—if you still want to. If it still matters to you."

"It still matters." We drove for a while in silence. I wasn't aware of thinking anything. My brain seemed coated in hardening cement. I felt suddenly exhausted. Not just tired or sleepy, but every particle of my being strung out, collapsed.

"I'm going to have to punk out on you for dinner, Trip. I'd fall into the plate. I need to go home."

It wasn't till we made the turn down off the canyon road, toward the beach and the house, that Trip asked the question I'd been expecting. "This Sister Magdalene—she involved in killing Mike too? Sounds crazy."

"It *is* crazy. No, she had no part in killing Mike, but he was killed because of her."

He pulled around to the front of the house and cut the engine. "You set out to get the bad guys. Sounds like they've been gotten. Why don't you just drop it all here, buddy? Give your agent a call and go back to work?" The earlier anger was gone from his voice, replaced by a note I hadn't heard since the time of Evan's illness and death.

Fleetingly, I saw myself dialing Bernie's number, letting him bawl me out some more about the missed Spielberg opportunity, and then waiting excitedly, fingers crossed, for him to come up with something—maybe another delicious crack at one of his scorned "dead Norwegians." And I wanted it. I wanted it so much.

"I would if I could, Trip. Believe me, I would if I could."

CHAPTER
THIRTY

I hardly realized that I was back in the house until the next morning. I'd let Trip help me into bed, dressed except for my shoes and belt, and fallen instantly into a deep, drugged-feeling sleep. I woke slowly, by degrees, at dawn. An initial sense of well-being—familiar bed, crispy-clean sheets, comforting smells of lemon oil and Windex—followed by a gradual, sinking reacquaintance with catastrophe. Mike wouldn't be jogging in from his morning run, a glass of squeezed orange juice in his hand. The sheets, the smells lied. All they meant was that Trip had called Aggie, the cleaning woman, and told her to come yesterday.

I lay there and let the tears flow as freely as they wanted to. No sobs, no wrenching anger this time—these were the tears of despair.

After some time, I pulled myself out of bed and bathed my swollen eyes and numb face in cool water. Then I pulled on sweat pants and shirt and headed out to the morning-fogged beach. I returned an hour or so later, back in the present, panting with the exertion of the run—a bit more difficult because of my heavy-hanging, bandaged arms—and the debate I'd had with myself while I was doing it. But my head felt clear, and I knew I would carry through with what I'd come home to do: face Teresa MacNiff.

I marched to the kitchen, ready to eat and drink anything I could lay my hands on. But first I reached for the phone and got Nurse Carruthers on the line in my grandmother's room. She reported that Gem had had a good day and a quiet night's sleep, despite the "excitement" of my visit, and had just been taken down for an MRI. I wasn't exactly sure what that was, but didn't ask. Though Carruthers's tone was correct, it let me know that she had not forgiven my behavior with her patient. "Doctor said to tell you that in another forty-eight hours, if she continues as she's doing, she can transfer to rehab." I told her to tell Gem congratulations—that I expected no less of her. And to send my love.

I spotted a note from Trip lying on the counter. "Coffee ready to go, just push button. O.J., English muffins, and butter in fridge. You're a crazy bitch, but net net you'd be hard to replace. Maybe we should just stay best friends. I will if you will. T." Oh, I will!

Half an hour later, I was nourished, washed, and rooting around in my closet for something to wear. Was there some code of dress, I wondered, particularly appropriate to the occasion of meeting your parents' killer? I pulled out a dark green skirt and decorous matching high-necked silk blouse—an outfit I often wore to auditions. It covered my arms and the residual bruise on my neck, the one that Trip had noticed, left over from the subway incident. Battle scars. Maybe I should leave them visible: full shock value. I saw Dev shaking his head slowly, heard his ironic voice: "Vanity, actress. Just vanity."

I looked in the mirror to comb my hair, and it happened. No warning at all. It just happened. Celia looked back at me, begging me to love her, urging me, just this once, not to let her down. I felt the twitching jumps begin in my gut; the shakes. *I'd hear that voice. I'd look in its face. And I'd kill it.*

No! Subversively, for just a moment, I felt trapped in a scene from the wrong movie. Trapped—needing to get out! Then the second passed, and the movie surrounded me, bringing me inside.

The room tilted slightly and I groped at the wall for

support. Almost dreamlike, I made my way to Mike's bureau and felt around in back of the socks, where I knew the gun was. I dropped it into my shoulder bag. Done, I thought. Done. I looked at Mike's watch. Eight-twenty. I'd get to St. Anthony's Hospital by nine-thirty, even given rush hour traffic.

When I reached St. Anthony's, a young southern nun, whose headdress gave her the look of a fragile child playing dress-up, told me it was Sister Magdalene's day off. I laughed. I gripped my heavy bag tight in two hands and rocked back and forth with laughter. Funny, so funny. Emily Silver: Queen of the Anticlimax.

"Miss, uh . . ." The young nun's initial look of alarm elided into one of nurturing. "I don't know, but if it's really important, maybe you could find Sister Magdalene at our house."

She motioned me over to the nurses' station, where she provided meticulous directions, written in a painstaking, round hand, to Issenheim, a tiny town I'd never heard of thirty-two miles south of L.A. The convent—also called Issenheim—was situated in a sparsely populated valley. "It's named after an old convent in France," she said proudly, her soft drawl making her seem even more childlike. "We're part of the Order of Saint Anthony, just like the hospital here. That's Saint Anthony the *Hermit,* you know, not Saint Anthony of Padua." I nodded, impatient to leave, now that I knew where I was going. She accompanied me to the elevator. "He lived alone deep in the desert, Saint Anthony did, and treated the sick. Miraculous cures, well, sometimes at least. I pray for his spirit to come to our people here—I surely do."

I drove, forcing my mind off the doubts that kept creeping under its tent. Would I kill her? Could I actually kill? What good would it do anybody? I thought of Gem, of Trip, of Dev. And then I made all three of them go away, and turned to my mother, trying to recapture the fury.

* * *

If you weren't looking for it, sharp-eyed, it would've been easy to miss the turnoff to Issenheim. The twisty road down into the valley was fairly steep and no other cars were on it. At the crossroads, a grocery store/video rental combo and an Exxon station—that was, as far as I could see, the town. I followed the carefully mapped directions onto Convent Road, where, after a little over a mile of nothing, I finally saw a tall, curlicued wrought-iron fence and a Gothic-lettered sign that read "Issenheim."

My wheels crunched their way along a picturesque gravel entrance road that rose gently toward a large, simple Mission-style stone building. I did not see any sign of a human being outdoors, even though it was almost eleven o'clock and pretty decent weather for February. It occurred to me that it would be just my luck if the whole damned place was off on some kind of retreat.

I parked near what looked like the front door, mounted a small flight of stone steps, and pulled a hefty bell cord harder than I meant to. After a long minute I heard footsteps. Then the heavy oak door was thrown open by a tall, gaunt woman in her sixties, dressed in an unadorned, sober gray dress.

"Good morning?" she announced in a lively voice surprisingly at odds with her appearance. The uptilt of the greeting asked me pleasantly to state my name and reason for being there.

"Good morning, uh, Sister. I'm here to see Sister Magdalene."

"Ah. Well, the sisters are in chapter just now. I'm not one, you see—not a real one. I'm merely a lay sister. Josephine." She held out her hand. I shook it. "And who might you be?"

I hesitated, but saw no reasonable alternatives to the truth. "My name is Emily Silver," I said quietly.

I saw the recognition on her face and thought for a second that I'd blown it. "Oh yes! *Emily.* Sister's been expecting you." *Expecting me?* "I'll tell her you're here, just as soon as chapter's over." Even though my brain was reeling with surprise, the word "chapter" had a familiar ring to it. Of course! I'd overheard her say something about chapter that night in the movies. It had meant nothing to me, but . . . "Why don't you walk over to our chapel, and I'll have Sister meet you there just as soon as she's free." Her tone was that of a pleasantly authoritative schoolteacher. The chapel was not a suggestion.

"Fine," I said obediently.

I took an exploratory walk around the carefully tended grounds. Some of the sisters obviously liked to garden, cultivate around them the brilliant colors they weren't permitted to wear—purple alyssum, red tulips, creamy daffodils, arranged in riotous borders around lush bushes of golden forsythia and acacia. The chapel was bigger than I'd expected, a full-sized church really, built of heavy gray stone along simple, squarish lines. I took my time about entering, giving the whole scene another look. And as I took in the vivid flower beds, acres of tall trees, bushy shrubs, charming walking paths, my anger rekindled itself full force.

Holy Sister Magdalene, God's good girl! She'd carved out a pretty nice life for herself—considering that she'd killed two people. You've done well, Teresa MacNiff. Pretty place to live, important work to do. No men for you, of course, but then maybe you lost your taste for them anyway, after my father.

I stepped inside the cool shade of the chapel. I smelled the burnt-out candles, the faint trace of incense, and felt an unexpected, strong flashback to my brief but intense childhood passion for the Catholic Church. Genuflections, dips of the hand into small pools of water designated as holy: signals of membership in an exclusive society. Candles lit by hopeful hands, flickering wishes, intentions, tributes up to the heavenly authorities. Confessions whispered secretly to God's delegate, hidden behind a screen. Penances repeated gratefully, the ritual all the more comforting for its formal language. I'd wrapped it around me like a magic cloak. And then, abruptly, I'd cast it off, feeling both betrayed and guilty.

The altar was dominated by a series of large, vividly painted panels depicting the usual key scenes in the life of Jesus. But with a difference. I stared at the center panel, couldn't take my eyes off it. A Crucifixion scene with nothing idyllic about it. This was a real man dead in torment: blood pouring out of suppurating wounds; dry, whitened lips stretched in pain; chest distended and ready to burst open. A mild-faced lamb stared up at him. The lamb itself was dying, a large cross stabbed clear through its neck, blood flowing out into a gold chalice. A woman in white, half fainting in grief, stood to the side, supported by a thin young man. A tattered woman with long yellow hair knelt beseechingly at Jesus' feet.

Then I noticed other panels: a richly dressed bearded man, obviously out of place in a desolate forest, talking to another man, a Robinson Crusoe dressed in reeds and leaves. In the panel next to it, the same richly dressed man was being tortured by fantastical, devilish beasts. An agonized creature, sore-covered body wasting with disease, lay in the bottom left corner, while an undefined deity, pink and gold and radiant, looked down from the heavens, doing nothing that I could see to help the situation.

"Our founder, Saint Anthony."

I froze. I was conscious of wanting to turn around, to look, but I couldn't make myself move.

"He lived as a hermit in the desert. And he nursed the sick," the killer voice explained as though to a party of tourists. "A terrible plague. They called it the Fire of Saint Anthony. It was really a nerve disease from infected grain. The symptoms were very much like AIDS, in some ways. Anthony cured some. Most died, but he cared for them, eased their pain. In the painting you're looking at, he's being attacked by devils. They almost killed him, but you see up there? God is driving them off. These are just reproductions, of course. The originals are in Europe. They were painted by Grünewald in the sixteenth century for the order's first convent at Issenheim. That convent doesn't exist anymore. This Issenheim is the only one in the world now. The panels are in a museum in a city called Colmar, in France. I hope to go there and see them sometime before I die."

"Stop it!" I screamed, the lock on my body abruptly released. I spun around and looked at her. *Now, Emily. Now do it!* But my hand made no move toward my bag.

What met my eyes was unsettling. Mackey's daughter. Unmistakable. Short, sturdy. Flattish, pan face, small dark eyes. Yet as different from Mackey as was possible to imagine: Translucent skin, alabaster-clear. A mouth thin, naturally red like her mother's and brother's, but curved softly upward at the ends in gentle goodwill. Eyes innocent—as though they'd never seen the things I knew they had. She wore a long-sleeved, dark gray dress that reached almost to her ankles. It had a broad bib of starched white, which matched the triangulated headdress that rested on her short chestnut hair.

"I'm sorry. This must be awful for you, Emily."

I clenched my fists hard, sending waves of soreness coursing through my arms. I welcomed the pain—its focusing power. "I don't need you to sympathize with me."

She nodded understandingly, the innocent eyes continuing to transmit their silent mild message. I found myself willing her to speak again, to go on with the damned history of Saint Anthony. Anything. I needed to hear that voice, get used to it—expunge its mystique, its power to awe. My silk blouse felt warm and constraining as an overcoat.

"Don't you make yourself sick, even a little? All this pious bullshit." I dragged in the word quite deliberately, to break the spell, to foul her tidy nest. "And meantime the body count keeps piling up, all because of sweet little you?"

"Yes," she said, the hoarse voice thinning to a metallic whisper, "sick is the word. I make myself sick, more than a little." She extended her hand, thick and square like her

mother's. It trembled slightly. "We must talk. Maybe outdoors would be . . . better."

She turned and strode quickly to a side door and opened
it to reveal a cloistered walk around a cool, green quad-
rangle. I followed her out. I noticed her straight back,
springy step. She had not developed Mackey's heavy, plod-
ding gait, nor Mac's disappointed stoop. No, the Teflon nun
remained unscratched. It all bounced off onto other people.
Great pair they made, she and my father.

"Nice place you've got here," I said, the sarcasm under-
lined in red. "God's reward for a job well done?"

"God is merciful. He doesn't deal in rewards or punishments in that way. Do you mind if we walk, Emily?"

So we did, two women strolling a pleasant, shaded path
on a pleasant California day, talking of graves, of epitaphs.
What the hell was I *doing?* "How did you know to expect
me?" It was hardly the most important question on my
mind, just the most accessible.

"Andrew phoned. He told me he couldn't be sure, but
he thought it wouldn't be long before you found me. And
my father called, too. My mother is distraught. She's hor-
rified by what she did to you."

"I *understand* what your mother did. That was passion,
hatred, instinct to protect her child. I don't like your
mother. I think she's a dreadful, sour, crazy religious fa-
natic. But I get her. It's *you* I don't get. How were you able
to just walk away from what you did, and let all these other
people explode their lives apart covering up for you?"

She nodded again, as though processing my words on
some slow-operating inner computer. "You're right," she
said. That ghastly whisper again. "People have suffered
because of me. People have died."

"Why don't you get out of the passive, *Sister*? You have
also *killed* people. They happened to be my parents.
Remember?"

"I will never forget," she said slowly, each word a separately considered item.

"I heard you that night. I heard you shoot them dead. And I heard you coming after me. *And no one would do anything about it.* Your squad of protectors saw to that. Even my grandmother chose *you.*" My throat felt swollen, sore, as though corroded by the words passing through it.

"Your grandmother has made some hard choices. She cares for you very much. You may never know how much." I turned my face away, not wanting her to see my suddenly wet eyes. *I do trust you. Remember that.*

"I can see how frightened you must have been hearing the shots, hearing this witch's voice of mine. I can't tell you how sorry I am that I was there that night. I should not have been. You must know I wouldn't have hurt you, Emily. I was terribly worried about you."

"I'll bet you were."

"All these years later, I was somewhere else I should not have been. I vowed to God and His Blessed Mother that I would never try to find you, but I gave in to temptation. I went to that movie to see how you'd grown up. I broke my vow and look at the result: disaster."

She'd needed to see me. Could that be true? I wanted it not to be.

"If I could exchange my life for Michael Florio's, I would," she said. "I pray for him—and the men who killed him. And for Frank."

"*How dare you!* Don't you say his name. Forget your prayers. Mike doesn't need your fucking prayers!" I was screaming now, the sound echoing back in my ears. "Want to know how he looked? *Do you?*" She stared at me mutely. The suffering in her eyes was clear enough, I just didn't give a damn about it. "He looked worse than that painting in there. He suffered like your precious Jesus suffered. More." I stopped, not to let up on her but because I couldn't bear the pictures in my own head. I shut my eyes, wanting to clear the screen, and stumbled, catching my balance just in time to avoid a fall.

I felt her hand touch my arm and recoiled as though it

held her mother's knife. She backed off. "I'm sorry. There, right behind you—perhaps you want to sit down."

I sat on a rough stone bench carved into the wall. Teresa placed herself on its twin, at right angles to it. I stared down at the leather shoulder bag at my side. If I reached inside, I'd feel Mike's gun—heavy, solid.

"I think . . ." She hesitated, the voice soft, foggier now. "I think the best thing to do is to tell you all of it. From the beginning. And then you can decide what you think is right."

"Right? Right would be for you to die, Sister Magdalene." I used her assumed name like an epithet. "See, I have things that I believe in too. I believe in personal responsibility. I believe in an eye for an eye. I believe in the death penalty for murder." Her face was tense, but it showed no return anger, no shock, no protest. "Well, *talk, why don't you?*" I snapped at her, afraid suddenly that she'd change her mind, not tell me. Not let me hear it from her own lips, in that voice.

She nodded just slightly and began. "I was very immature when I was seventeen. Even for a convent girl, I was immature. It probably came from having older parents, a much older brother—everyone babying me, even the nuns. I guess they all felt sorry for me about my voice. The other girls were uncomfortable with me—you know how girls in groups can be—so I spent a lot of time alone, a lot of time thinking. And God and His Blessed Mother became like friends to me. Oh, I don't mean I ever had illusions that I was . . . No, I mean that they were with me all the time in a comforting way, so you see, it didn't matter so much about not having girlfriends. I had *better* friends. But I didn't get to learn much about people.

"I'd never met anyone like Tuck Otis. Your father was . . . very unusual. I'd see him at your grandmother's sometimes when I was home on school vacations. And then that summer, he suddenly seemed to notice me for the first time. He began to come almost every day, just to see me.

Mrs. Otis didn't like it, but for once I didn't care what she thought—or anyone thought. We talked. No one had ever wanted to be with me, talk to me that way. The voice, of course—it always made people nervous. But not him. We spoke about belief, about God. He told me his theories— about how people could make holy communion with each other, about how it could be full and sacred, almost in the way it was with Jesus." She saw the grimace of disgust cross my face. "I can see how all this must sound to you. You're asking yourself how I could have been that naive. How he could have been that calculating. But he *wasn't*, you know. Not really. He was as caught up in the excitement of what we had as I was. I'm sure of that." I don't know what kept me from shouting out how wrong she was. I thought of my father's letter to Gem—the one I'd found in her closet. He'd been nothing if not calculating. But something did keep me quiet.

"Our communion was painful at first, but I was pleased for the suffering. It made the ceremony all the more . . . important." My father, I thought, had deserved to die. "And after a while the pain lessened. It grew almost pleasurable. When I returned to school, Tuck would come to see me—every week at first, and then less often, every two or three weeks. It was my mother who noticed when I came home for term break in February that I was pregnant. The doctor said it was five months."

"So you and Andy came to tell my mother, confront my father." My mother. My luckless mother. "What did you want? For him to leave her and marry you? A divorced, failed Protestant with his crazy sexual religious rites—great match!"

"Oh no! I never would have wanted to break up their marriage." Her face was shocked, as though the possibility hadn't occurred to her before. "I . . . I wouldn't have gone at all. But Andrew said we had to—that it was only right."

"Did he also think it was right that you grabbed his

gun and killed them? I can see how you'd want to kill him. But why *her?* Why my mother? What did she ever do to you?"

She took a long time to speak. I watched her face grow even paler, her eyes seem to sink deeper in their sockets. When she spoke at last, it was jerkily, the ghastly voice veering from metallic to furry and back: "Your mother began to scream at me, call me a whore. I yelled back that I wasn't. Then Tuck joined in and called me names too. I . . . I saw Andrew's gun there in his jacket. He'd taken the jacket off and hung it over a chair. I grabbed it and shot. Just to stop the words." She dropped her head to her chest and crossed herself, the motion so small and fast it was hardly noticeable.

And that was it. Everything else, all the death and destruction, had come from that. A seduced teenager's horror at being called names.

Something in my head seemed to click into focus. It vibrated through me. I felt strange, not myself. Yet, in some way, never more myself. All my villains were gone now. All my heroes, too. And I knew I would not kill her.

"The baby?" I asked.

"I don't know. She was born. She was adopted. It was part of my vow never to try and find out. It was self-indulgent even to let myself know that it was a girl. But I'm glad it was. I dream about her. I can't keep myself from doing that."

"Why didn't you just marry Frank Strohmeyer? He was so madly in love with you."

"Poor Frank. I blame myself for not being able to make him understand. I did try to tell him, dozens of times, but he wouldn't hear me. I never wanted to marry—not Frank or anyone. I've always wanted to be just what I am, a nun." The tinge of color had returned to her face. She looked relaxed now. At peace. "You said you believe in an eye for an eye, Emily. Does that mean you intend to kill me?" She asked it calmly, without fear.

"No," I said, making myself meet her eyes. It took me a long time to formulate the word. "It's over." I felt myself deadened, no satisfaction—just ashes, disintegrating at a touch, bitter to the taste. I stood up and took a deep breath. "Goodbye, Sister Magdalene. You can put it all out of your mind, or try to. You won't see me again."

CHAPTER
THIRTY-ONE

I stood outside the chapel with an odd feeling tugging at my chest—a whisper that there was some part of what had just happened that I didn't understand. Not at all.

I made my legs move—one, then the other—with conscious effort. My body seemed unfamiliar to me: new, yet remembered from a long time ago. The sun had come out full force. It shone harshly, making my eyes blur and ache. I was like someone venturing outdoors for the first time after a long illness. I rubbed my fists against my eyes to clear them.

When I lowered my hands I saw him on the other side of the grounds—maybe a quarter mile away—coming toward me: a slim, medium-sized man in jeans and a black shirt. He walked with a limp.

A yell of sheer joy formed itself somewhere deep in my gut, and I let it rip as I ran on rickety stork legs to meet him. He was alive. In the moment, everything else was scrubbed from my mind by the elation of that. *He was alive!*

We wrapped our arms around each other hard. "Thank God," I found myself whispering. "Thankgodthankgod"— the mantra having nothing at all to do with belief. After some time, Dev's hands moved to my shoulders and he stepped back to look at me.

266 · *Carol Brennan*

I took a good look at him, too. His face was pale, golden skin haggard and sallow. The purple eyes were shaded with worry.

"You look awful," I said.

"You're no oil painting yourself. How are your arms doing?"

"They'll be okay." They had probably suffered from being flung so hard around him, but I'd been beyond noticing. "If you know about my arms, you probably know a lot more," I said, the elation of the previous moment collapsed. "All of it?"

He nodded. "Except what happened when you found her." His voice was controlled, tense, wary—prepared for bad news. Not expecting it, exactly, but prepared.

"I left her intact," I said dryly, my cheeks unexpectedly switching on hot with shame. "What did you think?"

"That. But I wouldn't have bet my life on it. *She* did, though. She was eager for your visit. I wanted to come, intercept you when you arrived, make sure. She wouldn't let me. She promised to call me when you came, but only if I agreed to wait outside. Said it was between the two of you. She's an unusual woman, Sister Magdalene."

I opened my mouth to speak, but nothing came out. He put his arm around my shoulder. "Come on, Emily. Let's get out of here." We began to walk slowly.

"How did you know where to find her, Dev?" I asked finally.

"Wasn't all that hard. I figured I was looking for a nun. Mike's phone messages confirmed that for me. Those calls from Mother Saint Sebastian. I mentioned those to you— twice, just to be sure you had no idea what it all meant. You didn't."

"But *you* did. And Mike did. Here I was thrashing around on my odyssey of discovery, and all the while you had it down cold. Smart boys, dumb girl, huh?"

"*Catholic* boys. And don't knock your odyssey. It did what you needed it to."

"Yeah, it did. The price was too high though. I'd rather have Mike back."

"Not a bargain you get to make." I remember with a twinge that I'd've made the same bargain to have him, Dev, back. "Catholics don't have a monopoly on the word 'mother,' " I said, "or 'chapter,' for that matter. What the hell *is* chapter, by the way?"

"The meeting they have once a week in monasteries and convents, where everybody discusses their own faults, and each other's. No, not those words by themselves, but when you put them together with 'wooden altar' and 'plain chants,' they ring an unmistakable bell."

"Wouldn't alter. Plain chance." My ear had heard the words, and my tongue, repeating them, parrotlike, uncomprehending, had handed Mike his death sentence. I took a deep breath and let it out very slowly. "Why didn't you tell me? Why did you run off out here without letting me know? I thought you were dead."

"You know the answer to that. I didn't tell you for the same reason Mike didn't. You're a wild card, actress. You've been running this revenge movie in your head for so many years I was scared shitless of what you'd do."

I flushed hot again, the weight of the gun in my purse heavy as a cannonball. "I went to see my grandmother in the hospital," I said quietly, my eyes down, fixed on the gravel in front of me. "She had a stroke. But then you probably know that." He nodded. "She said she trusted me—asked me to remember that. It was the last thing she said before I left. She knew I had to go see Teresa and she trusted me not to kill her. I brought a gun here. Right here in this bag—Mike's gun. So Gem was wrong, wasn't she? And you were right."

"I don't know," he said after a beat. "Looks to me like the other way around. In fact, you didn't kill her."

"No, I didn't kill her. But you thought I might. You've never really trusted anyone, Dev, have you? I mean against the odds, against all reason." I thought of the third story

in his book, the one called "The Man in the White Hat."
The one about the day his father beat him and broke his
hip. "Except Mike," I added.

"Except Mike."

"I read your book," I said, and watched the purple eyes
widen for an instant in surprise. "I searched your shelves
for it and took it. So you see, you're right not to trust me.
I'm a snoop as well as a potential murderer."

He shrugged. "Keep me on my toes."

"The book was wonderful."

"If you tell me what a crime it is that I'm not writing
now, I will flatten you." His eyes said that he was only
partly kidding.

I smiled. Not a big smile, but a smile. "I wouldn't blame
you. Last thing a writer needs is a pep talk. It wouldn't do
squat for an actor."

He smiled back. "I like you, Emily Silver. Worse luck, I
think I may love you. Now if you have any sense, that ought
to make you run the three-minute mile in the other
direction."

"I don't remember anyone ever accusing me of having
sense. Yesterday I really thought you must be dead, and I
couldn't bear it, not to ever . . . Hey, talk about running
the three-minute mile. You're the one who ought to be
doing it."

"Gimp like me. No, I think I'll stick around."

"Not wise. You're right about me. I *am* a wild card. Also,
I come out of a pretty tainted gene pool."

"Oh, well, then the deal's off. Liam Hannagan is, after
all, the elite. Not to mention poor Mim, who must've been
some kind of depressive." He reached over and put his
hand very lightly against my cheek. "I want the nightmares
to be over for you, Emily."

I stopped walking, brought back with a jolt from the
delicious moment of bantering love talk. "I don't know that
they ever can be. I keep thinking of my mother. Such a
tragic life. Things you don't even know. And then to die

that way. It wasn't her fault! Oh Dev, it's all such an awful *irony*. The powerful, evil voice. My omniscient arch-villain. Some villain—a terrified pregnant teenager who went nuts for a second and grabbed her brother's gun." His eyes blazed sharp in what looked like astonishment. I thought he was going to speak, but he didn't. Then he looked away.

But not before something in me jarred loose. And I knew. No fireworks, no blinding flash of light. I just knew with the certainty that says calmly, "This is the truth." I think that somewhere inside I'd known for a while.

"Wait for me, please. Right here," I said.

He spun quickly to face me. "You figured it out."

"Yes."

His arm went around my shoulder, warm, firm. "I'll go with you."

"No. No, this is just her and me. I want to do it alone." I took his hand and squeezed hard for a second, and then broke away and ran top speed back toward the chapel.

I found Sister Magdalene on her knees, rosary in hand, in front of the painting of the Crucifixion. I stood behind her for a moment before I spoke.

"Asking forgiveness for telling a lie?" I asked.

She rose and turned to face me, her face coloring just slightly.

"Thank you," I said softly, tears filling my eyes. "I . . ." I stopped, the thought dissolving on my tongue.

"Did Mr. Hannagan—"

"No. No one told me. It just finally got through on its own. I had all the clues I needed, but I was learning so much so fast. Everything I'd believed, believed *in*, turned upside down. I knew when I left you that something wasn't right. I just didn't know what. But of course, your story didn't add up at all. Your brother was a cop—a seasoned cop. He never would've taken off his jacket with his gun sticking out in plain view and hung it on a chair in my father's house." I ran the back of my hand over my eyes. "Do you want to tell me what really happened, or should I tell you?"

Her smooth brow furrowed. She didn't speak. Her eyes remained locked on mine.

"Okay," I said, "this is the way I think it went. Andy broke the news to my mother, while my father stood there and did I don't know what—kept quiet or probably *didn't* keep quiet, knowing him. He probably tried some charming explanation. And my mother went crazy. She was always on the edge. I always knew that about her—that she had the capacity for violence. I just couldn't let myself . . .

"She probably rushed at your brother, tried to claw him, hit him—make what he was telling her not be so, even though she knew it must be. What happened then? His jacket swung open and she saw the gun?" I waited, my eyes insisting on a response. Somehow, I needed her to say it. Yes.

"Yes." She mouthed it soundlessly.

"And grabbed it."

Silent yes again.

"All these years. All those lies. Not just to protect you— to protect my mother."

"To protect *you*," she said, the weird voice oddly gentle. "Mrs. Otis was firm on that. She wanted to protect your memory of your mother. She felt it would be unfair for you to blame your mother, to think of her as a murderess. Tuck was to blame, she said. He was the one who deserved to lose your love. Your mother deserved to keep it."

But my mother had never had my love to keep, only my pity. And Gem had sacrificed everything for her idea of justice. If such a thing existed.

"Goodbye, Sister Magdalene."

"I will pray for you, Emily. I always do anyway."

"Thanks. I need all the help I can get."

* * *

Dev was waiting where I'd left him. I walked slowly, savoring the anticipation of reaching him.

"Now's your last chance to run, if you want to," I said, my fingers lightly tracing the outline of his mouth.

"Only if you'll run with me."